AF253203

HATS OFF TO LOVE

KATHRYN ANDREWS

be re-sold or given away to other people. If you would like to share this book with another person, please purchase an additional copy for each recipient. If you're reading this book and did not purchase it, or it was not purchased for your use only, then please return to your favorite book retailer and purchase your own copy. Thank you for respecting the hard work of this author.

For my readers.

1
———

If you ask anyone to describe the great state of Kentucky, odds are they'll most likely answer you with "Bourbon and horses," but if you ask me, the only thing I'll ever respond with is "Derby hats."

Big hats. Small hats. Elaborate hats. Simple hats. Elegant hats. Vintage hats. Statement hats. Bright hats. Pastel hats. You name it, I love them all. Every. Single. One.

I'm not sure when or where I was the first time I saw a Derby hat. Growing up in Louisville, they've always been a part of life. From the first Derby back in 1875 to today, every spring, as the dogwoods blossom and the tulips bloom, so begins the Derby season and so begins the quest to find the perfect Derby hat. After all, the Derby might be the most exciting two minutes in sports, but before and after the race, it's all about the parties and the fashion. The who's who of the thoroughbred racing industry will step out dressed to the nines, along with the many celebrities and influential individuals who come to be seen.

It's my absolute favorite time of the year, and because of that, I've always known I would one day open my own Derby hat store. Now, at twenty-five, my dream has come true.

"Do you think it's too big?" asks the woman standing in front of one of the shop's ornate silver full-length mirrors as she twists her head from side to side to get a feel for how sturdy the hat is.

"Honestly, you're asking the wrong person. To me, a Derby hat can never be too big." I smile at her while smoothing down a long black feather from another hat she tried on.

Her eyes find mine in the mirror, and she smiles back. "I suppose you're right. Plus, they all seem to be about this size." She glances at the counter where several hats she's tried on sit, varying in color and style.

It was after many months of planning and preparation that I opened Rosie May at the beginning of the year. Yes, I used my actual name, but I love it, and in many ways, it defines the Derby.

My mother grew up going to the Derby and has always loved the "run for the roses," which comes from the blanket of roses they drape over the winning horse and is how I acquired my first name. Since our last name happens to be May, the same month the race is run, it's really just perfect for my little boutique shop in the East Market District of downtown, which is also referred to as NuLu for new Louisville.

Could I have come up with a fun hat shop name? Absolutely, but I want Rosie May to be a brand, a label that one day is recognizable and sought out.

"Okay, I think I'll take it." She beams as she claps her hands together.

"I think you're going to look stunning," I tell her, and I mean it. She selected one of my favorites this season, a navy hat with arranged navy and pink feathers. On one side there is navy netting that supports the smaller feathers as they alternate in color to resemble a full gorgeous flower, and then there are the long feathers that arc up over the hat to complete the look.

"Now I just need to find a dress," she murmurs with a laugh. She's completely delighted with her selection, and my hat-loving, people-pleasing heart squeezes with pride and satisfaction.

It used to be that women would find the dress first and then the hat, but the tide is shifting with the elaborate ways hats are being designed. The declaration is the hat, not the outfit or dress, which sounds great to me.

She hands me the hat, and I carefully take it to the back counter to pack it up in a large light pink Rosie May hat box. She swipes her finger across the purchase screen and lets out a delighted squeal as she reaches for the thick satin twisted cord of the box.

"Thank you so much for coming in, Kelli. I really appreciate your business."

My gratitude is sincere. When someone opens a business, odds are they really have no idea how it's going to go. I wasn't sure what type of reception I would be given this Derby season, and I've had many sleepless, anxious nights. It's my first season, and I'm a brand-new, no-name shop. With every purchase, I still find myself surprised people came here to buy one of my hats. It's humbling, but it also gives me confidence in this risk I took.

"No, thank *you*! I'm so excited I can barely stand it. I knew I'd find the perfect hat here."

"That means a lot to me." I lean forward as if I have a secret to share, and she mirrors my posture. "Don't forget to send in your friends."

She stands back up and laughs.

"Let's do one better—take my picture?" She turns and points toward the front of the store where I covered a section of the wall from ceiling to floor in roses of varying shades of pink. It's the perfect backdrop for social media pictures and includes a neon sign that says, *A rose is a rose is a rose. -Gertrude Stein.*

"Of course! But it's better if Molly takes it—she has the eye for these things."

Upon hearing her name, Molly pops up from one of the four tables I have placed in the middle of the store where she is working on her laptop. In addition to people coming in to try on the hats, I wanted to enhance the experience, so I added the tables with matching high-back light pink patterned chairs and hung a gorgeous crystal chandelier over each one. For a small fee, the customers can order a pot of tea and a scone, which I buy daily from the bakery down the street, complete with Devonshire cream and jam.

I love the charming and classic feel the tea time brings to the store. It's an ode to my mother and one of my favorite childhood memories. We used to dress up in our Sunday finest, don our most favorite hats, and drink tea.

"Great, you can be in one with me," she says as she makes her way toward the wall.

"I do love taking photos," Molly says.

Molly is my best friend and also runs her own marketing company. Of course I hired her, and what she's done with the Rosie May branding, the logo, the website, the ads, and social media—all the stuff I have no clue how to do—it's amazing.

I watch as she perfectly places Kelli in front of the wall, has her extend her arm straight out in front of her so the hat box dangles off her fingers—putting my name front and center—and takes the photo.

It's brilliant.

I jump in one with her, she gives me a quick friendly hug, and then she's on her way.

"I swear that wall was so worth the time we spent mounting each rose. The tags and hashtags alone have made my job so easy," Molly says just after the door closes.

"Right?! There's nothing better than free advertising."

I'm always surprised by the number of followers some of these women have. Right now, the tags don't even show the hat, just the store, the wall, or the box. I can't wait to see what kind of action will happen once the hats are revealed.

I walk back to the counter and pull up the full digital catalog I created for this year's inventory, and I mark the navy and pink one as sold. I worked really hard in the months leading up to opening the store to build up my stock, and there are very few hats that look similar to each other. Part of the shop's mission is that when you come to Rosie May, your hat will be one of a kind.

"I think I'm ready for some lunch," Molly says as she closes her laptop and gathers her things off of the table.

"I could definitely eat." I've never met a meal I didn't like, and lunch is kind of our thing. Mornings are always busy for both of us, and as for evenings, Molly still lives at her family's farm, which is about thirty minutes outside of town, whereas I live above the shop. It just so happened that the previous shop owner also rented the two-bedroom apartment over the store, and when they decided to relocate to another town, both spaces became available. It could not have been more perfect.

With her belongings in tow, Molly heads to the office in the back of the shop. Meanwhile, I pull out my large day planner and cross off today's date. There are eight weeks left until the Derby, and I couldn't be more pleased with how things are going. So far, the last two months have exceeded any expectations I had for myself and the shop, and if things continue like I think they will, it's going to be amazing. The income from the season will be enough to sustain and prepare the shop for next year, and in my book, I'm calling that a success.

I'm so close, I can almost taste it. As long as customers keep coming in, at this halfway point, I'm not sure what could go wrong.

The bell rings over the door, announcing a new customer's entrance. I glance up, and there with the sun at his back providing a deceptive halo, striding toward me with long muscular legs wrapped in navy suit slacks, a swagger that can only be found on one man, and a smirk I'd know anywhere is William Stokes Whitlock III.

2

____

can't even say anything.

That joyful moment I just had—it's gone, instantly swept away. The mere presence of him in my vicinity increases my blood pressure and has my face flushing with annoyance and my hands balling into fists.

What is he doing here?

I can't think of one possible reason he would ever need to step foot in my shop, yet here he is infecting the space with his arrogance and uptightness.

Molly comes strolling out of the back office and lets out an audible sound at the sight of him.

"Molly," he says, addressing his sister first as she comes to stand next to me.

That's right, his sister. It's the one and only negative in my over-a-decade-long friendship with Molly.

She doesn't answer him. Instead, her eyes narrow as she knows he's just entered the lion's den.

One corner of his mouth tips up even further as his smirk grows at her irritation, and then his eyes land on me. I feel like I've been shot with two invisible laser beams.

"Thorney," he says, his deep, smooth voice rolling over my skin. Thorney is a nickname he gave me not long after meeting me, and I've hated it ever since. I thought about returning the sentiment, but the only nickname I could conjure to go with Stokes is Strokes, and well, if I had so much as even uttered the word, I know without a doubt he would have indefinitely had a field day with snide, suggestive remarks.

No thank you. I never would have lived that down.

"Do you see what I see?" I ask Molly, never once taking my eyes off of Stokes as he comes to stand directly on the other side of the counter. He's tall, foreboding, and unfortunately incredibly handsome—that is until he opens his mouth.

My teeth grind together as I take him in. I rarely see him on weekdays, mostly just the occasional weekend or holiday, so I forget he can look like this, and I swear this man can wear a suit like no other. It's actually not navy, rather a shade lighter with a little gray in it. His shirt underneath has a pale gray pinstripe on it, and he's wearing a tie that has a mixture of blues, grays, and pink. His shoulders are wide, his biceps can easily be located under his sleeves, his stomach is completely flat, and his waist is wrapped in a nice black belt. He looks like a *GQ* model, and my insides ache at the unfairness of the world.

"Yep," she answers, popping the P.

He raises a brow at her closed-off demeanor, but then again, he should know after all these years, Molly and I stand in solidarity when it comes to him.

"Do you think he's lost?" I ask her, tilting my head to the side to study him as if he's an endangered species, which he is. He has no idea how many times I've come close to taking him out.

"Lost his marbles, maybe," she replies.

"And his rocks," I state.

We both snicker, and he briefly closes his eyes, letting out a long sigh that says he's already bored with us and wishes he were somewhere else.

When I was thirteen, my father suddenly died. So did theirs.

Coincidence? Yes, and the loss set each family on a different trajectory. My mother suddenly found herself needing a job, and their mother suddenly found herself to be the sole owner of the third largest thoroughbred racehorse farm in the state. To say a lot of people had a lot of opinions about what she should do with the farm would be an understatement, so to mute the noise, she fired a handful then hired my mother, an outsider, to be her personal assistant.

We moved to the farm, and that's where she remains today.

Taking a step back, Stokes turns and slowly looks around the store, the store I designed all by myself. When something means as much as this place does to me, it feels like being looked at naked with the way he's analyzing and taking it all in, and I'd rather die than ever be naked in front of him.

"It looks good in here," he says, his shoulders dropping just a little. It's a compliment, and I'm not quite sure how to take it from him.

"It looks the same as it did when you came to the grand opening party," Molly reminds him.

He did come—showed up with a bottle of champagne and demanded we put down our swords for the evening to toast to the future success of the shop. It was one of the few times I can remember him ever not looking at me as if I were placed on this earth just to be an annoyance to him.

That's the thing about Stokes—he really is a nice guy, at least he is to everyone but me.

Which makes him even worse.

It's like I'm forced to know the real him, the good and the evil, and for that I hate him.

I hate how he turned out to be the perfect height and build for a guy. I hate how his light brown hair always looks sexy and disheveled, but there's not a hair out of place. I hate how he wears a suit so well it molds to his body as if it's hugging him. But I mostly hate how he has the most perfect hazel eyes, and when they look at me, they scream, *I know something you don't know.*

"What do you want?" I ask him.

He evades the question and begins walking around. I've known him long enough to know when he's pacing, he's thinking hard about what he wants to say and how he wants to say it. I already have this sinking feeling in my gut that it isn't going to be good. Nothing good ever comes from Stokes when he paces. I wait and watch him take in the details, one by one.

I know there are other hat shops in town. I don't have the benefit of being unique in that aspect, but I wanted to create a unique experience for my customers, which is why I decided on boutique and intimate.

The store isn't small, but it's not large either. It's in a two-story brick building that houses two storefronts on the first level and an apartment over each. The other is a succulent store and gallery. They offer over two hundred different types of indoor/outdoor plants, as well as wall art made by local artists. In the apartment across the hall from mine is a newly married couple. She is a teacher, and he is a sommelier in a wine bar. They keep to themselves, which is perfect for me.

This store is my life.

Which is why it's so weird to see him casually wandering around my space.

"The whitewashed bricks do look better than I thought they would," he says, coming to stand back in front of the counter.

I'm not sure how to take this.

"Okaaaay." I drag the word out, unsure where his mind is headed.

"But I still think you should have left them the color

they were. You disrupted the integrity of the walls," he states.

Molly sucks in air at the insult, but I just roll my eyes because that's so Stokes. He is an old man in a young man's body. He's always been serious. I swear he has zero sense of humor, and from what I've witnessed over the years, he has a hard time with change.

"Stokes! Really?" Molly chastises.

"It's okay," I tell her. "I understand that Stokes would break out in a rash if he actually had to pay me more than two compliments in a row. He can't help it."

He looks at me and frowns. Those two little lines strike between his eyes, and I'm surprised they're not permanent at this point. It's his go-to expression when looking at me. I'm used to it, although I wish I weren't. I seriously have no idea what I ever did to him to make him dislike me, but I'm not one to roll over and take it. I can give as much as I get. In fact, I can give more.

I actually put a lot of thought into the interior of the store. Yes, the brick walls were in their original state of brown, but I wanted the store to be brighter, to have that antique feel of the bricks but be modern at the same time. So, I whitewashed them. All the shelves are glass, and I found a company who makes black velvet mannequin heads to hold the different hats. On the outer wall of the building, the shelves run the full length of the shop to hold the large hats. Ceiling to floor, they are evenly spaced, with a light pink pillbox hat box in between each one. The store logo is, of course, on display. In the back of the shop is the checkout counter on one side and a fitting room on the other. Outside is a platform to stand on surrounded by three silver-framed mirrors, and on the interior wall, I have it broken up into thirds. The front third is the social media wall, in the middle I've set up a selection of headbands, crowns, and fascinators, and the back portion is all fascinators. Also, hat stands are strategically placed around the shop, stocked with color-coordinated hats and fascinators.

I love the image I've created. From the tables to the chandeliers and the black, white, and pale pink color scheme, it's perfect and it's me.

"Would you just spit it out already? We all know you didn't come here for a social call. What do you want?" I cross my arms over my chest. It's a defensive stance, one I am certain he's picked up on, but I don't care. So what if I have to protect myself? I've learned over the years to be on guard when it comes to Stokes Whitlock, from the condescending glares and comments to flat-out insults. Oh, and I'll never forget the pranks, or as he calls them, "jokes."

Standing at the end of the counter closest to Molly, he leans one hip against it, faces me, licks his bottom lip, and says, "I've been thinking you should be my date to the party."

No hesitation. No doubt. No inflections in his words. No hopefulness.

Just assuredness.

Simultaneously, my jaw and Molly's drops.

And then I laugh, because he really, truly has lost his marbles.

Only, he isn't laughing with me. He's looking at me strangely, almost expectantly.

Every year, on the eve of the championship series two races beginning, their mother hosts a large party at the farm. It has become one of the social events of the year for locals. It's a different kind of party from other Derby events as it is still far enough out that outsiders not from the Louisville area won't venture in that way, and the other farm owners and employees can come together for a night as friends. It's a huge party, but, in a way, private.

Turning around, I make sure there is no one else behind us that he might be talking to, and then I look at Molly, who is now looking at me too.

What is happening right now?

"Well?" he asks, impatience starting to seep through his relaxed-against-the-counter demeanor.

This is when I tell you I am so happy I installed video surveillance of the shop, because I will forever have a video recording of Stokes asking me to be his date to an event. This is blackmail material at its finest.

"Not in this lifetime or the next would I ever be seen as your date," I tell him in the most bored tone I can muster.

Something quickly flashes across his face, but just as it appeared, it's now gone, and the ever-present scowl has slipped back into place.

Straightening, he pulls on the lapels of his jacket then runs his hand down the center of his very broad chest to flatten his tie. "That's fine. I just thought it would be good for you to be seen with me."

My ears start burning, and next to me, Molly bristles.

"What's that supposed to mean?" I all but snarl at him.

"Exactly what I said. Think about it—it could be good business for the store," he states, as if I'm an idiot and should already know this.

I'm so confused.

"Since when do you care about me and this store? Are you sure it's not for you because LuVu Tea named you the most eligible bachelor of the season?" I close my planner and tuck it back under the counter.

His eyes sharpen, his nostrils flare, and then he lets out an irritated sigh.

LuVu Tea is a gossip blog that has an account on every social media platform available. Anything and everything is open season to the writers, from the happenings at the college to scandals with the horse farms, politics, and the city's socialites.

"That's it! I knew it," I crow, taking a step back.

Letting out a groan, he runs his hand through his hair. His eyes quickly scan over the length of me then he glances at the ground and back up at my face. His mood is shifting with his irritation, and so is his eye color. They're now more hazelnut than moss green.

"Fine. You're right. It would be beneficial for us both," he says, sounding like it pains him to do so. "I could potentially help you with spreading the word about the shop, and you could"—he looks me over again—"help me keep away unwanted advances."

"Molly." I'm whispering as if he can't hear me, even though he's standing right in front of us and our eyes are locked on each other. "Did you hear him?" I reach blindly to pat her on the shoulder. I'm smiling so hard from giddiness my mouth aches. "He actually admitted I was right."

Stokes is not amused, and Molly giggles.

"Well?" he all but demands.

"No," I say flatly, but I'm so giddy on the inside I feel like a caged animal ready to bust out of its enclosure.

He rolls his lips in between his teeth, blinks once long and slow, and then says, "Give me a reason why not."

And this right here is Stokes to the core. He knew I would say no, and he was ready for it. He is a lawyer and loves to debate. Granted, he primarily practices equine law, but that doesn't change the fact that he can argue someone into the ground. All he needs is an opening, and within three minutes he'll debunk any and all statements made.

I pause for dramatic effect and watch him as he watches me.

"I did. I said no."

He lets out another long sigh. This one is resigned and almost as if he's counting in his head the minutes he's been away from his office and wasted his time.

"Suit yourself." He dismisses me and turns to look at his sister. "You coming to dinner on Sunday?"

"Have I missed one yet?" she asks, still reeling from our conversation as her gaze, which unfortunately is almost the same shade as his but a smidge lighter, bounces back and forth between the two of us.

He pinches his lips together.

"Well, I guess I'll see you." His eyes slice my way. "Both of you then."

With that, he turns on his heel and strides right out the front door.

LUVU TEA

MOST ELIGIBLE BACHELOR OF THE SEASON

Ladies and gentlemen, loyal Louisville readers, with the series one championship races officially underway, we are pleased to announce it's time to present to you this year's most eligible bachelor of the Derby season.

As we are celebrating our tenth anniversary here at the Tea, it's only fitting that this year we aim high to crown our king. After sorting and contemplating many nominations, there seemed to be only one who stood out from the rest. And stand out did he . . .

Coming in at six foot three, not only is he tall, he's lean, strong, and built just like those gorgeous stallions he raises on his farm. His family has deep roots in our beloved town and the thoroughbred racing community, and dare I even say their name is a household one. With light brown hair, hazel eyes, and a brooding stare, he's not only a beauty—he has brains too. He completed his undergraduate degree at the University of Kentucky, graduated top of his class at Harvard Law, and is currently working as an attorney at Collier, Pierson, and Bilella.

While he does an impeccable job keeping his life private, sources have told us he is kind, driven, loyal to those closest to him, and would be the ultimate catch.

Now, who is this magnificent man? He is LuVu Tea's finest yet, as even his name has us shimmying in our boots. So run fast, ladies—we'll be watching and reporting, and we can't wait to see if there'll be a winner in this year's race for Stokes Whitlock's heart.

3

$\mathcal{W}$hitlock Farm sits on almost two thousand acres and is very much heaven on earth. From the endless rolling fields of bluegrass to the woodland pastures and miles of white plank board fences, there's always something so comforting and therapeutic about turning down the long tree-lined driveway. No matter what is going on in my life, my heart settles into a calm state. This place may not belong to my mother and me, but it is my home, and I can't imagine a time when it won't be.

The farm has the main house, thirty barns for breeding and boarding, and several on-property homes for staff members, trainers, and security. All the buildings are white with black shutters, a black door, and a green roof. The consistency and beauty of it all continually makes me breathless, and I'm proud to have grown up here.

Pulling up to the main house, I park next to Stokes's

large, expensive black SUV. I'm not surprised he beat me here; he often spends Sundays talking to the staff, going for a long ride, and generally overseeing the property. For as much as he is a hassle in my life, there is comfort in knowing he doesn't take this gift he's been given for granted and loves the farm as much as I do.

Well, that's not fair—he loves it more. After all, it is his.

Walking up the front steps, I breathe in the sweet blooming jasmine and smile at the perfectly polished black rocking chairs and pots of spring flowers. During the Derby season, visitor tours run daily, and Mrs. Whitlock, who goes by Birdie, prides herself on how well kept the farm is and how well taken care of the horses are.

Opening the front door, I hear voices inside and realize I'm the last to arrive.

For as long as I can remember, the second Sunday of every month has been family dinner. I think Birdie and my mother cooked up this idea together, wanting to create a new tradition for Stokes, Molly, and myself that we could all depend on. I don't mind. It doesn't always work out that we are all in town at the same time, but when we are, there's an unspoken expectation that the three of us will be here. That's right—forced proximity to Stokes, twelve times a year, though sometimes less if I'm lucky.

I can't really pinpoint exactly when Stokes and I became enemies. It was more of a gradual thing as time passed. Well, I'm pretty sure he disliked me the moment he met me, but he was never obnoxious about it. In true

Stokes fashion, other than Molly, he's never insulted or harassed me in front of others, keeping those moments just for us and in private. He knows his place; he's the only son and the oldest heir to Whitlock Farm, and his station in life demands that he act a certain way, which he does.

"Hi, everyone!" I call out as I walk through the foyer.

"In the kitchen," my mother replies, and that's where I find all four of them, plus Grayson, the lead trainer.

This kitchen is my favorite room in the house. It's large, the windows overlook the fields behind the house, which are all misty in the morning, and Molly and I have spent many hours here making a mess of the island and learning how to cook. Everywhere there are memories, and as I look around at them laughing, my heart swells with fondness.

That is until my eyes land on Stokes, and he's scowling at me, as usual. He's washed up after spending the day here, his hair damp and his clothes looking crisp and clean. He's wearing a light gray Henley, comfortable-looking jeans, and brown lace-up boots. He's holding a glass of iced tea, and with a mockery that's meant to get under my skin, he points toward his ridiculously expensive watch to let me know he knows I'm late. By four minutes.

I'm not a klutz, but at this moment I wish I were. I'd purposely bump into him hard enough to spill that tea all down his front. Then again, I'm wearing a cute light blue and yellow babydoll-type dress with a matching decorated headband, which of course I made, and I wouldn't want it to get stained.

"Don't you look cute." My mother beams as she comes

over to kiss me on the cheek. We are exactly the same height, and both of us have brown hair and brown eyes. There's no question that we are related, and I'm pleased to know when I'm older, I'll look like her and not a troll.

"Thank you. I came from the store and didn't run upstairs to change."

"Rosie, just darling like always," Birdie says. I can't help the grin I throw Stokes's way as his mother wraps me in a hug.

Molly is showing Grayson something on her phone and just whips her hand up in a wave without looking at me to say hi.

"Okay, I think we're ready," my mother announces, pulling out two sheet pans from the oven with six individual cast iron dishes filled with what looks like chicken pot pie. "Grab a plate, and I'll place your dish on it. Be careful, they're hot," she tells us.

Stokes grabs his plate and moves to stand behind me. I don't like that I can't see him; I don't trust him as far as I can throw him, which isn't at all. I glance over my shoulder and have to look up to see his face. I always forget just how tall he is until I'm forced to stand right next to him. A stodgy mixture of green grass and whiskey stares back at me, and I hate that he gets me so worked up by just being.

"You know," I whisper, and he leans down a notch to hear me. "When you bury a body and cover it with endangered plants, it's illegal to dig it up," I tell him animatedly.

He jerks upright, his nostrils flare, and that bored expression drops into its natural state of a scowl. He says nothing in return, just regards me with disdain. I give him a wink then spin around to go get my food.

Walking into the dining room, I smile at the familiarity: green damask wallpaper, white wainscoting below, long sheer white curtains framing the windows, and two antique light fixtures that hang over the table. I've eaten so many meals in this room, from Sunday dinners to holidays, that even with Stokes's presence lingering nearby, he can't squash my good mood. I take my usual seat across from Molly, and Stokes takes his between us at the end of the table. He's at one end, his mother at the other. Years ago, they firmly divided the children from the adults.

"So, how's business going?" Grayson asks, glancing my way as he takes his seat.

Off and on over the years, he's joined us for dinner, but recently he's been to all of them. I've often wondered about him and Birdie. They would make a striking pair, and I would love to see her happy.

"It's going great," I tell him as I reach for the large salad already on the table and scoop some into the bowl next to my place setting. "Business is steady so I can't complain, and I'm anticipating the rush for next month. It's going to be exciting."

And it is. I spoke to another hat shop in town a while back, and, granted, they are bigger and their operation model is different than mine, but she hinted that they sold thousands of hats in April. Now, I don't have thousands of hats made to be sold, but I feel I have enough, and well, if the inventory runs out, I'll be thrilled.

"How's Ace doing?" I ask him in return as everyone is settling in at the table.

Ace—or Ace of Spades, which is his race name—is the only three-year-old thoroughbred from the farm running in the Kentucky Derby this year. Bloodlines and breeding have become such an intricate science for horse racing, and when his mother, Dash of Spring, a Whitlock Farm Grade I stakes-winning filly, was bred with The General from Seven Stallions Farm and Ace was born, a male, everyone in the barn cheered.

"He's doing very well. Every time he runs, he gets faster, but that could be because he knows there are treats at the finish line." He chuckles.

I have never seen a horse more spoiled than Ace. From the second he was born, he was hugged, petted, and stroked from head to tail. His legs get massaged, his face gets kissed, and he immediately became acclimated to humans. Now he's a thousand-pound ham, and he soaks up any and all attention given to him.

"Well, I'm not a runner, but I'm sure with the right incentive at the finish line, I could be persuaded to go faster too." I smile at him.

Beside me, Stokes lets out a sound, and I shoot him a dirty look. He returns it with one of his own, only his expression is blank, uninterested.

When I cut into the pot pie, steam wafts out along with the delicious smell of chicken, vegetables, and pie crust. I try to remember the last time I had a nice home-cooked meal, and I'm pretty certain it was when I was here last month. I've been so busy I've been living off of coffee, take-out, and toast. I have a thing for toast, all kinds of toast: avocado, ricotta, eggs, jam, tomato, melted cheese—you name it, I love it.

"I don't understand why the two of you don't ride out here together. You live so close to each other, and it just makes sense," Birdie says, not picking up on the fact that I want to stab her aggravating son with my fork.

Stokes, who acknowledged his mother when she was speaking, now slowly shifts his gaze my way. This time it locks with mine. This room is brighter than the kitchen, and I suddenly feel as if he's magnified. His light brown hair looks super soft, his eyelashes look long and thick, and since it's Sunday, he has a weekend stubble across his jaw, framing his full lips. The double lines between his eyes that are ever present when he looks at me make an appearance at my perusal of him, and then it's like I can mentally hear him say, *"Go ahead, Thorney. Tell them why you won't ride with me."*

I stare back at him as if it's a challenge, one I refuse to back down from, and I mentally reply, *"And why would that be? Because I'd rather be eaten by bears than be stuck in a confined space with you, or because I'm afraid for my life as I can see you pushing me out while going eighty miles an hour?"*

We've done a great job of keeping our feud between the two of us over the years. I'm certain both my mother and his suspect there's no love lost between us, but that doesn't stop them from wanting or pushing.

Realizing I'm not going to give in, he eventually blinks and looks away.

I turn to look at Birdie. "Stokes comes out earlier than I'm able to, at least for right now. I'm keeping the shop open later during the season."

"Well that makes sense," she says, taking a bite of her pot pie and redirecting her attention to my mother. "This is delicious."

The two of them begin talking about the recipe, and I turn back to look at him and pop one eyebrow.

His eyes narrow then spark with mischief.

Oh no.

"Actually..." He pauses for dramatic effect. "I did ask Rosie if she'd like to be my date to the party," he announces. "But she said no."

Across from me, Molly drops her head and shakes it in disbelief. Meanwhile, my mother gasps in disapproval, lowers her fork, and looks over at me. I mentally count down the minutes until I can leave, go buy oranges, and then smear them all over his smug face.

Stokes has a crazy allergy to oranges. The minute the citric acid in the juice hits his skin, it starts burning. In fact, it doesn't even have to be oranges. There's a whole lot I can do with lemons and limes too.

"Why did you say no?" my mother asks just as I subtly kick him in the leg.

He jerks a little and fake drops his napkin. But instead of just picking it up, his warm hand lands on my leg, and I freeze, still looking at my mother.

"And ruin his opportunity to embrace being one of the most eligible bachelors of Louisville? No way. This is the perfect time for him to find you a daughter-in-law, Birdie."

His hand slides from my calf over my knee and up my thigh until it reaches the edge of my dress, and suddenly the room is a thousand degrees. Why did it get so hot in here, and why is he touching me?

Birdie looks to Stokes. The window is behind her, and if I look at her just right, her entire face blacks out. Oh wait, maybe that's me just losing my vision and my mind.

"I was sent the link to that article, and I thought it was rather nice. She's not wrong—you may meet someone you might not have met before."

Grayson chuckles, but Stokes's nostrils flare, and his cheeks turn a slight shade of pink. I'm certain mine are pink as well, but for an entirely different reason.

I mean, what is he doing? And why? I can't think of any other time he's ever touched me in the dozen years I've known him, except for maybe flicking my ear or pulling my hair.

"Mother, I have zero interest in finding someone to marry," he declares in that bored haughty tone he uses.

His fingers dip under the edge of my dress just before he slowly drags them away. A small gasp slips through my lips, a ringing starts in my ears, and I feel lightheaded. I cannot believe he just did that. Why? And did I like it?

Wait...

I did not just ask myself that.

No. Nope. Not going there. Ever.

Absolutely not.

I glance his way, but his eyes are on his mother, and he looks as unfazed as a lazy cat lying on the porch. Meanwhile, I'm so confused I can barely breathe, and I certainly can't compose an actual sentence.

My eyes dart around the table to see if anyone noticed anything, particularly me as I'm sitting here freaking out, but no, they're all fine and eating their dinner.

Ever faithful and loyal, Molly chimes in to remove the pressure from Stokes. "You'll never guess who called Rosie at the store last week." She grins, and I force a bite of food into my mouth so I appear as normal as possible. The bite is large and so hot it's burning.

"Who?" my mother asks, angling more toward me in her chair.

"Avery Layne," Molly says proudly, smiling at me and then at the others around the table.

Is it suddenly even brighter in the already bright room? I swear the light fixture over the table is working overtime, and I feel the need to squint as heat radiates off of my neck. I'm sweating and can feel my hair sticking to my skin.

"The pop singer?" my mother asks.

"Yes! Isn't that so exciting?" Molly responds.

Avery Layne is a pop singer who has a classical twist to her songs. She's brilliant on the piano and is also with Will Ashton from the band Blue Horizons. They are like music royalty.

My mother looks at me, stunned. "Why?"

I swallow the food, and it goes down like a rock.

"Because someone showed her my personal Instagram page where I posted those progression photos last year while I was in New York. She wanted to know if I would design something for her."

I'm shocked she saw the pictures. Granted, I did have hashtags on the designs so anyone could find them, but to have someone like her reach out to me—it's been surreal.

"Really? That's incredible. Just think of the exposure," she says.

And I have. She will be photographed, and the pictures will be everywhere.

I went to college for fashion. After I received my bachelor's in fine arts, I took advantage of the postgraduate programs and completed a one-year internship under a famous milliner in London and then another year under a milliner in New York City. While I was in NYC, I combined my education, and under her direction, I designed my own collection of five gowns with five matching hats. To me, the end product was artwork and spectacular.

"So are you making her a dress and hat like mine?" Birdie asks. Birdie commissioned me to make several things for her this season: for her party, a dress and matching fascinator, and then a hat for the Derby.

"Not quite. She and her husband were given two tickets to the Met Gala, so what we design together will be more high-end fashion and more elaborate."

"Isn't that amazing?" Molly has stars in her eyes. She's

already begged me to let her be there when Avery comes in. How could I say no?

"Do you have enough time for this?" Birdie asks. "Isn't the gala the first Monday in May?"

I shrug my shoulders. "Who needs sleep?" I look around the table and, against my better judgment, look at Stokes. Both his hands are now on the table. He hasn't chimed in to the conversation at all, not that I expect him to, and he has not one emotion or expression on his face. It's as neutral as always. Oh wait, his lips are now pressing into a flat line as I continue to look at him.

I turn back to the parent end of the table. "I know it's a lot, but it's just for a couple of weeks and then it will all suddenly come to a halt. I have to do this. The more I can get my name out there, the better for next year."

I glance at Molly, and she is grinning with full support.

What would I do without her?

"Well, I'm so happy for you," my mother says, and she is. Her support for my hat shop has always been one hundred percent.

But as I sneak another peek at Stokes, it seems I might now have to figure out what to do with him. He's up to something with that little stunt he just pulled, I'm certain of it, only I'm not sure why he's thrown me of all people into the mix.

4

—————

They say if you love what you do, work isn't actually work, and they aren't wrong. I love getting up each day and knowing I'll be spending it in my shop. If the farm is heaven on earth, my getaway oasis, this shop is my daily happy place.

However, since the dinner—well even before that, since last week when Stokes randomly appeared in the shop, I feel like I have been anxiously waiting for the other shoe to drop.

And by drop, I mean him reappearing here, in my space.

In a way, I guess he has—he's in my head space.

Curse him.

I'm certain that was his goal all along. He probably hasn't thought of me once, whereas I've been obsessing over what his next move might be, almost like the childhood game of pop and scare. It's like I know he's out there, beyond my brick walls, and he's lying in wait to make his next move.

For what reason, I have no idea, but he rarely does things without purpose. He can't help it. It's his strict, controlled, decisive personality.

AKA . . . boring.

Coming from the back, I'm carrying a tray with three pots of tea and a two-tiered stand that holds all the food goodies. While my shop is open to the public, I also set up times where people can book private events or private appointments, which is what I have right now. For one hour, these three ladies have the store to themselves. They can try on hats or embellish one that's already made, or we can design one from scratch. Then they can sit down and relax with a cup of tea.

"Here we go, ladies. Please let me know if you need anything else," I tell them as I drop off their refreshments and make my way to the back counter to give them some space. Unconsciously, I glance out the window to the street. This seems to have become a bad habit, almost like a tic, as I know he's out there somewhere, and it's driving me crazy.

The three women let out a delighted hum. I can't say I blame them; the tea selection I stock comes from a local organic tea company, and the smells coming from the three pots are mouthwatering.

"Even the teapots and cups have roses—just perfect," Mrs. Rupp says as she carefully picks up her pot and begins to pour her tea.

Besides Birdie, two other farms who have horses that will race in the Oaks and in the Derby have reached out to me about making a custom hat. While I limited the number of custom hats this year, it's the three for the farms that I'm most excited about: Whitlock Farm, Sterling Bells Farm, and Bluegrass Fields Farm.

Today, Mrs. Rupp, the wife of the owner of Sterling Bells Farm, is here with two of her friends.

"I definitely think you should have Rosie make you that grand hat," the friend on her right states as she scoops some sugar into her cup.

"Me too," the other agrees.

In hopes of situations like this, I specifically stocked hats and embellishments to match farm colors. Whitlock Farm is green and white with an accent of blue, and Sterling Bells Farm is burgundy and silver. I also have dyeable fabrics so I can make a necktie or bowtie to match.

"I don't know…although it would be lovely, it seems kind of pointless this year. Maybe I should have her downsize it more to a modest fascinator." Mrs. Rupp twists her cup in its saucer, a frown gracing her perfectly enhanced lips.

Downsize?

"Nonsense. Just because you don't have a Derby contender doesn't mean people won't be looking at you and for you. You still need to represent your farm." Her friend pats her on the arm.

Cue record scratch.

What was that? Did I hear her right?

No contender for the Derby?

Without making it obvious, I discreetly turn down the cafe music I have playing in the background so I can hear them better. Should I be eavesdropping? No, but this is some front-row gossip. After all, Sterling Bells Farm is one of the oldest and most prestigious thoroughbred farms in Kentucky, and they have a top-three trainer. Every year—and I do mean every year—they have a horse racing in the Derby. They've had four Derby wins in the last twenty years.

"It's just so crazy. Bill is beside himself. They've gone over and over what could have made those horses lame. They aren't overworked, they aren't obese, the floors in the stalls of the barns have rubber mats, their food is specialized—it just makes no sense," Mrs. Rupp declares.

"What about the bloodlines? Was there any documentation or disclosure of laminitis in the purchase paperwork?" the friend on the left asks.

Laminitis—yikes. Crippling foot pain from inflammation between the hoof and the bone that takes several months of gradual healing before they can go back to work. Even then, once a horse has one episode, they're likely to get it again, and she said horses, as in plural. I wonder how many. Just thinking this hurts my stomach.

"No, none. Those poor horses. We were so certain Big Red was going to go all the way this year, too," she says as she picks up her cup and takes a sip.

"I can't believe you waited three weeks to tell us," says the friend on her right as she takes a sip of her tea.

"Bill is worried if it gets out, it might affect breeding and boarding for next year. He's gone into damage control, so y'all must keep this between us." She looks them both in the eye and then over at me. Of course I anticipated this, so I'm on my laptop looking completely disconnected from them.

"Absolutely," says the friend on the left as she reaches over and places her hand on Mrs. Rupp's back.

"Regardless, it's just one year, so you should definitely let Rosie make you that hat. It's going to be stunning."

"It really is, isn't it." She smiles softly.

I've often wondered what all these women do with their hats when they are done with them. Do they keep them boxed up in their closets, or do they donate them? I can't imagine them being thrown away, but after so many years, it would be a large collection.

"Isn't this place just the cutest?" Mrs. Rupp asks her friends as they finally make it to the checkout counter. The two women have each chosen a hat off the wall, while Mrs. Rupp has commissioned me to make her one with burgundy, silver, white, and pink. This way she can find a nice white dress.

"It really is. We may need to come back here during the off season just to have a pot of tea," the woman who sat on her left says as the two friends grab their boxes and the three head for the door.

My heart thumps with excitement. This is exactly what I've been hoping for. Maybe during the off season, I can get the bakery to supply me with a few more items, and it can be more like a high tea with sandwiches, scones, and petit fours.

From the back office, Molly hears the bell over the door ring, signaling that the women have left, and she makes her way out to help me clean. We both agreed that although the farms around Louisville have a long history of friendship, during the season, for the private appointments, it can become a little tricky, so she stays in the back unseen. Even though the results depend on the jockey and the horse on race day, it doesn't make the different farms any less competitors until it's over.

"How did it go?" she asks as I stack all the dirty dishes on a tray.

Part of me wants to tell her about the injured horses, but part of me doesn't. If I want customers to come in and feel like they have a safe space to talk, the secrets told need to remain within these walls. There's no way Molly wouldn't tell her mom about the horses from Sterling Bells Farm, and then it would trickle out from there, even if she didn't mean for it to.

"Great. Mrs. Rupp is having me make her a custom hat, and her friends each bought one too."

"Woohoo! That's wonderful." She leans over the table to spray it with cleaner. She has a potential client coming in; she loves to meet them here. It's usually quiet, they can have a cup of tea, and there's nothing better than surrounding someone with the product of your work.

"You know," she says, eyeing me warily and tucking a piece of hair behind her ear. "I've been thinking...Stokes is right. It would be great exposure for you to be seen with him. Yes, I know you will be at the party, but it's different. He's someone people look at, and I think you should be his date."

What?

My gaze fogs over at her words. She can't be serious.

I stand up straight, holding the tray with the dishes, and frown at her. "You must be kidding. You know how I feel about him—how he feels about me!"

"I do, but come on, he's not that bad, and it might be fun for you two to go together." Her face morphs into something hopeful, and all I can think is pop and scare. He's not even here and *POP*, there he is, only this time he's somehow cast a spell over my very loyal best friend.

"He is that bad, and as far as 'fun together,' I equate that to getting a root canal." I turn and head to the back of the shop. Inside our office we've installed a mini kitchen, and I set the dishes next to the sink with a frustrated sigh.

Why she thinks I should be saddled with him for an entire evening is beyond me. I can already see it now, me standing there while he charms the socks off of people in his own unique way while ignoring me, and then when no one is looking, he insults something about me, perhaps how much or how little makeup I'm wearing or my height —while I'm not super short, I'm definitely not tall. Maybe it's whether or not he thinks my shoes are appropriate, and let's not forget the many, many times he's made snide remarks about my hats, fascinators, or headbands. It's like he thinks they have a personal vendetta against him.

No thanks.

"Poor Stokes," she mumbles with big Bambi eyes as I come out of the back still feeling stung by her suggesting this.

"Poor Stokes? Poor me! Do you not remember the time he told me I was like a stray dog that just wouldn't go away and was always begging for his scraps? There's nothing like being compared to a homeless, starving, dirty animal."

"Rosie, he was eighteen. Boys say dumb things when they are eighteen. And besides, you know he's all bark and no bite."

I want to tell her Stokes is not. He's very particular about his choice of words and who and when he decides to share them. She may think he's all bark, but that day I felt his teeth as they pierced my soul. It really hurts being made to feel like you don't belong.

After my mother and I went to live at the farm, Birdie decided it would be a good idea for me to attend Stokes and Molly's private school. Of course she footed the bill, not that she minded, but every day I would slip into the required uniform, make my way to their house, and wait for us to be driven to school.

I felt like I was living in an alternate universe, and although Stokes rarely said anything to me, his gaze and deep scowl made his feelings on the matter known. He didn't want me there. Even now, there's his ever-present disdain and the way he looks down at me. While I'm over it and really couldn't care less, he still knows I know exactly how he feels.

"Well, I don't particularly like barking dogs. I much prefer them quiet, compliant, fluffy, and snuggly." All of which Stokes is not.

She giggles, and I'm saved by the bell as her soon-to-be client walks in.

5

———

oday, the city is rainy and business is slow. I didn't expect much for a Monday, but with the cold late-winter air—spring doesn't start for a few more days—it's left people feeling verklempt with unwanted winter blues. When a touch of spring peeks its way out from behind the clouds, people are ready and completely over dark and gloomy days like today.

"What is it about Thai restaurants that are so good?" Molly asks.

I snuck out of the shop to meet her for a quick lunch. It's not that I think customers will flood in during the thirty minutes I choose to take a break, but it always leaves me just a little anxious.

Then again . . . lunch.

"I don't know, but this place is my favorite." My eyes slide shut, and I breathe in the delicious scent of curry.

A waitress comes over, recognizes us, smiles, and says, "The usual?"

We both smile back and say, "Yep."

Totally my kind of place, and the fact that it's just two blocks away makes this the perfect spot.

Picking up her phone, Molly smiles at something she sees and then looks across the table at me. "When was the last time you went on a date?" she asks me tentatively.

Umm...

Horror flits across my expression, and I ask her the same. "When's the last time *you* went on one?"

"Saturday." Her smile widens.

"What!" I whisper and lean closer to her. "You didn't tell me."

"I know. He's the friend of a client, and I wasn't sure. I first went out with him like a month ago. It was kind of like a blind date, and at the time there wasn't much to say, so..." She trails off, grinning from ear to ear.

"But now?"

"But now, I'm thinking there's a lot to say."

"Oh my." I lean back in the booth to look at her very happy face.

"Oh my, indeed." She blushes. "Which is why I want you to go out with someone, too. We could double date, and it would be so fun. We've never done that before, and well, now's the perfect time."

"You do realize you are wanting the impossible right now, right? The only thing I plan on doing for the next six weeks is focusing on my shop. That's it. That's all I've planned for, and it's all I want to do. I mean really, when and where do you expect me to meet someone?"

"What if you already know him?" she asks.

"Who do I know who is available and would want to date me right now? I'm the most unavailable person until the Derby is over."

Her eyes lock with mine and sparkle.

Uh-oh.

"Stokes."

"You said someone and just suggested your brother, who is not a someone. He is the spawn of the devil who's been sent to earth to ruin me."

"You are so dramatic. He's not that bad, and he already asked you out."

"I guess you've somehow forgotten that last Christmas he bought me a bag of tools for the shop and a how-to book for dummies."

"Those tools were really nice."

"Maybe, but I'm not a dummy. I know how to use tools. He just thinks I'm incompetent at life and constantly shoves that in my face."

"I disagree. I happen to love my brother and you too. Seems like the perfect setup to me. Besides, if not him then who?"

"If my options are him and, say, anyone else, I'll take the latter."

"Seriously, when was your last date?" she asks as the waitress drops off our drinks.

I have to think about this and then feel my cheeks heat up. Ironically, my last date was a dinner date with Stokes in New York. He was in town for work and all but demanded I let him take me to dinner. He claimed his mother would be disappointed if he didn't, and well, I agreed because I was an intern and it was a free meal. We were told twice to keep our voices down as we flung insults at each other for ninety minutes.

Before that, I don't remember. I've been busy and focused, and I've moved four times: college, London, New York, and now back to Louisville. It's not that I don't want to meet the perfect guy and settle down one day. I do, it's just that since my life plan has unfolded, this really doesn't line up for a few more years. In the meantime, I'm content with romance novels and Hallmark movies. There's nothing like a super-romantic grand gesture to make the heart sigh.

"Last year when I was in New York," I tell her, hoping she doesn't press for details.

"Exactly, last year."

"So what? You know I've been one hundred percent focused on the shop."

"Well, in just a few weeks, after the Derby, your focus can shift."

I can't even think about that time yet. I want to drown in my first season and enjoy every moment of this unknown.

"Maybe," I murmur to pacify her for now.

We've just finished eating our appetizer of soup and an

eggroll when a dark shadow falls over the table. Looking up, I don't know why I'm surprised, but I am.

POP!

For crying out loud, what is with this guy?

"Stokes! What are you doing here?" Molly asks, all cheerful as he runs his hand through his damp hair to shake out any rain left behind.

My eyes narrow with distaste at him and then her.

Traitor.

"I thought I'd join you two for lunch." He slips out of his charcoal gray suit jacket. His shirt is light blue and his tie is plaid, and I hate how good he looks. He bends down and slides into the booth.

On. My. Side.

"Umm, excuse me," I blurt out at his blatant rudeness as I press up against the wall, putting the tiniest fraction of space between us.

His eyes flit my way. "Sure, no problem," he says as he drapes his jacket over one leg.

Unbelievable. Who does this guy think he is?

"How did you know we were here?" Molly asks, ignoring the death glare I'm sending his way and picking up the menu she placed next to her in the booth after we gave our order. I allotted myself thirty minutes to be away from the shop, and now my nice, relaxing time is not only disrupted but ruined.

"I have my ways," he states as he flips the menu open.

I let out an unflattering snort, and he turns to look at me and flatly says, "To find both of you, actually."

What the what?

"This is one of my favorite places, so I thought I'd join you," he says, as if being here casually lunching with us is an occasional occurrence.

And it's official: I can never come here again.

I also need to destroy my phone, seeing as how he's somehow hacked into it and invaded my privacy.

About this time, the waitress sees him and scurries over to take his drink order. Like the boring person he is, he orders water. Meanwhile, I pick up my Thai iced tea, which is next to my Diet Coke, and take a sip.

"How's work going?" Molly asks him.

"Same as always." He lets out a sigh. "Contracts, disputes, and fraud claims," he says, as if those things are the most mundane in existence.

"Better you than me." She grins at him just like a younger sibling who has not even an ounce of the responsibilities he has.

Stokes never questioned taking over the farm. Since the day he was born, his father, the one I never had a chance to meet, talked to him about the ins and outs of running the operation that would one day be his. At fifteen, feeling overwhelmed by his dad's sudden death, Stokes buckled down on his destined path. He got an accounting degree to understand the money side of the farm and then went on to law school to understand the business side of dealing with thoroughbred horses. Does he need to work at this law firm? No. He could already be at the farm, but him making these commitments shows the thoroughbred world he's serious about his role for when it's time for him to step in.

He gives her the barest hint of a smile, and I wonder why I'm even here, trapped against the wall.

Molly flips her gaze my way, her expression turning to one of hopefulness. It better not be hopeful about her brother and me, because not in this lifetime will that ever happen.

"Well, I actually asked Rosie to meet me today, because I have something I want to show her." She reaches into her bag and pulls out her laptop. After a few seconds of turning it on and connecting to the restaurant's Wi-Fi, she glances up, looks at me sheepishly, and then turns it around to face me—well, to face us, as he is right here all up in my personal space.

And I hate it.

I hate it because he's the one person in this world I can't relax around. I feel like I always have to be on guard, because I never know what type of mood he's going to be in or what's going to come out of his mouth. Both are unpredictable, until they aren't.

"We haven't talked about this," Molly says, "but I got to thinking after the last Sunday dinner, and this is something you do and are brilliant at, so I decided to add a new page to your website. When we first started, you said I had full control of creative liberties, and I just think this is one more thing to set you apart from the others."

There in front of us is the Rosie May website, a website I absolutely love and can't believe is mine. It is so pretty with how she designed it using the store colors, the brand name, fonts, and photos. All the images have a filter over them so they are cohesive, bright, and beautiful.

Stokes shifts his big body next to me to get a better look. He moves one arm to stretch along the top of the booth behind me, and his leg brushes up against mine.

Irritation crackles down my spine.

He flusters me, and I'm certain he knows it.

"I added a page for couture designs. You have the five you created in New York, plus my mother's dress for the upcoming championship series two party, and now with Avery Layne, there's no reason you shouldn't be advertising these as well. After her debut, you could price your designs higher and do really well. This could be another source of income during the off season."

Molly kept the home page simple. She wanted all categories to be present on one screen so customers don't have to scroll down to find what they're looking for: hats, fascinators, weddings, events, couture, custom orders, about, and in the news. I click on the large word couture on the home page, and it jumps to a new page.

Molly's phone rings, she picks it up, and her face lights up. It has to be the guy—I didn't even have a chance to ask her his name.

"I have to take this, but I'll be right back," she tells us as she scoots out of the booth and heads outside to stand under the awning.

Silence descends over the table, and I pretend Stokes isn't even here as I study the layout, images, and text she added. It looks so good, and sometimes when I look at things like this, I feel like it's for someone else's business and not mine.

"I like it," Stokes says.

I say nothing in return but realize the heat from his nearness is smothering me, as well as his peppermint breath.

Ever since he mentioned that he wanted me to be his date, I've had a sinking gut feeling that I might have made the wrong decision. Stokes is someone whether I like it or not. He runs with the type of people I want buying my hats, and although he and I don't really get along, it would have been a great strategic move for my business. Don't get me wrong, though—I will never admit this and will take these thoughts to my grave, especially after he mentioned it again at dinner and mocked me.

Of course the whole idea *is* completely preposterous and just nonsense, but that feeling has me regretting my quick reply otherwise. Then again, on principle alone, I can't, won't, and shouldn't even entertain the idea.

"What do you like about it?" I lean back against the wall to put a sliver more space between us and put him on the spot.

"The pictures and the content are gorgeous, the layout is easy enough to understand, and I like that she put a call to action button at the top and the bottom for people who have an interest in you designing something for them."

"Hmm," I mutter in response as I look back at the webpage. He's right about the *Inquire more here* and *Inter-*

ested in a consult for your very own custom gown? buttons. The only other place she's added a button like this is on the custom orders page for hats and fascinators where she states I am offering limited designs.

Beside me, Stokes reaches for his water. I watch as his mouth makes contact with the edge of the glass and he takes a sip, my stomach involuntarily dips, and I get angry with myself, because I should be watching him warily as if he's a snake about to strike.

"What are you really doing here? You never leave your office, the weather is horrible, and this can't possibly be one of your favorite restaurants."

His eyes drop to my mouth for a split second and then cut away. Needing him to know I'm not some helpless prey he's strategically cornered, I grab the lemon off the glass of my Diet Coke and suck it between my lips. He jolts away from me just a little and frowns, while I smile conspiratorially.

"Clearly I do leave my office, as here I am, and it is one of my favorites. The duck fried rice and beef pad thai are exceptional."

"You venture all the way from your office downtown to eat at this little hole in the wall?" I ask as I toss the lemon back in the glass.

His brows pull down, and he shifts a little to face me as he studies me. "I do on my way home from work."

"And where is home?" I tilt my head and examine him as he's literally two feet away from me. His hair is drying, his eyebrows look perfectly shaped even though I'm certain he does nothing to them, and while his eyes are hazel, from this vantage point, it's easy to see where the green ends and the whiskey begins.

He looks at me strangely. "Across the street." He waves his hand in that direction.

"What?" I'm so confused, and he registers the shock stamped on my face.

"Molly never told you where I live?" The two lines between his eyes make an appearance.

"No, why would she?" I state with an attitude so he understands he's an uninteresting topic to us.

Molly and I rarely talk about Stokes. In fact, up until two weeks ago, we never talked about him at all.

"Huh." He looks down at the table as he ponders something.

No wonder Birdie asked why we don't ride together to Sunday dinners. Apparently everyone but me knows Stokes and I are literally a stone's throw away from each other.

Letting out a harsh breath, I grab the iced tea and take a long pull on the straw. I feel like my world has just shifted on its axis. For the last three months, this little neighborhood was mine and it felt perfect, and now I feel like it's not. Now I feel like I can't even go outside without wondering if I'll run into him. Five minutes ago, I felt free; now I don't. This is just the worst.

Clearing his throat, Stokes decides to change the subject. "So, you mentioned at dinner that Avery Layne is coming in. When is that scheduled?" His eyes lock onto mine, and my chest starts to squeeze. The laser beams are attacking me, and suddenly I feel super claustrophobic crammed in next to the wall. There's nowhere for me to turn to breathe.

"What is this? Small talk?" I ask him, taking air in slowly and counting to five.

"You are familiar with the concept, aren't you?" he fires back, and while I don't see red, everything is slightly tinged with a shade of pink.

I stare at him.

He stares at me.

And then I feel my hair move.

The hand on the arm that is draped across the back of the booth has moved, and he's slipped his fingers into my hair. Heat travels from my hair to my scalp, and it burns.

What is he doing?

This guy is unhinged and drives me bananas.

His eyes fall to my shoulder, and I watch his face as he rolls my hair between his fingers. It's a little bit contemplative, a little bit sincere, and a little bit offended. This is the weirdest moment I've ever had with him. It surpasses the hand on my leg at dinner, and all I can think is *What is happening right now?*

And that's when it hits me. I jerk out of his reach, swat his hand away, and glare at him.

"So that's it—this is your game. You think if you act a little bit civilized, I'll cave and agree to be your date? Touch me here, sit by me there, talk to me like I'm an actual person and not a splinter in your ass—you think two weeks of good behavior will instantly replace twelve years of bad?"

"I'm not playing a game," he says flatly in that haughty tone of his.

"You forget I've known you since zits and braces. Nice try."

His jaw tenses as his face drops into a scowl, and at that moment the waitress brings over his soup and eggroll, along with my lunch and Molly's.

I turn away from him, pretend to ignore him, and start eating. Of course he's got me so riled up I can't even taste my food. Worst lunch ever. I should have just stayed at the shop.

His gaze lingers on me for a little longer, and man do I wish I knew what he was thinking. None of this makes any sense.

He makes no sense.

Eventually he removes his arm from behind me and begins eating as well.

Good riddance.

6

$\mathcal{M}$olly and I are standing behind the counter when a large SUV pulls up in front of the door to the shop at exactly two o'clock. Adrenaline and nerves are racing through me as I'm about to meet Avery Layne. Part of me feels like I need to pinch myself because this can't be my life.

Yet here we are, and Molly is in no better shape than I am.

A tall woman in all black gets out of the passenger side, looks up and down the block, and then walks through the front door. She eyes both of us, as I'm certain we look like a couple of deer standing in direct headlights, and asks, "Ms. May?"

I raise my hand like I've just been called on and forget to say hello.

The woman nods then proceeds to walk back outside

and open the back door of the SUV. Avery slips out, and Molly gasps.

My sentiments exactly.

Everyday Avery (versus performance Avery) is in what looks like sweatpants and a hoodie, with her long blonde hair all wild and curly. She says something to the person in the car and then the door closes.

"Do you think Will Ashton is in the car?" Molly whispers. "Do you think she was talking to him?"

"Let's pretend he was, but I'm not sure I could handle both of them in the same day," I whisper back.

The same woman who was in the front passenger seat again opens the door to the shop for Avery to come in and then stands there to prevent anyone else from coming or going. My jaw drops.

"You have a female bodyguard?" I ask.

Yes, folks. These are the first words that spew from my mouth when given the opportunity to meet a celebrity. My face heats, and I'm certain it is flame red.

Avery grins. "I do. And let me tell you, no one wants to cross her." She makes her way to where Molly and I have moved out from the counter and are now standing next to the tables.

"That. Is. Amazing," I tell her.

"Her name is Blair. She's been with me for a few months now." She turns her head over her shoulder and very obnoxiously says, "And I love her."

Blair shakes her head like Avery is crazy but smiles anyway.

Turning back to face us, she looks at me and says, "You must be Rosie. It's nice to meet you." She holds her hand out, and I take it as if I can only move in slow motion.

I'm. Touching. Avery Layne.

"It's nice to meet you," I say with a voice that's much steadier than I feel.

We both look at Molly, but she's just frozen. She's smiling, but she's frozen.

"This is Molly, my business partner," I say to help my friend out.

"Hi, Molly," she says, offering her hand.

Molly looks down at it, then at me, and then back down at her hand, and she tentatively returns the greeting.

"Sorry," she says, looking back up at Avery. "I'm trying really hard to remain calm, but you should know my insides are throwing a wild party right now. It's so nice to meet you." She smiles like a kid in a candy shop, and I want to laugh.

Avery just grins at her and takes her craziness in stride. I'm sure this is a common occurrence for her.

"Can I make you a cup of tea? Or get you a bottle of water?" Molly asks.

"Oh, I'd love a cup of tea. If you have something fruity, that would be perfect." She sets her bag and her phone down on the table.

"We have peach vanilla and triple berry jam."

"Triple berry jam sounds delicious."

"Coming right up." Molly turns and heads to the back of the shop.

Avery watches her leave then finally surveys her surroundings. Her eyes are wide with wonder, and my heart swells as I can tell she loves it here.

"Oh my gosh. This place is something else." She spins in a circle to take it all in. "I loved it online, but this . . . I love all the details, and the hats—oh my. I want to try on every single one."

"I'm okay with that." I smile proudly, and she laughs, delighted.

Moving toward the fitting room, I wave Avery toward the three mannequins I've set up. The theme for this year's gala is Roaring Twenties. Avery said she didn't care how I designed the dress as long as it was theme appropriate and she was able to move around in it, but that didn't stop me from sending her a questionnaire to find out some preferences like her favorite color or desired color to wear, short or long, tight or flowing, train or no train.

"Based on your feedback from the sketches I sent over, here are three different mockups. Obviously, they aren't even close to being finished, but I wanted you to get an idea of what each gown would look like in shape, size, feel, and concept, and then we can go from there."

She stops in front of them, and her eyes grow as large as saucers. Nerves crawl their way inside me. It is very unsettling to have someone look at something you've created and judge it, especially someone like her. I hope she will love them, but there is the off chance she'll hate them.

"Oh my God, these are just beautiful."

A large exhale slips past my lips.

"Don't get me wrong, I love that you make all these gorgeous hats, but you should definitely be designing and selling gowns, too." She turns to look at me in awe.

I did think about it at one point, but my dream was always the hat shop. I think anyone who has an area of interest they love tends to be good at several different aspects of it, and designing dresses just happens to be one of mine. I could design more of them, but what would I do with them? Owning a couture dress shop feels a lot harder than owning a hat shop. Plus the number of dresses I would need to make to stock a shop doesn't sound fun to me.

Instead, I draw them up as a hobby, and then when someone I know needs a dress, like Birdie or Avery, I'm available to make them one.

"I do in my spare time. Currently, I have three dresses this season. Yours, Birdie Whitlock's of Whitlock Farm, and mine for the Bourbon Ball after the Oaks race."

While I haven't decided for certain if I'm going to the ball yet, Molly and I did talk about it. Then again, I'm not so sure now that she's dating Austin.

That's right, his name is Austin, and he is an accountant. He owns his own business, and from what she says, he's doing very well. I've asked her when I get to meet him, and all she says is "Soon."

Immediately Avery gravitates to the silver dress as Molly returns with the tea. She sets it down on the table near Avery's bag then comes to stand next to me. We both watch as she lightly touches the silver feathers of the bodice and the large Swarovski-crystal-studded sash that ties around the waist to the back of the skirt. This dress is one I drew out while I lived in New York. I didn't complete it as it really didn't match the theme of the other dresses for the collection, but I did start the bodice once I moved back to Louisville.

"This one," she says, voice just above a whisper as she reaches out to touch the front of the skirt. "It's stunning."

Her words call up a memory for me, and my heart compresses as I remember Stokes saying the exact same thing.

After the disaster of a dinner we had in New York, he insisted on seeing me home. My apartment was a tiny studio, about six hundred square feet on the Upper West Side. Instead of it looking like a place someone lived, it looked more like a craft room as I kept things strewn all over the place, including the wall that held all the drawings of dresses I was conceptually working through.

He pointed to it then looked back at me. "You drew these?"

"Yes," I told him, waiting for the insult to follow.

Only it didn't come. Instead, he took his time and looked at each and every one. There were eleven hanging up, and once he got through them all, he went back to this one and said, "If you make this, it will be stunning."

Here's the thing about creative people: we need constant reinforcement. It doesn't matter if you design houses or dresses, paint murals or write novels, there's an insecurity that incessantly lingers, but with each and every positive word, it shrinks and doesn't feel so debilitating. That one comment coming from him, even after he told me I lived in a pigpen and not like an adult—it restoked my fire to buckle down, finish my collection, and be proud of it.

"I've always loved this one," I tell her, moving to the mannequin. "This dress is actually two pieces, the bodice and then the skirt." I untie the sash. "This will have crystals sewn over the entire length and will hook in the back once we measure you." She lets out a pleased hum as I lay it to the side then continue. "The bodice is composed of silver feathers laid out in a full alternating pattern until they reach mid-chest and then will arch up over each breast. The feathers will wrap around your back where we can do a lace-up enclosure or a zipper, depending on your preference. The bodice, once complete, will be sewn onto a bodysuit to keep it flat and in place."

"I love the feathers," she says.

"There will be more of them. I just wanted you to get an idea of the pattern and the design of how they will lay. Also, the same feathers and crystals will be used in your headpiece."

"It's just so beautiful." She holds a hand to her chest.

"Thank you," I tell her, and I see Molly smiling from ear to ear. "As for the skirt, you can pick any of the three here. I'm open to suggestions, but if I had to choose, it would be the one I paired with it."

The skirt is a bubble skirt. It is very full, but I made the front short, hitting at mid-thigh, and then as it wraps around the legs, it gets longer until it drags on the ground, and there is a small train.

"Oh, I agree with you. I love this one because I'll be able to move my legs around and they'll feel free."

"If you want, we can make the whole skirt short and then add an additional piece that hooks in the front and back under the sash and kind of acts like a cape. The look will still be the same with the train, and then once you're off the red carpet, you can take it off if you want."

"I think I like that idea as it will be easier to sit and eat in."

"Perfect. All right, let's get you changed. There are bodysuits in the fitting room, go ahead and find the one that fits you the best and ignore the shoulder straps. They will be removed. From there we can start measuring and decide on any changes we want to make."

"Sounds good to me."

"Hey, Blair," I call out, and she turns to face me. "The curtains"—which are currently swept back to each side of the store and anchored by holdbacks—"they close. Will you pull them so no one can see in?"

"Got it." She moves and pulls the white sheer curtains. They are thick enough to keep people from seeing in and thin enough that natural light can still shine through.

"Is it okay if I document this and take pictures?" Molly asks tentatively. "You can delete all the ones you don't like before you leave."

"Okay." Avery smiles at her as she walks over to the tea and takes a sip.

"Should I get Blair something to drink, too?" Molly asks Avery.

"Yes, I think she would like that."

As everyone starts moving, my cell phone vibrates on the counter. I walk over to pick it up and see I have one new message. Swiping it open, I see it's from Stokes:

Good luck today.

I'm shocked he remembered this was today, but what I find more shocking is that I'm glad he remembered. It means he's thinking about me and hopefully it's ruining his day. I can feel the devil horns sprouting from my head as I smirk at his unfortunate misery. Taking the high road despite my feelings, I text him back:

Thanks.

After a solid hour of laughing, drinking tea, trying on hats, and taking more measurements than I will possibly ever need, Avery looks at me with a twinkle in her eye and asks, "Shall we take a photo?" She's pointing toward the rose wall.

"You want to take a photo with me?" I ask her, feeling shocked and flattered.

"Absolutely. All three of us can be in it. Blair will take it, but we have to pick out hats to wear."

You would have thought Avery just handed Molly a million dollars with the way she flushes and lights up like a Christmas tree.

We each select a hat, Avery stands in the middle of us, and Blair takes our photo. There's a series of us laughing with each other and then smiling nicely. She texts the photos to me so I can post them on social media and says she'll do the same, then, just like when she arrived, the car pulls up and she's gone.

Molly and I are still standing just inside the door, and it isn't until a solid five minutes of silence have passed that we turn to each other and scream.

This is one of my proudest professional moments to date.

In my pocket, my phone buzzes. I pull it out to see that Stokes has texted again:

Just saw the photos, well done.

I show Molly the text, and we both just stare at each other. It's only been five minutes, and she's already posted them. Neither of us comment on how or why Stokes has already seen them, but instead we open up the social media app and see the shop tag. There under the pictures of the three of us is the caption: *Just wait until you see what Rosie May is designing for me.* She added the heart eyes and rose emojis.

Behind us, the shop phone rings.

7

―――――

oday is April first. It's been three days since Avery was in the shop, and it's the eve of the first race of the series two championship races and officially my busy season. It's crazy how just overnight, the number of people in my shop doubled. I don't know if it's because Avery posted about my store or if this is just how the next month is going to be, but Molly joked that we were going to need a ticket system for April, and she might not be wrong. She's offered to help me this month as an employee, and I immediately said yes. I know she still has her own clients to work with, but I am going to pay her handsomely.

Next year, I'll have a better idea of whether I need one employee or two. Maybe I can even talk my mother into working a few hours a week during peak times. It would be fun to have her with me, just like now. I arrived at her house two hours ago. First, I needed to drop Birdie's dress off, and then I made my way here where we always get ready together for the Whitlock party.

"What did she think of the dress?" my mother asks.

"She said she loved it." She wouldn't tell me otherwise, but the cut and the color do suit her perfectly, and she's going to look beautiful tonight.

"I'm sure she does. You have an eye for making things that compliment anyone's size and shape," she tells me proudly as she leans closer to the mirror and applies her mascara.

The first series two championship party Birdie hosted was ten years ago. After her husband passed, investors and breeding buyers slowly started slipping away. The party was her way of showing them that Whitlock Farm is as grand as it ever was.

I remember sitting outside the tent with Molly, hidden in the shadows, and watching as the guests arrived. Birdie stood at the entrance, so regal and classy, and it was the first time I thought to myself, *I want to be like her when I grow up.*

People shook her hand, a few air-kissed her, and those who had approached with skepticism on their faces became spellbound by the air around her.

She was now the boss. She was and is the head of the family, the matriarch, and although Whitlock is an old English surname, it took no time at all for her to be revered and respected as if she was in charge of an Italian family.

That was what I wanted, and what I decided I would one day be: my own boss.

As for Stokes, being seventeen at the time, he stood next to her like the prince he is. Where people admired Birdie, they viewed him with open curiosity. No matter how he appeared in public, it's the boy behind closed doors that had them wondering what type of son or benefactor he would truly one day be. When there's as much money as there is in racehorses, a lot of thought goes into investments.

Year after year, as Stokes has stood by his mother's side, he's become beloved to the community and the doubts have slipped away.

Well, all but mine. It seemed with each passing year, his animosity toward me grew, and although I would lie in bed and dream of the day he smiled at me like he did everyone else, it never came, just the permanence of a scowl and the disdain of my existence.

I hate that even now, all these years later, he still makes me feel as if I'm unworthy of him, his time, and his respect. I shouldn't let it get to me the way that it does. After all, I'm proud of who I've become and how I'm running my life, no matter what his highness thinks of me.

I am my own boss.

I am a woman.

Hear me roar!

"Rosie, did you hear me?" my mother asks, startling me and pulling me from my thoughts and straight back to her bathroom.

"No, I'm sorry. What did you say?"

We're almost done getting ready, and I twist and turn in the mirror to see how I look, loving how this fuchsia pink short strapless dress I found in a boutique one block over from the shop looks.

"I asked if you heard about Shaded Oaks Farm." She picks up a pretty pair of chandelier earrings I found to go with her black dress.

"No, what happened?" I ask as I look at her in the mirror.

At some point over the last couple of years, my mother has transitioned from being more my mother to more my friend. I guess that happens to most the older we get, and I've loved it. We've always been close, especially since my dad died, and although we don't talk every day anymore, it's still fun to catch up and gossip when we do.

"Barn fire," she states, and both of us grimace.

"Where?" I pick up my pink gloss and perfectly apply it. Should I go with a dark color like my dress? Maybe, but with the feathered headband I'm wearing and the dress, I feel like there is enough to stand out without accentuating my lips more too.

"In Black Bandit's barn," she says, hooking one of the earrings in her ear.

Chills race down my arms. Just the thought of something like that happening to Ace's barn makes my stomach turn.

"How?"

"Well, it rained that night so they are saying it was a

lightning strike, but one can't help but wonder if that's the truth."

She's not wrong. With being just a couple weeks out from the Derby, stranger things have happened, and everyone knows to be on guard.

"How sad." I think about the family and how lovely they are and Black Bandit. I saw him in a pre-Derby championship race, and he was such a pretty horse.

"Yes. There were over a dozen horses that didn't make it out."

I gasp at the heartbreak Mr. and Mrs. Heikkinen must be feeling. "What about Black Bandit?"

"He was one of the lucky ones. So was Daffodil"—the filly they had planned on running in the Kentucky Oaks—"but both suffered severe smoke inhalation and won't be able to run."

Barn fires rarely happen anymore. I guess anything can eventually catch on fire, but with advancements made to the thoroughbred barns, it's unlikely. Then again, Shaded Oaks is one of the oldest farms in the area. Their history is what makes them so popular for tours, and I know they've kept a lot of the original integrity of the farm for appearance's sake, but it just blows my mind that a fire can still happen in a structure housing millions of dollars' worth of horses.

"Was the barn still made out of wood?" I ask her, leaning against the counter.

"I'm not sure, although a lot of barns still are."

Ace's barn is brick and mortar, with concrete blocks for

the interior and exterior. Each stall has a metal gate, lighting, and a sprinkler system in case of something like this happening. It's also continually updated as advancements come out for the health and safety of the occupants.

My heart sinks. Those poor horses.

At the front of the house, the doorbell rings, and I force myself to push away the devastation.

My mother leans in to kiss me on the cheek. "Go ahead with Molly, I'll meet you there," she says, giving me one of her motherly smiles.

After one last hug, I quickly make my way to the front and open the door. There on the other side are Molly and her new beau Austin. Their arms are wrapped around each other and both are grinning at me. I grin back, my gaze halting on Molly's.

Sometimes she looks so much like Stokes it catches me off guard. Granted, she highlights her light brown hair, making the color different, but when it's pulled back and her eyes are homed in on me, the similarities are uncanny.

Tonight, she's so happy she's glowing, and my heart expands for my dearest friend. It's easy to see how much this new guy means to her, and how much she wants everyone to welcome him.

"You look like a nerdy Clark Kent," I tell him, looking him over from head to toe, and he chuckles.

He has on a sharp black suit with a black tie. His hair is dark, slicked to the side, and he's wearing a pair of black-framed glasses.

"You must be Rosie," he says as he steps forward to shake my hand.

"The one and only." I return the greeting and smile at him.

Molly is so smitten I swear she is looking at him with hearts, wedding dresses, and babies in her eyes.

"Are you ready to go?" she asks, rolling up on her toes in excitement. Her dress is gold, and the two of them look incredible together.

"I am!" I reach down to grab my bag.

Tonight is going to be a great night.

8

———

When I was sixteen, Molly and I decided we were not going to hide behind the tent, but we were going to actually attend the party. Without telling either mother, we bought dresses and got dressed in her room, and twenty minutes after the party started, we walked up to the entrance of the tent like we owned the place.

Of course Birdie was surprised to see us, but she told us we looked beautiful and welcomed us with open arms. Stokes, on the other hand—I'm not so sure I'd ever seen him frown so hard. His scowl bordered on murderous, but I felt so pretty I didn't even care. I wasn't going to let him ruin my night, and just to stick it to him, because I knew he wouldn't even dream of stepping out of line with all of the industry people around, I danced with some of his friends.

Tonight, that same scowl is directed at the three of us as we approach the tent. Rather, I should say it's directed toward Austin, who is walking between us and now arm in arm with both of us.

"Mother," Molly says as we stop in front of them. I let go of him so Molly can properly introduce her new guy. "I'd like you to meet Austin."

She smiles at him warmly and holds out her hand. "Hello, Austin. Call me Birdie."

He takes it and returns the greeting. Meanwhile, I shove Stokes in the arm, and as his eyes flash to mine, I mentally tell him to knock it off and not ruin this for her.

He lets out a sigh, and his shoulders droop a little.

"And this is my brother, Stokes. Stokes, Austin. Austin, Stokes."

"Hey, man. It's nice to meet you," Austin says, holding his hand out and grinning like he's just found his new best friend.

Stokes plays his part. "It's great to meet you too," he replies, even though I know he's gritting his teeth.

"Wonderful!" Molly claps her hands together, beaming. "Now that introductions are done, we're going inside for a drink." She wraps her arm back around his to pull him in, and as I go to follow, Stokes reaches for my hand.

"Wait," he says.

Instantly, my eyes zero in on his hand wrapped around mine. His is warm and completely foreign, smooth, but still marked with callouses where he holds the reins from riding. Someone calls for Birdie, and suddenly it's just the two of us standing here.

"What do you want?" I pull my hand away as it tingles strangely, and I watch as his fingers curl into his palm.

Looking up at Stokes, I trace the lines of the shadows playing across his face. His jaw looks more chiseled, his lips fuller, and his eyes are full-on hazel—the perfect mixture to make my stomach suddenly flip.

"Reconsider," he says, taking a step toward me and almost entering my personal space.

"Reconsider what?" I ask, looking up at him.

"Tonight. Me," he says, as if that's the simplest explanation in the world.

His face is so open and skirting on vulnerable that I almost say yes, but let's be real here—he's never vulnerable. He's Stokes Whitlock, the golden child.

"What is wrong with you?" I ask, and in an instant, shutters flip down, closing him off. He pauses for three breaths as he watches me, but he knows the rejection is coming. He takes a step back and shoves his hands into his pockets.

"Never mind," he says, more to himself than to me. That response is shrouded in disappointment and irritation as he dismisses me and looks over my shoulder and out into the night.

I stand there and give him two seconds to take back the attitude he's just thrown my way, one I didn't deserve, but he doesn't. Instead, he ignores me as if I'm not even there. My emotional wall pings as if it's been hit. Why, I don't know. He's always treated me this way, and he wonders why I said no. Whatever. Shaking my head, I let out a disconcerted sigh and wander off into the tent, leaving him at his post.

I can't help but look back at him, suddenly feeling bad for telling him no, even though I have every right to. Birdie hasn't returned and he's standing there alone, and for the first time, I actually wonder if he likes his life. Has he embraced it? Yes, but has anyone ever asked him if it's what he wants? They say it's lonely at the top, and right at this moment, he looks really lonely.

Then again, he made his bed—he can lie in it.

Turning, I take in the scene before me, and it's just breathtaking. There's white gauzy fabric draped around the perimeter, high top tables decorated with green, blue, and white arrangements, too many hurricane lanterns to count illuminating the space in the most magical way, an eleven-piece band toward the rear, and a large bar where I find Molly, Austin, and a few of our friends.

Once Stokes left for college, I was finally out from under his thumb, and for the first time since moving to the farm, I made friends other than Molly.

Thirty minutes later, Stokes joins us, and while he doesn't outright acknowledge me, he also doesn't leave my side. When people approach me, he turns and stands there as if he is a part of the conversation. When we go off to dance, he follows and stands near me at the edge, and when people approach him, he somehow maneuvers me in front of him and forces me to participate in the conversation versus ignoring him and being rude.

Even though I shoot him a gazillion dirty looks, he

pretends he doesn't see any of them, and this goes on for a solid hour.

Having had all I can take, I grab Stokes by the sleeve and pull him through one of the tent flaps so we are standing on the outside and no one can see us. He shakes his arm free the minute we are alone.

"Seriously." I grit my teeth. "What is your deal? Why are you hovering so close to me?" I growl up at him.

His eyes roam my face, and it feels oddly intimate. I mean, what is he looking at?

"Stokes?" I all but demand he answers.

"Well, I guess because you're disposable if I need to save myself," he replies, his pompousness shining brighter than the moon.

"Really? That's what you have to say to me? You are unreal," I hiss while mentally grabbing that expensive tie around his neck, yanking, and twisting.

He says nothing, but the way his chest is rising and falling lets me know he's breathing harder than normal.

"Stop hovering and leave me alone," I mutter just loud enough so he can hear me.

He continues to stare at me, and then in a firm voice, he says, "No."

"What do you mean no?" I throw my arms out. "This isn't up for discussion." I've already told him several times that I don't want to play the role of his date tonight.

His hard gaze bores into me, and then he lets out a long sigh as he again tears his eyes away and aims them to look across one of the fields. It's dark out here, and I watch as he blinks and his long lashes fan against his cheek. The two ever-present lines slip between his eyes as he shakes his head in anger. Anger at me? I don't know, but I'm officially over it and him, and I have to fight to keep my body under control.

Exasperated and done waiting for a response, I storm away and walk back into the party.

"I need a drink," I mutter to myself as I make my way toward the bar, which is on the opposite side. Then someone grabs my arm and spins me around.

Stokes. Again.

He's officially driven me to the edge and I could scream, but Stokes has gone completely rigid, his hand is tightening more by the second, and he swears under his breath.

"Rosie." His eyes lock onto mine, and there's an unexpected desperation in them. "Just this one time, will you please play along?" he asks, his lips barely moving.

"What are you talking about?"

Just then, he steps forward, wraps his hands around my face, and moves his lips just a breath away from mine. I'm two seconds away from flapping my arms like a wild bird needing to flee when his forehead presses against mine, and he breathes out a "*Please.*"

Have I thought about what it would be like to kiss Stokes? Absolutely, only every day of my teenage years, but then I grew up and reality set in. That unrequited love I held for him, that slow-burning ember . . . it finally winked out, and I let it.

Seeing my hesitation and taking that as a yes, he tilts my head and settles his mouth on mine.

Oh. My. God.

What is happening?

My eyes are wide open and so are his, my brown to his hazel. He's watching me, and I'm watching him, and I'm completely frozen.

"Kiss me back, Thorney," he mumbles onto my lips, all commanding, and against every fiber of my being, I give in and do.

Without even having to think about it, my body knows exactly how to proceed. I rise up on my toes, and my arms wrap around his neck, one hand slipping into his hair as I lean into him. My eyes shut, and I revel in the feel of his soft, full lips hoping to become acquainted with mine.

He lets out a sigh, almost like it's a long overdue sigh, and one of his hands drops from my face to my rib cage where he wraps his large palm around me and pulls me further into him. I can feel all five fingertips and the heat from his body as it warms mine. I'm also engulfed in his smell. He smells like melons, sage, and smooth leather. It's exquisite, invoking a thousand memories from my lifetime at the farm, and

I don't know if I can do this. It's too much.

I try to pull away from him, but Stokes just tightens his grip to hold me in place.

"Stokes," I whisper, and he shakes his head.

"No. Not yet." He tilts my head just a little more and

deepens the kiss in a way I never ever thought I'd be experiencing with him.

The world slips away, and I allow myself to be lost in the slowest most decadent kiss I've ever had. The way his tongue takes its time, licks against mine and the way his teeth graze both of my lips. The way I can feel parts of him pressing into my stomach I never imagined I'd feel and the way his large hand slides up a little higher and his thumb gently brushes the underside of my boob. Right now, no matter what has ever been said or done between us, it doesn't matter. He is all in for this kiss, and apparently so am I.

A kiss with the enemy.

Well, maybe not a full-blown enemy, at least not anymore.

That's when ice water trickles into my veins, dousing the flames that had wrapped around us in this heated and very hot moment, and I gasp.

Pulling back, I look up into his face, a face that's so close to mine, and all I can think is, *What have we done?*

What have I done?

Taking a step away, I break eye contact and look at the ground. My hands involuntarily clasp at my heart, and one of his slips to my elbow to hold me in place. I can feel him watching me as I try to regain my composure.

A throat clears next to us, and my head jerks to find Molly staring at us with wide, shocked eyes. We are, after all, standing under the middle of the tent, and that kiss happened in front of everyone. The most intimate moment

I feel I've ever had was in plain sight, surrounded by mostly his people: other thoroughbred farm owners, some of his colleagues, and his friends.

This is horrible.

And humiliating.

"What's going on here?" she asks. The color has receded from her face. I'm not sure if it's from shock or displeasure, but she's clearly struggling, just like I am. Austin is standing right behind her, confused and watching the scene between the three of us play out.

My gaze flies back to Stokes. His hands are now off of me, in his pockets, and as he watches me, his "Rosie face" has returned.

"Nothing," he answers. His cheeks are pink, but his jaw is locked tight.

More humiliation crawls up from my stomach to my throat, and I think there's a real possibility I'm going to be sick.

"Nothing," I parrot, whispering more to him than her, that word seemingly hurting my soul way more than I should be allowing it to.

Whatever he sees on my face has the hard look in his eyes shifting to almost remorseful, and his Adam's apple bobs as he swallows.

"Heather was headed this way, and well, now she's not," he says quietly, his stare still locked on mine.

Heather.

Right.

I know Heather, and I remember her from New Year's

Eve. The Blantons hosted a party at their farm that most of Louisville's social scene attended, and once she set her sights on him, he was done. It was like instead of having two arms, she had eight. They were octopused all over him all the time, and no matter how hard he tried to get her to leave him be, she was there pawing at him until he eventually got fed up and left.

"So you decided to kiss her?" Molly whisper-shouts.

He doesn't answer her. In fact, he's full-on ignoring her as his attention is locked on me and my reaction to what just happened.

Did he just take the kiss? No.

But that doesn't mean I actually wanted this.

Yet, I conceded.

This is terrible.

Recognizing the meaning of the lump crawling its way up my throat and the burning behind my eyes, I spin on my heels and make a beeline for the exit. I smile at people as I pass them, and I realize, with horror and clarity, people are staring at me. They saw that kiss. It will be talked about.

Why this matters to me, I don't know. It's just . . . it's Stokes.

Cool air hits my face the second I leave the tent. I didn't notice it before, but now I do. My skin is burning, my eyes are welling even more with unwanted tears, and I just need to get out of here.

So much for a great night.

"Rosie, wait," Stokes calls after me.

I don't. Bending down, I slip off my heels, grab them, and run.

Of course his long legs eat up the distance between us, and he keeps pace next to me all the way to my mother's house where my car is. All of my things are already in my car because I wasn't sure how late we would be up tonight, and I didn't want to bother my mother in case she had gone to bed. I'd also rather be at the shop in the morning than here and have to drive in.

"If you're going to apologize, there's no need," I tell him through labored breaths. I just want him to go away.

"Apologize? Why would I do that?" he asks, and I turn to face him, shocked. I know he sees the traitorous tears that always come when I'm mad, because he sucks in air like I've personally wounded him and suddenly looks so bereft it's almost comical.

Down by my sides, one hand tightens around my shoes and the other clenches the fabric of my skirt. "Maybe because you just kissed me against my will. You're a lawyer —you should know that's harassment."

He doesn't answer right away. Instead, his gaze continues to travel over my face and trace the tracks of my tears. Then, as if my words have finally registered, he chuckles in that dark delicious way of his that has my eyes dropping to his mouth and now sends my toes curling.

No.

This cannot be happening.

"Don't you mean sexual assault?" he mocks as he takes a step closer, and I lean back against my car.

Hearing him say the word sexual has my lower stomach tightening. Truth is, he and I both know he didn't assault me; I was a willing participant.

Willing and stupid.

Looking up at him as he's barely left any space between us, I mentally curse the moon for highlighting the angles of his profile, making his face even more handsome.

"I hope you enjoyed yourself, because it will never happen again," I say through gritted teeth and a few more tears.

He raises his arms, and both of his hands land on my car, bracketing my head. I watch as he slowly lowers himself even closer to me and his smell, which I now realize is as familiar as home, wraps around me.

Squeezing my eyes shut as his warm breath brushes across my cheek to my ear, I shiver. I should be shoving him away, but I can't. I'm frozen and stuck on the fact that he's just so close to me.

After a beat, he gently wipes away the moisture with his thumb, his temple comes to rest against mine, and, voice low, he says, "Yes, it will."

And then he's gone.

LUVU TEA
WE'RE OFF TO THE RACES

Good morning, dear Louisvillians! We are up and running at full speed today as the season begins not only its series two championship races, but apparently also the race for our most eligible bachelor's heart!

Last night, Whitlock Farm hosted its infamous annual season party. Dripping in grandeur and refined taste, Mrs. Whitlock outdid herself on creating an enchanting night. While we were intent on sharing all of the most delicious tea, none of what landed in our inbox is as tasty as this. It seems we have a filly who's entered the race—the race for our bachelor, that is.

As you can see from the images provided, Mr. Whitlock and his date very much enjoyed each other's company and the party last night. The pair were seen talking, laughing, dancing, kissing, and even leaving early. So who might this little filly be? A local by the name of Rosie May. Rosie owns a hat shop in NuLu and can be found on all major social media sites.

Sources tell us Stokes and Rosie are childhood friends and have known each other most of their lives. While their friendship has been unique, time and time again, the two have always gravitated back toward each other. Be still our romantic hearts. Friends to lovers is a trope we definitely stand behind here at the Tea. Is that what this is? Is this their time? And are you going to get a front-row view of their fairy tale? I hope so, but there's only one way for you to find out—hit that subscribe button and come steep along.

9

———

The first time I saw Stokes was actually before we were introduced.

We had only been at the farm for two days. My mother and I, both still deeply grieving the loss of my father, were living more side by side than we were together. We were both quiet, internally dealing with all the sudden changes, and while she unpacked our new house, I spent time outside wandering the property. No one told me I couldn't, and I found the endless fields of bluegrass and fresh air therapeutic.

That particular day, I had wandered off into the trees and found a stream running through the property. I was lying in the shade staring up through the leaves when I felt the ground vibrate. It was the telltale sign of hooves pounding against the earth, and as the seconds passed, it got stronger and stronger.

Sitting up, I did my best to blend in with the trunk of

the tree just as a horse went racing by and then came to a sudden stop. There was a boy with light brown hair on the back of it wearing a black T-shirt and jeans. No shoes, no saddle, just him and the horse.

At the time, I didn't know it was Stokes. It could have been anyone's kid, but as I watched him slip off the horse, stand next to it, and yell as loud as he could into the trees, I knew it was him. My mother had told me about him and Molly.

Over and over, he yelled, sometimes bent at the waist with his hands in fists, ready to fight, and other times with his head thrown back like he was calling to God. In the end, he fell to his knees, slumped over, and cried. I cried with him because I knew exactly how he felt.

I never told him about that moment. It was meant to be private, but I felt bonded to him in a way he would never understand, and I thought of him endlessly as a kindred spirit.

When we did finally meet, a few days later on their front porch, although his height and hair color were the same, he was not. This boy was quiet, controlled, stoic. While Molly was excited to meet me, he just stared at me as if he was completely indifferent and it was a waste of his time. The strings on the bond I had created between the two of us began to unravel at a rapid rate, and I felt foolish. He inadvertently hurt my feelings, and he wasn't even aware of it.

Although that might have been the first time my feelings were hurt by Stokes Whitlock, as we all know, it certainly wasn't the last, which is why it should come as no surprise that I have dark circles under my eyes and a raging headache this morning.

I didn't sleep a wink. How could I?

Never have I been more mortified as a result of my actions or, quite frankly, his. I still have no idea what he was thinking planting his lips on mine, and I have absolutely no understanding of why I agreed.

It's insane.

I'm insane.

That must be what is happening to me—I'm going insane.

And what does any insane person do? They obsess over false realities.

I can't stop thinking about his hands on my body, the feel of his face and his hair under my fingertips, his tongue as it so expertly moved against mine, tasting as much as he could. Stokes has unknowingly ruined any other kiss I will ever receive from anyone else going forward. It was so good and so life-altering that just replaying it in my mind is causing unwanted heat flashes.

So. Unfair.

Bursting through the door at two minutes after ten, Molly waves her phone like a crazy person. Yesterday, she said she'd be here when the shop opened, but considering how much fun she was having with Austin last night, I wasn't expecting her until at least noon. Then again, we haven't had a chance to talk about what happened last night.

"Did you see the Tea?" she half-yells at me. No *Hi, how are you?* or *Are you okay?* Part of me was even expecting, *What in the world took over your body and possessed you to kiss my brother?*

I groan, and my head drops to my arms, which are draped across the counter.

Not only did I see the Tea, now aside from just the people at the party, the whole world has seen Stokes kissing me.

I mean, it wasn't even that long of a kiss, at least I don't think so, but there we are headlining, front and center this morning for the article breakdown of last night's party.

"Molly, this is horrible," I whine into my hands.

I'd like to say I'm above all this and can be nonchalant about the whole thing as if it were nothing, but I can't.

I'm traumatized.

Again the bell over the door rings, and my head pops up to find Stokes casually striding toward us. Where I look like I've been run over by a semi, he looks as fresh as a daisy in a dark gray sweater and jeans.

"Oh, big brother, you've done it now," Molly teasingly warns as she moves to stand next to me.

He comes to stand on the other side of the counter from us and sets down three coffees and a bag. Without saying a word, he opens the bag and pulls out a clear plastic to-go box with the most heavenly piece of toast I've ever seen. It's large and covered with smashed avocado, pickled radishes, crumbled goat cheese, and salt and pepper.

My mouth waters as he sets the box and one coffee My front of me.

Instantly my arms wrap around them, and I pull them closer as if the items don't already know they're mine.

"Peace offering," he says, his light eyes meeting mine.

My stomach dips and swirls at the connection, and I hate that right at this moment, I have to remind myself that he and his perfect kiss are not my friend, but a foe.

"Whitlock, I appreciate the breakfast, but you must know there will never be peace between us, only war, especially after that stunt you pulled last night."

Next to me, Molly grabs her coffee. She mumbles about liquid fuel and how much it's needed as Stokes and I continue to stare at each other like we're about to participate in a gun-slinging showdown.

He shifts so he's leaning against the counter and facing me. "While I'll agree with you that it wasn't my finest moment, need I remind you that you neither challenged nor resisted me?"

He brought lawyer Stokes with him this morning, and I just don't have it in me to stand tall, fix my ponytail, and spar with him. I let out a groan and drop my head again so I don't have to look at him. If I do, I'll be swayed to look at his lips, because, again, I'm going insane, and I refuse to give him the satisfaction.

Next to me, Molly cracks the lid on her coffee, and the smell of hazelnut hits us both. She murmurs, "My favorite."

"You realize this is a good thing, right?" he says to me, ignoring his sister.

"How do you figure?" I ask, inhaling a deep breath and finally lifting my head.

Will I ever be able to look at him and not think about his hands on me, how well he kisses, how he tastes, and how he feels pressed against me?

"Because now I'll be left alone." His eyes are bright with delight, and he's giving me his version of a smile, lips closed with one corner tipped up higher than the other. "Well, mostly."

He'll be left alone. Part of me wonders if there's something more going on with him than we know, but then again, he's a lawyer and should be able to handle these things.

Ignoring him, I open the box, and as I'm swiping my finger through the avocado spread, a thought hits me, and I find I'm now wondering about the spontaneity and legitimacy of that kiss after all.

"Did you plan this?" I ask, looking back up at him and sucking the spread off my finger.

His eyes watch the movement of my mouth, color rises to his cheeks, and then his gaze comes back to mine, a smidge darker than before.

"No, but I wish I had. It's brilliant. You can be my girlfriend until the season is over," he says so smoothly and in a way that is meant to leave no room for discussion.

Having just taken a sip of her coffee at that exact moment, Molly starts to choke, coughing loudly. He looks at her with concern pressing his brow down as she grabs a napkin to wipe her mouth, and then his eyes shift back to me, waiting for a response, only all I can hear echoing in my head is *my girlfriend.*

Girlfriend.

I'm speechless, and I'm never speechless. The sad part about all this is if it were anyone else, I would have said yes in a heartbeat. I'm loyal to my friends, so loyal I'm like a puppy that rolls over on command or will bring the shovel, if you catch my drift, but you have to be a friend to have friends, and Stokes has made it clear time and time again that he is not mine.

"I mean listen," he says, "I firmly stand in the camp of a woman can do what she wants, but you're trying to build a reputation here. You might want to think about which reputation you want to be labeled with." If the knife that came with the toast were anything but plastic, he'd be lucky if I didn't aim it at his chest like I'm playing darts and throw it.

No, he did not.

"Oh my God. What is wrong with you?" Molly yells at him.

"There's nothing wrong with me." He looks back and forth between the two of us. "All I'm saying is Louisville is in many ways a small town. People saw us together, it's gone viral, and no matter what might or might not have happened, assumptions are being made."

I hear him. I do. I just can't help but wonder what he stands to gain from this. Is he being sincere, or is he doing this just to somehow get an advantage over me, and if so, for what purpose?

"Why do you want this so bad?" I ask him.

"I have my reasons," he says, tilting his head up a little and refusing to elaborate.

"Maybe you should enlighten us," Molly says, but he ignores her.

Letting out an annoyed sigh, he turns away and walks toward the front window, where he tucks his hands in the pockets of his pants. I know he's just a guy—a guy I can't stand—but even though he's not in a suit today, it's still easy to see how large he is, and not just because of his size. Just standing by the window, he has this air about him. It's broody but powerful, arrogant but solid. He is someone, and I need to remind myself of that while I unfortunately contemplate this.

"I'd rather not," he replies, his words clipped.

"You are so infuriating," I yell at him across the store.

The thing is, I have no idea how we would even be able to pull this off. We aren't friends. We really never have been. We're forced together through circumstance, but even then, we barely tolerate each other. He's always being condescending or dismissive to me. We're spiteful to each other. I love to point out how he's so boring and a stick in the mud, and he loves to remind me that he thinks I'm nothing more than a hot mess and a nuisance.

We are different.

We are different in the way we think, the way we live, and how we work.

There is no place on this earth where I think we can coexist and not kill each other.

Turning, he looks at me one last time before he walks out and says, "Just think about it."

Yeah, pal, I think not.

10

It's a little after six when my phone pings with an incoming text, and I'm up in my apartment in the second bedroom I use as a workshop. My plan had been to keep the shop open until eight each night this month, but since Avery's picture and the article in the Tea was posted a couple of days ago, I have been swamped and am suddenly worried I might run out of inventory.

Stokes was right.

Granted, he's rarely wrong, and just the thought of his smug face makes my blood boil. He will forever be silently gloating over this. He won't even need to say a word; he'll just raise one brow and his point will be made. Being seen with him is good for business. For that I hate him.

I reach for my phone, and the locked screen shows a message from Stokes. Instantly I grind my teeth together. Swiping it open, I see it says:

Bringing over dinner, be there in twenty.

So not invited.

So bossy.

Ugh.

Moving into my living room, I give it a once-over. I pick up a few things that are lying around and load the dishes that were in the sink into the dishwasher. I'm not sure why any of this matters, but for some reason it does, and as I'm wrapping up, the buzzer rings for the downstairs door.

With a deep, resigned sigh, I hit the button to let him up, and because he's not a small guy, I can hear every step he takes coming up the stairs.

Then there's a pause as he stands outside my door.

What is he doing?

Tiptoeing over, I peek through the eyehole and see him standing there with one hand wrapped around a bag and the other on his hip. He's looking down, I'm not sure at what, but as his spine straightens, it's as if his brick walls, which keep him so stiff, are falling into place one at a time. He runs his hand through his hair then roughly knocks, which causes me to jump.

Taking a deep breath, I open the door, and we both stare at each other. I'm wearing a pair of athletic shorts and a tank top. He's wearing a Kentucky Wildcats T-shirt and jeans. He looks so casual I feel like I'm looking at someone completely different.

Without a word, I open the door a little wider, and he

tentatively steps inside while taking a slow, long look around.

It was bad enough to have Stokes perusing my shop, but to have him in my apartment somehow just feels wrong. Maybe it's because, aside from the day I moved in, I haven't had any guy here in my space.

This apartment is pretty standard. The living room and kitchen is one large space, and then there are two bedrooms. The master has its own bathroom, and there is another in the hallway. It doesn't have much character, pretty basic except for the outer wall being brick just like downstairs and the vaulted ceiling.

He clears his throat. "This reminds me of your apartment in the city."

"It should," I say, closing the door behind him. "I'm the same person with the same furniture."

He levels me with a flat look before walking past me and into the kitchen. Of course I follow, and he's barely opened the takeout bag when I catch a whiff of curry. He brought Thai food, which I never said to him was my favorite, and I can't help but wonder if he somehow already knew this. He at least knew he was playing it safe by bringing something he knows I like.

"Would you like a beer? Water? Wine?" I ask him, reminding myself to take the high road and be polite.

"A beer would be great," he says, looking at me over the kitchen table. "Thank you."

Thank you. Looks like he's going to be on his best behavior too.

I grab two beers from my refrigerator along with two plates and silverware then make my way to the table. If someone had told me Stokes Whitlock would be in my apartment tonight, I would have laughed them right out of town, bet the bank, and declared them mental. Yet here he is, and somehow the space feels smaller.

He sits down at the table then looks around the apartment again.

"I like it. It looks like you."

Is that meant to be a compliment or an insult? One can never tell with him.

"And what do I look like?" I ask, feeling somewhat defensive. It's not meant to be a test, but I am curious if he'll be kind or not.

His gaze falls to me as I start unloading the to-go boxes, and I can feel the heat climbing up into my cheeks. If he notices, he doesn't let on. I'd hate for him to get the wrong idea and think his opinion of me matters when it doesn't. It stopped mattering a long time ago.

"Colorful. Comfortable. Familiar."

So he went with kind. Smart boy. We both know he's here because he wants me to be his fake girlfriend, and he's bright enough to know he can catch more flies with honey than vinegar.

Sitting down across from him, I empty half of one container onto my plate and then reach for the other.

"I wasn't sure what you like. I remembered the panang from lunch, so hopefully these will work," he says, grabbing the box I just had and scooping out the rest.

"Everything from there works. No matter what you get, you can't go wrong," I tell him, and one corner of his mouth lifts.

He's pleased to know I like what he brought.

"Noted."

Together we eat in silence, except for the country music playing in the background, but I don't hear it because my brain is too busy arguing with itself. The majority of it is urging me to tell him to leave, while the rest is saying I should hear him out. After all, I'm also trying to consider the success of my business here.

As he takes a sip of his beer, I have to force my eyes away from his face, his mouth against the bottle, and his neck as he swallows.

"So, have you thought about it?" he asks, leaning back in his chair and looking way too comfortable.

I could lie to him and say absolutely not, but he'd probably see right through me and know the truth anyway.

"I have," I tell him as I match his posture and wipe my mouth with my napkin.

"And?" he asks, his brows raised, hopeful.

I lean forward, pick up the beer, and take a sip before I answer. "I just don't know if I think it's a good idea," I say honestly.

He rubs the back of his neck as his predictable scowl is trying its hardest to drop into place, but he holds it off. "Tell me why."

Oh, here we go.

"First off, I'm so busy I'm not even sure how I could

help you if I agreed to this stupid plan. Second, anyone who knows us will know this is fake—there's no love lost between us. And well, third, I don't like who I am when I'm around you."

He frowns, and this time the scowl wins.

"Being mean is not a trait I possess around anyone else but you. I'm not built that way, Stokes, and after every interaction with you, I walk away with a stomachache. I don't like it. I don't like you. You are not nice to me, never have been. I honestly feel like I owe you nothing, and I have no idea how you expect us to get along in front of people for extended periods of time."

His lips press together, color dots his cheeks, and his eyes shift down and off to the side. He doesn't like what I've just said, though I'm not sure exactly which part.

"I can do better," he says sincerely, and then his gaze comes back to mine. "Look, it's not for that long, only four and a half weeks. Then the season will be over, and we can slip silently back into our normal lives with no one the wiser."

"Listen, I get it. I understand how the photos looked, and I understand that you are someone here in this town, and it could be good for my shop, but I'm just not sure I can do it."

And I mean that wholeheartedly. When I'm in prolonged situations where I'm uncomfortable, I become anxious, and it makes me turn inward and lose myself. I have too much riding on this season to feel emotionally off my game. I like the place I'm in now. I feel strong, independent, and like I'm providing value to the community and to myself. Being with him could very easily squash how hard I've worked, and I can't risk that.

"We'll only have to be together a few times," he counters, his bravado looking a little more shaken and less firm.

"Like how many and for what?" I start tearing the napkin on my lap.

"I have a work function coming up this weekend, and then there's the Oaks and the Derby. Three times. Plus, let me take you to dinner. It doesn't have to be a long outing. As long as we're seen, that should be good enough."

"I'm not planning on going to the Oaks. I have to work that day, and good enough for what? I don't understand. This is so extreme, especially for you."

Pulling out his phone, he opens one of his social media accounts and shifts closer to me as he flips it around to show me the inbox. Name after name, message after message from women—and some men—asking him out, wanting to know if he'd like to meet up and get a drink.

Then, he turns his phone back around to face him and opens his voice messages. Angling it my way, he scrolls down so I can see there are so many he hasn't listened to from numbers not on his contact list, but the dictations are basically all the same.

"All of this is because of the one 'bachelor of the season' article?" I ask, suddenly irritated for him.

"Yes," he says in that flat tone of his.

"How did they get your number?"

He lets out a frustrated sigh. "I have no idea. I'm half tempted to change it."

Then he pulls up his work email account. He slides the phone across to me, and I pick it up. There are more messages here, so many more messages, inundating his business account.

"But why?" I look up at him, confused.

"Who the fuck knows," he says, surprising me with the harshness and leaning back in his chair. He runs his hand over his face, clearly annoyed and tired. "Why do people do what they do? I don't get it. I'm not that interesting. I work all the time. Between the office and the farm, I hardly ever go out in public unless it's required, and I'm honest enough with myself to know I'm a boring guy."

There are many things in that statement that are true. He is a boring guy. He has a subdued personality and never gets overly excited about anything, but where he's wrong is that he is interesting. It's easy to see he is intelligent, loves his family, and is hardworking, and most know he comes from money. Oh, and don't forget that he is easy on the eyes.

"There has to be someone else you can ask to do this," I say. Surely he has a friend or someone willing to play along.

"Like who?" he asks like he's suddenly offended.

"How should I know?" I fire back. "I know nothing about your life."

"That's not true. I'm quite certain you know me more than anyone else." He stands and begins pacing, looking around my apartment, and then he stops at the front window and looks out. It never occurred to me that I might be able to see where he lives. Is that what he's doing, looking for his home and wishing he were there?

I scoff. "I find that hard to believe."

I stand as well and start to clear off the table. Dinner is over; I can't see him staying much longer. I mean, there's no reason for him to.

He turns to face me and crosses his arms over his chest. His biceps fill the space under the sleeves of his T-shirt, and I hate that I continually notice how nice his arms are.

"Seriously, what difference does it make?" He's frustrated. "It's not like it's a hardship for you to pretend to be with me," he says.

I drop the containers in the garbage and begin waving my finger back and forth between the two of us. "We don't like each other."

"I like you just fine." His tone says my statement is one hundred percent false and absurd.

Whatever expression slides onto my face has him letting out a long exhale, and his arms drop by his sides.

"I do like you just fine," he tells me.

I laugh because that remark is completely false, and I make my way to stand in front of him.

"A little less than a year after I moved to your farm, you found me one day on the back of the property sitting next to the stream by myself."

"Yeah, I remember. You were fourteen, and I was sixteen," he says, as if that memory was just yesterday.

"Yep. You rode up next to me on one of your giant horses, made fun of me for being there by myself, and when I cried, you called me a crybaby and told me to grow up before you rode off."

The muscles in his face slip and his lips turn down in a frown.

"It was the anniversary of my father's death."

He closes his eyes.

"When I was fifteen and in the tenth grade, you told the whole school not to talk to me, so no one did. No one, Stokes. The only friend I had for the longest time was Molly."

He looks away from me and down at his feet. More color blooms on his cheeks as he sucks in his bottom lip to chew on it.

"When I was sixteen, I spent a whole month saving my money and working on my very first Derby hat. I was so proud of that hat, and then when we all loaded up to leave for Churchill Downs, you said to me, 'You're not going to wear that, are you?' You made this disgusted face, and I'd never felt more humiliated. Need I go on?"

I hate reliving these moments. It's not that I think he truly cares about how he behaved or can even process how he made me feel, but he needs to understand I am not beholden to him for anything.

"Rosie." His voice is deeper and tinged with regret, yet he doesn't apologize. Why can't he just say he's sorry? The glow from the streetlight outside reflects off his sharp cheekbone. It's there in the way he's clenching his jaw; I can see it, but he won't give it to me.

"I just don't understand why you want me to do this with you or why you think, after twelve years of comments like that, I will?"

Twelve years of comments and apparently no apology.

My heart aches, opening old wounds.

"Well, I guess the way I see it, the damage is done. The pictures are out there, so why not?"

"The damage might be done, and yes, the pictures are out there, but you still haven't answered my question."

My hands find their way to my hips. I feel grounded, my feet planted firmly. I've kind of trapped him next to the window, and my words leave no room for the topic to turn in another direction.

His eyes lock onto mine, and he isn't just looking at me; he's imploring me to do this with him, his laser gaze aiming straight down into the heart of me.

"I am hearing you. I can see how, from your point of view, this might not be the best arrangement for you, but I promise I will be better. I do recognize my part in our dysfunctional relationship over the years, but Rosie, I'm begging you—you and only you. Please do this with me. I will not bother you, I will be there for you if you need me in any way, and I'll do my part by talking up your shop."

Curse my personality. The loyal side of me is screaming to help him, even after all the things he's said and done, and the insecure side of me is upping the ante by insisting it'd be nice to have some support outside of myself and Molly for the next couple of weeks.

But I know how these things go. Fool me once, shame on you. Fool me twice, shame on me. There will be no three strikes and he's out—it's one and I'm done.

"Fine."

"Yeah?" he asks, a small grin moving in. He looks so relieved it's almost palpable.

"But, I'm only going to tell you this one time." I point my finger at him. "No one is allowed to treat me badly, especially you. One wrong move and it's over. I don't trust you, and don't think for one second that I'll keep my mouth shut either. Just as quickly as this went viral, I can make your golden boy persona disappear. Do you understand what I'm saying?"

"I do," he says gently.

His words hit a tender spot deep in my soul, a spot I thought I washed away years ago, but apparently it's just lain dormant and covered with dust. Then, to top it all off, he smiles at me. It's not a fake smile, not one he uses for other people. It's not even one he uses for his family. This smile is one I've never seen and always wanted, and deep down where that spot lives, it recognizes that it's just for me.

This situation has nothing but disaster stamped all over it, and I realize he still hasn't answered my question.

11

———————

When we first moved to the farm, I was in awe of the fields, the trees, and the space, space I'd never had before. Granted, I was sad to leave my childhood home, but it was in an outlying neighborhood of Louisville, where the streets are lined with houses one next to the other. The two houses are about the same size, and while I hated leaving my friends, I didn't hate leaving behind all the stares, whispers, and pity.

Like my mother, I needed to move on and start fresh.

Hours and hours I spent wandering the property, breathing in the fresh air, and mending my broken heart. Of course scars remain, as that's what happens when a loved one dies—it's permanently with you—but under the trees and by the stream, little by little, pieces of happiness found their way in.

Occasionally, Molly would join me, but most of the time I was by myself. Well, that is except for when I discovered Stokes had followed me at a distance, sometimes on foot, other times on horseback. I never was certain why he was following me. It wasn't like I was going to get into any trouble or cause problems out in the middle of nowhere, but he was there lingering in the background, which always made me feel like I was doing something wrong, even though I wasn't.

All week now, with this fake title hanging over my head, I again feel like I'm doing something wrong. I know I'm not, but still. I'm an honest person, and in a way this feels dishonest. Dishonest to who? I don't know. I just feel strange, and he isn't helping matters at all.

He came over two nights ago, which was when we decided to do this thing until the Derby. Then yesterday he showed up with a huge bouquet of light pink roses, which of course was photographed outside my shop and almost immediately posted online, and then this morning he brings me coffee.

It's unnatural and confusing.

We don't even say anything; we just stare at each other. Well, I would say I more glare, but that's my default, and around him, I'm not sure how to be any different.

Yesterday, I was so shocked I barely uttered a thank you, and all he gave me was a small closed-mouth smile. Today, I was so mesmerized by the scent of espresso and caramel wafting out of the hole in the lid, I forgot he was there until he told me to have a nice day and left.

Of course Molly thinks this is hilarious and is loving watching her brother do nice things for me, but it's such a contradiction to the Stokes I've known for so long that for a split second, I wondered if he'd poisoned the coffee.

Coffee I savored until the last drop.

Now, hours later, as customers filter in and out, faces, hats, and colors are blending together. Every time I go to help someone new, I see Stokes's eyes instead of theirs, and when I stand at the counter, the memories of his strange newfound kindness and then his lips on mine threaten to overwhelm me. What have I gotten myself into?

"I just can't believe someone stole their horse!" I hear whispered animatedly from the counter adjacent to mine.

I frown as the dark-haired woman's words register, and I switch to eavesdropping. Who knew owning a hat shop would involve such gossip, as if it is a salon?

"Right! That horse is worth millions, too, from what they paid for the bloodline, the purse winnings, and the stud fees that were sure to come," the woman next to her says.

Someone stole a prize horse?

How is that even possible? And which farm was it? I glance to the other side of the shop to see if Molly heard them, but it doesn't appear so. She's helping two younger customers with fascinators.

I scan the women to see if I might have some sort of recognition, but I don't. Both appear to be in their forties, and both appear to have money as they are wearing and carrying brands like Gucci and Valentino. They didn't have an appointment, they just wandered in from the street to try on hats.

"What did Eloise say happened exactly?" the dark-haired one asks while picking up a red hat that is decorated with red ostrich feathers and pearl and crystal adornments.

Eloise.

The only Eloise I know of in the thoroughbred community is Eloise Blanton, and their farm is adjacent to Whitlock Farm. My stomach churns with unease. That's not to say there couldn't be another, but how often do you hear the words Eloise, horse, and millions lumped together? I think of Mrs. Blanton from the New Year's Eve party, and I feel just awful for them. They are such nice people.

The other woman picks up a bright yellow fascinator. For that one, I shaped a wide yellow sheer ribbon with starch into a bow so it would hold and surrounded it with navy leaves and long yellow feathers. She's already tried it on once and now must be considering it.

"They were headed to a friend's farm last week as they were going to race in the Florida Derby at Gulfstream Park. On the way, they were hijacked."

Darkhaired woman gasps with wide eyes, and I have to hold mine in.

"How did no one see this happening? It's not like the truck and the horse trailer are small." She frowns as she places the red hat on her head, and I can't help but think it looks really good on her. Some hats and colors are just made for people, and while I hate to say it, others are not.

"They took some random side road to get to the farm entrance."

She turns to look at her friend and tilts her head. "Then this had to have been planned. Otherwise how would the thieves have known exactly where they were going to be?"

"Right! That's what I said." She places the yellow fascinator back on her head and looks at herself in the mirror.

"But what about the horse? They should be able to locate it," the darkhaired woman says as she moves over to the wall and picks up a black hat.

"They removed the chip so he can't be tracked. Do you like this one? It's smaller than what I was thinking, but my eyes keep going back to it. The yellow is so pretty."

They removed the chip? I know from listening to Grayson that once they go in, they don't come out very easily. And what about a scar? I imagine there would be one, and wouldn't it be identifiable? How sad and how suspicious. I wonder if Birdie knows.

The dark-headed woman puts the black hat on then moves to stand next to her friend. They share a mirror and look at what they've selected.

"I really do. The yellow looks amazing with your hair color. There are so many dresses that would match it perfectly too." She takes the black hat off and puts the red one back on. "I kind of feel about this red one the way you do with the yellow."

"You've always looked good in red, and you know Anthony loves you in red lipstick," her friend says.

"He really does." She smiles. "Did Eloise tell you what they are doing to find it?"

"No. I was so shocked, and she was so distraught I didn't ask many questions. I just let her tell me the story." She takes off the fascinator and pulls her phone out of her bag to look at the screen.

"This is like the craziest thing I've ever heard. I'm not even sure what one does with a horse like this. It's not like you can call it yours and bring it into the racing community. People would know."

"Exactly." She tucks her phone back into her bag and picks it up along with the fascinator. "If we plan on meeting Christine by three, we should probably get going."

"Sounds good." The darkhaired woman returns the black hat to the wall and gently picks up the red one. "Was there a ransom?" she asks as they make their way to the counter.

"Not that she mentioned, but I can't see how those actually work these days anyway. Everything is traceable."

"True. Maybe their intent is to breed it and then in three years or so produce a winner."

The woman with the yellow fascinator hums, and they both stop talking as they reach me at the counter.

That has to be it. I mean what else would you do with a horse like that?

12

"Would you quit fidgeting?" Stokes says to me as we turn down the driveway of the home of the law partner who is throwing the party. I shoot him an annoyed look that says, *Don't tell me what to do.*

Twenty minutes ago, he picked me up, and we've barely spoken to each other. It's not that I think talking to him would be bad, I just don't know what to say. He asked me how the store is doing, and I replied that it's doing well. I thanked him again for the flowers, and he smirked and said at least they weren't black.

Right after he started his job at the firm, I sent him black roses as a congratulations. I might have made a comment about how the color matched his career choice and his soul. I couldn't help myself. Him reminding me has my cheeks flushing, although I'm not sure if it's with indignation or embarrassment—embarrassment that I never would have felt up until this week.

Just like Whitlock Farm, this house is also outside the city, but in the other direction. The home is large and well-manicured, and although there is a barn off in the distance, it's easy enough to see this is only a home and not a farm.

"He throws this party every year?" I ask him, ignoring his jab and smoothing down my skirt for the three hundredth time.

"Yes."

"And you've gone to it before?" I'm trying to gather some background information.

"Yes." He lets out one of his annoyed sighs.

"I guess I just don't understand why I need to be here. You already know all these people, and you've been to this party before. Wait . . ." I turn to look at him. "Do you always bring a date with you to these things?" It had never occurred to me that he might have.

He shoots me a look that says, *You can't be serious.*

But I am. Other than seeing Stokes once a month and on holidays, I really don't know anything about him or his social life. He doesn't strike me as the player type of guy with his pristine reputation, but who knows? I certainly don't.

"Well?" I ask as I turn to face him a little more.

"No, I don't, but you'll see why I need you today," he says as he parks next to the other guests who have already arrived.

Need.

Such a strange word to hear coming out of his mouth.

He turns to face me, and we sit in the car in silence and stare at each other. His face is tight, and there's something more severe about the way his jaw is clenched.

My eyes narrow as I take him in. He's wearing a black button-down, black slacks, black shoes, and a black belt. I'm not sure I've ever seen him in all black, and he looks like someone else, more outlaw and less preppy polo spectator. I'm also glad I chose to wear this black and white striped dress. We match, even if it was unintentional.

"Why do you look like that?" I ask.

"Like what?" He runs his hand through his hair and then over his face.

"Like you'd rather be stabbed repeatedly than go in there to spend time with your colleagues."

He lets out another deep sigh, and his perma-scowl drops into place. Breaking eye contact, he looks out the window. "You'll see."

"Is there anything you should be telling me before we go in there?" I flip down the visor to look in the mirror one last time.

He turns back to me as he opens his door. "Lawyers— be careful what you say."

With that, he gets out of the car and comes around the front to open my door.

"Thank you in advance for doing this," he says with low-level exasperation as he takes my hand to help me out then keeps holding it as he shuts the door. I can't tell if his irritation is because he's saddled himself with me for the night or because he doesn't want to be here. Meanwhile, I'm stuck on how Stokes is holding my hand, and I keep glancing down at his large palm wrapped around mine.

"Don't thank me yet. It's quite possible I let everyone know how you really are and ruin your reputation." I smile at him conspiratorially.

He tilts his head as his hand loosens so he can thread his fingers between mine. "And how am I really?" he asks as we start walking toward the front door.

It takes a second to register his words as I'm still baffled by the fact that we're holding hands at all, and now in an intimate way.

"Cunning, two-faced, mean—"

"What?" He jerks us to a stop on the porch, two steps away from the front door, and looks genuinely disturbed by my assessment of him. Why he is surprised, I have no idea. His favorite pastime is insulting and ignoring me, with a splash of kindness like the champagne at my grand opening.

I'm just about to answer him when the door flies open and there's a man in his early fifties smiling at us. Instantly, I feel on guard with the way he's staring at Stokes, and then his eyes fall on me. Stokes's hand tightens around mine.

"Son! So happy you could make it," he says as he takes a step forward and pats Stokes on the arm.

Son?

"I said I was coming," Stokes replies in that bored, uptight tone he's perfected, and I almost snicker.

"And I see you brought a date," he says. As his eyes shift to me, the hair on the back of my neck stands up.

Stokes releases my hand and wraps his arm around my shoulders to pull me in tight. Of course I go, partly out of wariness of this guy and partly because I know I need to play my part. Mine goes around his waist, his very firm waist.

"This is Rosie May, my girlfriend. Rosie, this is Dean Collier, the partner throwing the party tonight."

Girlfriend.

Air conditioning from inside rushes past him as I hold my hand out, and goose bumps rise on my arm. "It's nice to meet you. Thank you for inviting us," I say as politely as I can.

His cold hand wraps around mine, and it feels gross.

"Of course. Can't imagine a firm get-together without Stokes attending. Although, I must admit, you are a surprise, my dear," he says as he eyes me suspiciously.

"Well, if you give me an empty beer bottle, a few napkins, some Bacardi 151, and a lighter, I can be a whole lot more surprising," I tell him, grinning.

Mr. Collier's face morphs into confusion and then horror while I glance at Stokes and see one side of his mouth is twitching.

"Right." He takes a step to the side. "Well do come in. The party is out back on the patio."

Stokes thanks him as we make our way past, through the house, and to the outside bar.

"You kill me," he whispers in my ear from behind as we stand in line, his hand moving to rest on my hip.

"Yeah, well you knew what you were getting yourself into when you invited me," I say back as I look up into his face. His expression is one of consternation, and although the double lines are present, his gaze looks pleased.

"I did."

We move a step forward, and the pressure from his fingertips sears through the fabric of my dress. The weather is mild, which makes for a pleasant evening, and in general, the party is very beautiful. Whoever he hired to decorate and cater has gone over the top, and in addition to spotting the bars set up at each end of the patio, my eyes have drifted to the table holding the canapes. Even from our spot in this line, they look delicious and are calling my name.

Over and over, people come up to us to say hello, though we try to keep to ourselves. It's weird, because although this is a party and he sees most of these people every day in his office, it feels more like a forced fancy happy hour. People are here, but it's clear that it's out of obligation and not for fun. Then again, we are talking about lawyers—maybe they all share Stokes's gleaming personality.

In attendance are three partners, quite a few associates, junior associates, staff, a handful of clients and potential clients, and then of course the significant others. There are only maybe a hundred people here, which means everyone is talking to everyone, and everyone seems to be talking to us—or should I say it's me doing the talking. Other than pleasantries, Stokes is quiet with his dressed-in-all-black inscrutable look, forcing me to lead, and it's quite aggravating.

I meet his junior associate, a guy named Christopher who's been with the firm for ten months. I meet his secretary, who tells me she's delighted to meet me as Stokes is such a mystery to everyone. And I meet Suzy Collier, the daughter and the apparent reason why I am here.

Just like her father, she's startled to meet me, but that doesn't stop her from touching Stokes's arm, laughing at things he says that are not funny, and following us around like we're the best of friends.

In one of the rare moments we're alone, I pinch him in the side. "You should have told me."

"Would you have come?" he asks, his hazel beams scanning my face, painting my lips and making me feel all twisted inside.

"Probably. After all, I did agree to this sham, and I find it amusing to watch you suffer. How long has she been like this?" I glance past his shoulder and see her talking to a few of the other younger people here. She's tall, wearing a skintight beige dress, and quite frankly looks like someone I would expect him to be with.

"Since I started, although then I didn't have to see her much as she had just started law school. Now she works at the firm, and it's awful. Most days, the way Dean looks at me, I think he only hired me because of who I am. He's continually pushing her my way, and Christopher has had to intercede on my behalf several times."

I find this interesting. In all the years I have known Stokes, people have approached him more in a state of awe than one of determination. His birthright has given him prestige that most people crave, and I've certainly never seen anyone try to handle him. He's not someone who tolerates this sort of behavior, from anyone, and it confuses me.

"Do you like working for this firm?" I ask him. I've never even considered that Stokes might not like what he does or the path he's chosen.

He lets out a sigh and drops his gaze between us while running his hand down my arm to wrap his hand around mine. All evening he's touched me in one way or another, and while it should feel strange, it really doesn't.

"I don't know. I did at first, but now . . ." He trails off. I hear what he isn't saying and am pretty sure I understand why he feels this way.

"That explains why he calls you son," I say with a tone that lets him know I don't approve, and he presses his lips into a flat line. "But Stokes . . ." I look up so his eyes meet mine. Regardless of our history or how we feel about each other, in the big picture of life, these are truths he needs to hear. "You are an incredibly smart and dedicated guy. Your name aside, they are very lucky to have you."

Tiny spots of color dot the sharp edges of his cheekbones as he frowns and his brows pull down.

"What?" I ask, my gaze dancing back and forth between his eyes.

He pauses and then says, "Nothing," as he steps closer and lays his forehead against mine. My breath catches. This intimacy from him is foreign, and I'm not sure what to make of it. Is this how he is with someone he's dating, or is this all an act for the people around us? Public displays of affection don't really seem like the Stokes I know, but then again, I don't really know him like this.

Lifting my hand, he kisses the back of it. It's a sweet gesture, which has confused tingles moving up my arm, and I watch him as he watches me.

Something strange is happening here tonight. Something strange indeed.

A little over halfway through the party, needing a break from this overload of emotional stimulation, I excuse myself to go to the bathroom. I've just walked back onto the porch when I'm stopped by Suzy.

Oh, here we go.

"It's so nice to meet one of Stokes's girls," she says to me in a condescendingly sweet tone, a tone that hasn't been present all night until now. She tosses her hair over her shoulder then squares them off. Unfortunately, no one sees that I've just been accosted by a pit viper, and I can't spot Stokes or Christopher to give them a *Come save me* look.

"One of his girls." I laugh, letting her know I'm not intimidated but amused. Come to think of it, I've never met one of his "girls" so I have no idea what he's drawn to, and I'd bet the bank she doesn't either.

She bristles as if she was expecting a different response. "Well, Stokes and I go way back," she says. "He does love to surprise us from time to time."

Us? And who might that be? Her and her manipulative father? How exactly did Stokes end up working at this firm? She's also lying through her teeth, and I want nothing more than to put her in her place.

I tilt my head. "That surprises me. Knowing Stokes, I'm not sure how you would think anything he does is for you, or anyone else, for that matter."

Her eyes narrow. She's clearly not a dumb person, and I think back to Stokes's warning about lawyers. "And how long have you two known each other?" she asks patronizingly.

"Oh, we also go way back. Way, way back," I tell her so she can hear my tone as well and know she better watch what she says.

"Really now," she drawls, and I just smile in return. "Did you see the article in LuVu Tea? I can't imagine all the attention he's getting from being named the most eligible bachelor."

She's trying to get me riled up, but I refuse to take her bait. Instead, I smile wide. If she saw the first article, I'm certain she has seen the few after and is green with envy that it's not her.

"We did. We laughed." Well, I laughed at his expense. "Technically they aren't wrong—he's not married, so he is a bachelor. The attention is the same as always: gold-digging socialite groupies." I look her over from head to toe then bring my eyes back to hers and smile again.

She may not consider herself to fit that description, but she does, to a T. With her expensive dyed-blonde hair, puffed-up lips, and tight clothes, just because she has a law degree, that doesn't make her any different. All she sees is someone who can elevate her spoiled status even more.

"So how serious are the two of you? I mean he's never mentioned you. Ever."

I laugh, and this catches her off guard. He's never mentioned her either. "Well, that really wouldn't be any of your business, now would it? In fact, I think it's quite inappropriate for you to ask about his personal life. After all, aren't you just his boss's daughter?"

Her nostrils flare, and her eyes widen at the slight.

"And you do realize you are talking about Stokes, right? He holds his cards and those he cares for close to him. He's not an open book. Not to anyone."

"Except maybe to you," he says, coming up from the side.

Suzy sucks in some air and stands straighter. This poor pathetic girl. Clearly she's been handed everything she wants on a silver platter, and she can't imagine why someone like Stokes wouldn't want to be with someone like her.

"Sorry," he says to me, completely ignoring her. Bending, he runs his hand down my back and kisses me on the corner of my mouth.

My. Mouth.

Oh my word.

And just why?

My skin tingles, and I feel like I've been branded with a hot poker. I do my very best to not look shocked at the sweet gesture. Really, why do his lips have to be so warm and soft? And why do I react to them so? Instead of feeling like I've been kissed by a gross frog, my heart jolts, recognizing he's a prince. Only this isn't a fairy tale, it's real life, and I'm not his princess.

"Christopher had a few questions for me regarding a contract I worked on this week."

"No worries, although this is a party and you promised no work tonight." I lean into him and smile up at him adoringly, batting my eyelashes for good measure. He's amused by me and smiles back. It's not fake, it's not closed mouth, it's rare, and it's what I'm now recognizing as my smile.

"Rosabelle and I were just talking about you." Suzy runs her hand through her hair to fluff it then puts it on her hip while holding her drink in her other hand. Her eyes are glued to him, and she doesn't even realize he couldn't care less that she is standing here speaking. "I asked her how long the two of you have been seeing each other, but she wouldn't answer."

She's still pushing and trying to make a play off her words, *seeing each other.* I glance to Stokes to take cues from him.

He sighs as his hand wraps around me and grips my

hip. Every time he does this, I feel claimed, which is completely absurd. Suzy sees the movement, and in my peripheral vision, I see her shuffle on her feet.

"If I'd had my way," he says, still not really looking at her, gazing at me with his serious face again, "almost thirteen years."

What he's really saying is, if he'd had his way, he would have sent me back to whatever hole he thought I crawled out of almost thirteen years ago.

Suzy lets out some kind of shocked noise at his admission, and I turn to her and say with a huge, winning smile, "Way, way back."

She pauses as she looks at us both, like really looks at us. "It seems so," she replies in a defeated tone.

Finally.

"If you'll excuse me, I hear my father calling," she says and then walks off. The air around us instantly warms, and my shoulders drop as the tension I didn't realize had bunched up my muscles releases.

"Well, well, well," I say to him once we are alone, and I turn so I am still in his arms and our bodies are flush. "You are so going to owe me, Whitlock. This is the second time now I've had to save you from your adoring fans."

He grimaces and says, "I know," his gaze roaming my face.

And then he bends down to kiss me. It's not a deep kiss, but it's sweet, and also unexpected. It's not a quick peck either. He holds his mouth against mine and breathes in through his nose. Of course alarm bells are going off in my head, screaming, *Abort! Abort!* but I can't help the way my body melts against his. He's familiar in a way I wasn't expecting, and my heart pinches.

"This is so weird," I whisper against his lips.

He freezes then asks, "Is it?" while kissing me again and pulling my bottom lip in between his teeth.

Lord, have mercy on me.

My breath catches, and my stomach tightens with feelings that are unfamiliar when associated with him.

What is happening right now?

Eventually he drags his mouth across my cheek to my ear. "I told you I would kiss you again."

My hands tighten in the fabric of his shirt at his waist, his skin warm and solid underneath. "Yeah, well don't get used to it," I tell him, though really it's me who needs to not get used to it. I'm pretty sure kissing him could become addictive, and I can't have that, at least not with him.

"Oh, Thorney." His hand dips low on my back, anchoring me to him. "Why are you such a pain in my ass?"

I lean back a little. "Me? I'm the pain?"

He sees the flash of annoyance in my eyes and grins with triumph in his. "You know we're being watched right now, right?" he asks, tucking a loose piece of hair behind my ear. Shivers chase his fingers, and I hate that my eyes want to roll back in my head.

Instead of answering, I play my part by running my hands up his chest and over his shoulders, and I rise up on my toes so he can better wrap me in his arms. His eyes flare briefly at the contact, but then it's gone as I'm enveloped in sage, melons, and worn leather.

Maybe they are watching, maybe they aren't. All I can focus on is that I'm hugging Stokes and Stokes is hugging me.

What's shocking is that I don't hate it.

After a long moment of me having my head on his shoulder with my eyes shut while breathing in the familiar scent of him, he pulls back, looks at me fondly, and quietly asks, "Are you ready to go?"

My eyes search his. "Mission accomplished?"

He lets out a deep sigh. "God, I hope so."

LUVU TEA
CHOMPING AT THE BIT

Rise and shine, Louisville, have we got the best morning tea for you. So, grab your cup and fill it with black, green, or mate. I promise this photo will give you that extra little jump you just might need.

While we've had several sightings of our bachelor of the season entering and leaving Ms. May's hat shop with flowers, coffee, and to-go food galore, for the past week and a half, none have been of them together. Until now, that is.

Attending a season party, the pair stepped out in style looking sleek, sophisticated, and just remarkable together. Dressed in black with accents of white, the two were striking as they unknowingly stole the show. Little kisses here, lots of touches there—they were keenly observed to be utterly smitten and content with each other. Is this what's to come? More of this sweetness? Here at the Tea, we love to keep things mixed with honey, but we also enjoy a little spice. Be our eyes and ears, and send in those photos. We are just chomping at the bit for more and more.

13

______

$\mathcal{S}$tokes picks me up after work to drive us both out to the farm for family dinner. I can't believe it's already been a month, and I also can't believe all the things that have happened since the last dinner. I'm not sure why he didn't head out earlier, but who am I to complain? I'm already reaping the benefits of this so-called truce, from the coffee and the snacks to him driving me around. I'm tired; work was crazy busy this weekend, and then after I got home from his firm's party last night, I lay in bed awake and replayed different scenes of Stokes and me together and how Stokes is with his colleagues.

I'm pretty certain I've always been who I am with everyone I'm around. I'm a happy person. I'm lovable, sometimes funny, and I try to be positive. I trust those I keep in my circle, and really what you see is what you get. It's hard for me to hide emotions—they're usually plastered on my face—but with Stokes, it's the complete opposite.

He's a closed book, and on purpose. Yes, he's done well for himself, even I can see that. Aside from the success of the farm, he's worked really hard to identify himself as someone, and not once has he seemed to lounge back and enjoy the conveniences he was born into. But, he's so stiff around people, it just doesn't make any sense. Of course he can hold a conversation, and occasionally he laughs, but for the most part, he's hard to read, at least he is to ninety-eight percent of the world. Me, I've always thought I could read him well, but now I'm second-guessing that too. It's like I'm holding the last piece of a puzzle that is Stokes, and I'm so close to solving it. The words are right there, but they just won't materialize.

"You okay over there?" he asks, one arm draped across the steering wheel, the other playing with his cell phone, which is sitting in the center console. Tonight he looks relaxed and trendy in a navy blue shirt and gray pants like you'd find at J.Crew. His hair is mussed, he hasn't shaved, and I think I like this side of him more than I should.

"Yeah, it's just been a long week," I tell him, because it has.

He hums in agreement but doesn't say anything else. He lets me be lost in my head as I look out the window, and it isn't until we're sitting at the table for dinner with Mom, Birdie, Grayson, and Molly that I snap out of it.

"So, curious minds want to know: are you two dating?" Birdie asks point-blank, and my head pops straight up.

Tonight we're eating lasagna, and it's usually one of my favorites, but the ricotta is sticking to the roof of my mouth, and I'm having a hard time swallowing. Her question almost makes me choke, and my stomach bottoms out. Deep down in my gut, I knew they saw us at her party, or someone did and told them. Then again, those gossip articles are running wild.

I glance at Stokes, and he's giving his mother a look I can't decipher. In return she gives him one of her own.

"No, we are not dating," he says. The relaxed posture he had in the car is now gone, and tension has taken its place in his shoulders and all down his arms. "You know I asked Rosie to be my date to the party, and she's agreed, for appearance's sake, to be my girlfriend until after the Derby." His eyes—back to laser beams—flit my way and then move back to her.

It is what we agreed upon, and although it's only been a little over a week, I feel like it's been much longer. I've seen him seven of the last ten days. That's like seven months of Stokes time condensed, and I'm feeling affected, overwhelmed, and—I know it's strange—crowded. Having someone come into your life this much, it takes up space. I don't mind; it's just a lot in a short amount of time, and I'm having to adjust quickly.

Mostly adjust to it being him, the one who calls me Thorney and in general has refused to acknowledge me in life.

"Appearance's sake," my mother repeats, while his mother starts grinning.

What is she grinning at?

Running his finger inside the collar of his shirt, he leans back in his chair and asks her, "Why are you smiling like that?"

Great minds think alike ...

"Grayson, tell him," she says as she picks up her wine glass and takes a sip.

Grayson lifts his napkin, runs it over his mouth, and then picks up his glass of bourbon and water, his favorite. "Well, let's just say, recently the farm tours have been sold out," he says as he also takes a hefty sip.

I lean forward with my elbows on the table, not seeing the problem. "Okay. Well, that's good, right?"

He looks at Birdie and then at Stokes, and apparently I'm the only one not following.

"Good, yes." He hesitates, and then the hammer drops. "And the staff around here love that it's all college girls. Makes for an interesting time to say the least."

My vision blurs, and even though it's suddenly so quiet in the dining room you could hear a pin drop, my ears start ringing, and I've stopped breathing.

"Did you say college girls?" I ask him with narrowed eyes.

"Yep." He shifts his gaze to Stokes. The two of them have a silent conversation as they stare at each other, and my muscles suddenly feel strangely tight. Stokes is scowling hard, and Grayson—well, he just shrugs as if to say, *What do you want me to do?*

"Gross," says Molly from across the table, and my eyes dart to hers.

Without thinking, I blurt out, "So you think that's gross, but me fake dating your brother is not?"

All eyes fall to me, and my face burns deep. I'm certain my whole body has gone three shades of red.

"It's different," she says gently. She can see that Grayson's comment has affected me and I've gone into defense mode. I don't know why, though. Is it for him? Is it for me? I don't know, and that has me more confused than anything. "I know you, and well, random girls stalking our home hoping to get some time with my nerd of a brother is just ridiculous."

It is ridiculous.

"Speaking of stalking our home, the staff even found one girl wandering around the barns. How she got there, no idea," Birdie says.

I glance at Stokes, and his cheeks have also flushed pink. He's now looking down at his plate, just holding his fork, and he doesn't make eye contact with anyone at the table.

I really don't understand. Who just goes to someone's home and wanders around without being invited? That's not normal, and in what scenario does that ever work out? Did she think he would just find her and be like, *Oh, hey there. Want to have dinner with me?* Just no.

Another unwanted surge of emotions hits me right in the chest. I can't tell if it's extreme annoyance or jealousy.

Clearly there are pictures of us together floating around, and yet people are still coming after him. Lexington is over an hour away; it's just absurd.

His jaw clenches, and he swallows. With this one subtle move from him, my eyes flare as the puzzle piece drops in place, and I know all these years I've pegged him wrong.

I've always known he shows me a different side of himself than he does others. I assumed it was because he was playing his part of prince of the castle by day and villain to me by night, but I was wrong.

He's always been a bit of a quiet guy. Even when I was thirteen and had just met him, he didn't say anything, just stood next to his mother and stared at me. He's tall so he looks down at people, and with his ever-present scowl, he gives off a vibe of being broody and self-important, but now I'm realizing it's because, in general, he's shy.

He's an incredibly shy guy, but with me, he's himself—or at least he tries to be.

I am an idiot, and the urge to slap my palm to my forehead is fierce. If I apply this new image to what I already know of him, it changes everything.

Everything.

All. These. Years.

When we were kids, he would just follow behind me quietly. At past parties, he would stand next to his mother and let her lead the conversations. Last weekend, he shadowed me and rarely allowed himself to be in a situation where he might be stuck talking to someone he didn't want to talk to, and at his work function last night, the way he breathed as we were walking to the door and the way his hands were sweaty most of the night—it isn't that he thinks he's better than anyone else. He's just uncomfortable.

Which suddenly makes his desperation for this whole "be my fake girlfriend" situation because of that article understandable. People—strangers—going out of their way to meet him and contact him is so far out of his comfort zone, no wonder he all but begged.

It also makes sense now why he comes out here and rides by himself every weekend. He's decompressing or recharging, whatever, and he just needs solitude, an escape from his everyday life.

But if he dislikes it so much, why is he doing it? And why do I suddenly feel the need to protect him? It's like he cast a spell over me this week, and after one evening with him, just twenty-four hours later, my opinion of him has changed so much that I'm ready to storm those surrounding the castle and go into battle for him, this person who, for so long, I hated.

Well, if I'm being honest, hate is a really harsh word. It's more like I greatly disliked him, and now I suddenly have whiplash from doing a one-eighty.

All of this is disorienting.

Letting out a sigh, I tell Molly that makes sense then change the subject to direct attention off of us by asking Grayson about Ace. It's a topic he can go on and on about, and it was a good move as this gets us through the rest of dinner.

Yesterday was the last race for him until the Derby, the Blue Grass Stakes, which is held in Lexington every year. The points awarded were 100-40-20-10, and he came in second, earning 40, and secured his place in the top twenty to run the Derby. The horse who beat him, Windstar, came from Ocala, Florida, and is a real contender this year. With only one more race left, the preseason qualifiers will be over and the lineup will be set.

"Go for a walk with me before we head back?" Stokes asks almost hesitantly as we carry our plates to the kitchen, and my heart squeezes. He said he'd do better, and all week he has. I wonder if he thinks I'm doing better for him? I don't think I've been too confrontational. In fact, I think I've been quite amenable considering all of our "public" appearances so far have been for his benefit.

"Sure," I tell him, feeling a little bit optimistic, a little bit skeptical, and still a little bit disgruntled by how wrong I've been and the part I've played in our dysfunctional family over the years. I can't help but wonder if things could or would have been different between us if I'd paid attention to him more, and that makes me sad, especially since he is someone who has been a constant presence in my life for so, so long.

The sun has started to set, casting its golden hue across the fields and the barns. The fields are empty, and it's quiet. It's pleasant outside, and as we start walking, I can't help but sneak peeks up at him. The lighting amplifies the lighter tones in his hair and his skin. He's always been handsome, but tonight it feels like so much more, more in a way that being alone with him is somehow now making me nervous.

"Did you like living here?" he asks. Most of the roads on the farm are laid out in a grid fashion. Yes, some of them wind around, but ultimately the pattern is the same. The way he's guiding us, the full loop will be about a mile, and a part of me is wishing it were longer.

"Are you kidding? I can't imagine a better place to live." I truly can't.

A small smile curves his lips as he looks across the field to our left. My answer pleased him, and something slippery moves through my chest. He seems so ordinary—we seem so ordinary, like taking a walk after dinner is something we do all the time. He's relaxed here, and the stress that keeps him uptight and formidable seems to be gone.

Don't get me wrong, he's still far too attractive and there's nothing ordinary about his broad shoulders, his piercing gaze when it lands on me, or how he makes me just a little bit jittery, and yet after this past week, it's precariously easy to pretend we're more than we are.

To pretend we're friends.

"But what about London and New York City? Do you wish you could have stayed in one of those places?"

"Technically, I could have. I'm not tied to this town like you are, but Louisville is home. My mom is here. The farm is here." I glance over to see if he has a reaction to this, but he doesn't. "And my goal has always been the hat shop. Why? Do you wish you could live somewhere else?"

He tilts his head a little as he thinks this through. "I have thought about it," he says warily, as if admitting this is somehow a deep sin.

"Yeah?" I ask with a little enthusiasm, trying to let him know it's okay to talk to me.

"Yeah." He looks at the ground, and then he adds, "Yeah, even if just for a short time."

I hear what he's not saying, and I feel empathy for him. Two weeks ago, I would have mocked him by saying, *Oh, you poor little rich boy*, but not today. Today, I'm able to look past the animosity I've carried toward him for so long to see a man I know for certain loves the life he was given and wouldn't change anything but sometimes dreams of something different. I think that's true for most people, though, and it would be unfair of me to scorn him for his feelings.

"Well, maybe you should start by taking a vacation or two. I don't remember you doing so in a long time."

He sighs. "I haven't. There really hasn't been time. I started working right after law school, and I've barely had a chance to come up for air. Besides, who would I go with?"

The sudden thought of him living his best life and exploring the world with someone else makes the dinner in my stomach turn over. I know it shouldn't, but it does.

"Do you need someone to go on vacation with you?"

He glances at me. "I guess I don't, but I'm not completely immune to wanting company."

I think back to the party when I had that thought about him and it being lonely at the top. I've never considered that he might actually be lonely, though I don't know why he would be. Like I've said, to everyone other than me, he's always been charming and kind. He might not be an outgoing, boisterous person, but he is someone people like to be around.

"I know you have friends—I've seen you with them." I bump his shoulder with mine to attempt to wipe away the double lines between his eyes.

"I suppose."

"What about Jackson, Tristan, or Jacob?" These are the friends he brought home once from college. They've spent several weekends here over the years, and I know he keeps in touch with them because his mom occasionally mentions them at the monthly dinners.

"I saw Jackson in February—he's moved to Nashville— and Jacob is getting married. We've talked about a possible weekend somewhere, but it's hard to coordinate schedules."

"Jacob is getting married?" I know we are of the age, but I don't have any married friends. In fact, the thought of marriage almost makes me feel squeamish, but then I look at Stokes and that feeling drifts away. He will make a great husband one day, and for some reason that idea has my heart sinking and my shoulders drooping.

Lost in thought and not paying attention, I trip over a rock on the gravel road, and Stokes grabs me to keep me from falling. His hands are warm, and his brows pull down in concern.

"You okay?" he asks, running his fingers down my arm to my hand where he wraps his around mine.

I nod, unable to respond.

He starts walking again, only this time we're holding hands. The teenager inside me weeps. I'm not sure if it's over lost and broken dreams or because the possibility might still be there. Either way, I'm reeling and at the same time trying to take as many mental pictures of us as I can.

"Yes, he's getting married." He lets out a sigh, but it's content, not discouraged, and I know he's happy for his friend. "His poor fiancée . . . does she even realize what she's strapping herself to?"

I grin. "I'm sure she does. When is the wedding?" I have to believe Stokes will be a groomsman. At the thought of him and his tall masculine frame in a fitted tuxedo, baby butterflies stretch their wings in my stomach.

"August. Want to be my date?" he asks, his eyes seeking out mine. They are confident, sure, hopeful.

August.

That means he wants us to continue being friends like this when the Derby is over. Those little wings start to beat. Then again, why wouldn't we be friends? It's not like our lives are going to change any time soon, that is unless he finds someone he's interested in.

"So that's it, you're just going to default to me as your plus-one from now on?" I tease, but something begins to flit behind my rib cage. If I didn't know any better, I'd think wishfulness were trying to make its unwanted presence known.

"So far so good, right?" he asks, studying my face with an openness I don't usually see on him.

It makes me wonder, *Does he have this wishfulness too?*

14

"Good morning, Louisville!" the television host Carly says animatedly toward the camera, the softbox lights illuminating her skin and everything around us. "This morning, I am here with Rosie from Rosie May, and we are going to discuss all the details you need to know about Derby hats."

On Monday, I received a call from a producer at the television network. They had discovered I was a new business in town and wanted to come out to do a spotlight as part of their *Run for the Roses* series. It's only meant to be a few minutes long, but all morning my stomach has been in knots. Other spotlights include large sponsors, local destinations, the balloonfest, and the Derby festival marathon.

"As you know, tis the season, and we are just a few weeks away from the *Run for the Roses*. If you haven't secured your hat yet, now is the perfect time to run out as well, before they are all gone."

My smile grows at her play on words, and at the same time, she's not wrong. I'm not running low on inventory yet, but in another week to ten days, pickings will definitely be slimmer.

"Before we get started, I want to remind all of you about the other events that are coming up this week."

She continues to ramble on about different places they'll be and things that are happening, then I catch a glimpse of the shop door opening behind the crew, the bell tinkling as someone slips inside. Molly, who was watching us, breaks out in a large smile and quietly moves out from behind the counter to greet the person, and that's when Stokes comes into view. It's been four days since I've seen him. He had to go out of town to meet with a client, but he's back, and he's got a to-go bag draped across his arm and holds a drink carrier with what looks like three large coffees. Molly takes whatever he's brought, and he moves so he's standing off to the side and out of the way.

He brought us coffee again, and the thoughtfulness, combined with what I now know of him, has my baby butterflies turning into toddlers.

He's in a suit and tie, his standard business look, and it hasn't at all stopped being impressive. If anything, I can't help but appreciate it more. I've never considered myself to be someone who admires a man in a suit or finds it to be a turn-on, but now I'm thinking it might be. His hazel eyes find mine, and he smiles. I can feel it all the way down in my toes. It's not a huge smile, but a small one that's one of mine. It's personal and intimate between two people who know each other differently than they know others, and it calms me instantly.

"Rosie," Carly says, pulling my gaze from him to her. "This is your first season with your new shop, Rosie May, and we are excited to learn more about you and the gorgeous hats you make." She takes the one on the counter in front of her and puts it on. It's hot pink with one large hot pink flower and tall dark purple wisps that I've curled to point up versus out.

"Thank you, Carly, for coming by today. Yes, this is my first season as a shop owner, but I was born and raised right here in Louisville and think it's the best city in the country. I love having you here, and you're in luck because I also love to talk about hats."

The crew showed up over two hours ago. They filmed shots of different parts of the store, which I'm sure have already been diced and spliced to slip into our conversation, while I sat with makeup.

"Obviously, the Derby is about the horses, but amidst all the thoroughbred races, this one, ours, is famously known for its hats. Tell us about this one right here," she prompts as she holds up the baby blue fascinator.

"The hats here at Rosie May are one size fits most, but if the head is larger, we recommend a fascinator that looks like a hat." I show the top of the fascinator to the camera. It has a large brim, is appropriately adorned, and looks like a hat to the common eye. Then I tip it back so the viewers can see underneath it, revealing that the hat is attached to a headband. When worn, the hat will sit at an angle on the head and just be beautiful. "It's a way to give the illusion one might want, but it's also very comfortable and secure."

Carly takes it from me, removes the one she's wearing, and slips it onto her head. She faces me so I can make sure it's in place then turns back to the camera.

"You are so right! It is comfortable and looks incredible, don't you think?" She's asking the viewers with large delighted eyes. "But what if the head is smaller?"

"If they choose to wear a hat then there are ways to pad the inside so it will stay anchored." I pick up a hat that's in front of me, one we've already padded for demonstration purposes. Carly takes it from me and holds it out for the camera to zoom in.

"I had to do this to a pair of shoes once too. It worked brilliantly." She laughs as if she's funny and being silly. This reminds me of a sitcom show, when the producers want the audience to think something is funny and they press a button to dub in a prerecorded audience laugh.

It's fake and definitely confirms what I already knew: I could not do this job.

"Now, Rosie, if this is someone's first time coming to the Derby, what should they look for when buying a hat?"

"Well, there are three main embellishment categories that make up a Derby hat: flowers, feathers, and netting. While not all three need to be used, it is favorably looked upon, especially for those who are expected to be seen. The hat must be elegant but modern. It needs to be genteel but also one of a kind. Here at Rosie May, we've worked hard at trying to think outside the box when it comes to hat design and how to incorporate other elements to make it unique, such as wide ribbon, painted leaves, crystals, tulle, and curved brims. I think the most important thing to look for in a hat is how it makes you feel. From the color to the style, when it is put on, there should be a feeling of rightness. If that's there, that's the meant-to-be hat or fascinator."

"I love that," Carly says, taking off the fascinator and trying on another. "Tell me about this right here," she says, turning the original hot pink hat around to show the back and holding it out for the camera.

"One thing I have always wanted was some kind of marker on my hats that makes them stand out and identifiable as mine, something that makes the brand recognizable. Now obviously, the hat embellishments are usually elaborate and eye-catching, so I had to get creative with what that might be. Yes, I have the label on the inside of the hat, but what about the outside? I wanted people to be able to look at the hat and know it was mine.

"As you can see, what I came up with is a light pink Swarovski crystal that is affixed onto the back rim of the hat. If you look closely, you'll see they've been cut specifically for me to look like a rose. I wouldn't call them small, but they're not ginormous either. It's easily spotted if one looks for it or missed if they don't, and I love it. It's the signature color of the shop and the hat boxes and will definitely be one of those *If you know, you know* things."

To me she says, "Well, we all know now, and I will definitely be looking. I love it." Then she shifts back to the camera. "If you are interested in one of Rosie's hats or fascinators, make sure you check out her website or make your way on over to NuLu to see them for yourself. While you're here, you can enjoy a cup of tea and pose in front of her fabulous rose wall to share with all of your social media friends." She turns back to me. "Thank you, Rosie, for allowing us to stop by today."

"Thank you for coming," I tell her, genuinely meaning it.

She goes back to facing the camera, and I watch as the lens changes its dimensions to zoom in on Carly.

"Stay tuned, because after we come back from a quick break, we'll meet up with Jeanine at the Sweet Stop Bakery where they'll be teaching us how to decorate Derby cupcakes to look like roses—the perfect finishing touch to any hosted Derby party." She smiles big, and then it's over.

As I'm putting away the hats we featured, Carly beelines straight for Stokes, her high heels clacking across my floor like an unwanted mating call. I didn't even realize she saw him come in.

"Well, if it isn't Stokes Whitlock. How are you?" she asks in an overexcited southern tone while walking right up to him and wrapping her arms around him.

He visibly tenses then takes a step back from her. "I'm well. Thanks for asking."

I have to look away, because if I don't, I'll laugh. He's being dismissive; he doesn't inquire how she is, and his tone is crisp, bordering on rude. If she picks up on it, she doesn't let on. Instead, she pushes forward.

"I haven't seen you in months." She reaches over and starts rubbing his arm, as if she's a tiger and he's suddenly dinner. "Where have you been hiding, and what are you doing here so early this morning?" she asks, attempting to be flirtatious with him.

His lips have pressed into a firm line, and as his eyes briefly flit my way, I feel them burn into me with a pleading I'm now becoming accustomed to. I know I need to play my part, so I make my way over and move to stand next to him. Molly is talking to the camera guy about who knows what and doesn't see her brother's discomfort radiating in every direction.

"Rosie mentioned the interview this morning, so I thought I would drop in to cheer her on," he says as he reaches for my hand and pulls me even closer next to him, holding it a little tighter than normal.

I didn't mention the interview. Some things we talk about and others we don't. This little situation we've found ourselves in hasn't been going on long enough for us to braid each other's hair and share secrets.

"Right. I think I did hear somewhere that the two of you are dating." She quickly glances at me, and I smile in confirmation.

There's no way she didn't see the 'bachelor of the season' article or the one highlighting Birdie's party. People in the media live and die by gossip and drama, and then it occurs to me that maybe I got this interview because of him and how people perceive us, not because I'm new to town and am a fresh face amidst the businesses who've already done these interviews year after year.

"Yes," he says, not giving her anything more, and she glances back at me, maybe hoping I will, but I don't. If anything, I find I'm suddenly super irritated. She "heard somewhere" that we were dating and yet she turned on the charm right in front of me. What is with these women and him? I just give her a small smile then look at him with adoring Bambi eyes.

He squeezes my hand at whatever he sees simmering under my surface.

Recovering like the professional broadcaster she is, she says, "Good for you. After all these years, I've often wondered who would officially take you off the market, and well, Rosie here is just darling."

Darling. As if she knows me and wouldn't run me over if given the chance to be with him.

I grit my teeth, and my hand constricts in his.

"I think so," he says, looking down at me and smiling, only this smile is more of a smirk and says, *Take it easy, Thorney, she'll leave us alone in a minute.*

I smile back. *She better before I lose it.*

His eyes crinkle in the corners, and his grin grows.

"So how long have you two—"

Stokes cuts her off. "Well, if you'll excuse us, I'm going to steal Rosie for a minute before I head to the office," he says, politely letting her know this little meet and greet is over.

She blinks at him, clearly not used to being dismissed.

"Of course. Lovely to see you, Stokes." Out of courtesy, she gives me a glance, and then she wanders over to Molly and the cameraman.

"Another one of your many devout fans?" I ask through my teeth once we're out of earshot, feeling way more than I'd like.

His lips twitch as he tries to stop them from smiling, and his brows rise. Still holding my hand, he twists me, looks behind me at my back, and then runs his hand over me several times before facing me again and saying, "There. Better now?"

"What?" I twist to try to see what he was looking at while not embarrassing myself by purring at how good his hands felt on me.

"Your hackles—I've flattened them back down."

"Seriously?" I glare at him, and he chuckles.

"I've known her since college. She wasn't subtle about her interest in me then, even though I gave her no reason to believe I would ever return it. I've never understood why some people just can't take a hint."

I glance at her and then back at him.

"But why not?" I ask him, truly feeling curious. "She's clearly beautiful and driven. Why wouldn't you be interested in someone like her?"

He looks down at the ground as his thumb swipes over the back of my hand. "I just wasn't. I didn't have time for it, nor am I interested in someone being with me because of my name and what comes with it."

I tilt my head a little and observe him. His gaze comes back to mine.

"You've said this before. I didn't like it then, and I don't like it now. You are not just your name—you are so much more."

The double lines drop into place, and he frowns. Silence fills the air between us as his gaze drifts over the features of my face, and then one of his hands is pulling mine while the other gently lifts off the burnt orange hat I'm wearing. He brings me right into his arms, and my head falls under his chin. He lets out a sigh as the familiar scent of Stokes wraps around me, and my eyes fall shut. I breathe him in and revel in his heartbeat as it steadily knocks against his chest, the warmth from his skin heating up his thin dress shirt and the side of my face.

"You look beautiful this morning," he tells me, and a blush burns through my cheeks. I really did try with my baby blue dress and orange hat. I chose them because I wanted viewers to see that to look good, the colors don't necessarily have to match.

"Thank you," I tell him, feeling oddly sensitive to his kind words.

"Have dinner with me this weekend," he asks, just barely over a whisper.

And for reasons I don't quite understand yet, I instantly reply, "Okay."

15

For the rest of the week, I have been stuck thinking about Stokes. I'm loving that oddly affectionate moment after the interview and how it feels to be wrapped in his arms, and I'm hating it too, because I'm so busy with my life that having him invade my brain is still throwing me off.

Yesterday morning, he texted me his address and told me to come on over today whenever I decided to close the shop and was free. I've been trying to stay open a little later on Sundays, but really between the store and Avery's dress, I'm exhausted. I start at seven and haven't finished before eleven once this week. Molly decided to leave halfway through the day to go spend time with Austin, and well, what is one or two hours in the grand scheme of things? That's the whole point of owning your own business, right? To be able to make decisions as I see fit, even if somehow a six-foot-three, walking, talking distraction has hijacked my common sense.

Feeling anxious and out of sorts as I slip upstairs to change my clothes, I can't help but wonder if he is regretting the invite or has changed his mind. After all, we agreed to public sightings, and this isn't one. He's voluntarily asked me over, and my mind is stuck somewhere between the old Stokes and this new one. Other than that time in New York and the night he came over to basically beg, we haven't spent time together alone; it's not who we are. I mean, he lives so close, and I had no idea. He kept this detail from me for months, and on purpose, so I feel uncertain as to why now. Panicking, I shoot him a text, giving him an easy out.

> You know we aren't really dating—you don't need to invite me over. If you have work or something to do, I understand.

He immediately replies:

> Trust me, I know we aren't dating, but we both still need to eat, and I have food.

His words sting a little bit; I'm not sure why. I'm well aware of what this is, and even though I started the conversation, still . . . those toddler butterflies roll in their wings, and I remind myself that after all these years, we are just now becoming friends.

Friends with Stokes. Who would have thought? Certainly not me.

My stomach growls. Did he buy this food just for me, or did he already have it? Curiosity gets the better of me, and as much as I hate to admit it, I do want to see him and where he lives.

Okay, I'll be there soon.

Great.

Thirty minutes later, in a pair of trendy jeans and a long-sleeved slouchy green shirt with my hair in a braid, I'm standing outside his building. Stokes wasn't kidding when he said his condo was across the street from the Thai place, two blocks away. How I never knew he lived here is beyond me, and why it took months for him to drop into the shop, I don't understand either.

I take the elevator to the sixth floor, which also happens to be the top. It opens to a hallway where there is only one door. I walk to it and knock with an unwelcome anxiousness.

A few seconds later, it opens, and I'm face to face with my fake boyfriend. Tall, messy hair, weekend scruff on his jaw, and whiskey eyes ringed in green. We stare at each other for a beat too long. Those toddler butterflies wake up, liking being under his gaze, and the tension that is always present when we are together somehow shifts and crackles. He feels it too as his brows furrow, and without saying anything, he clears his throat then steps out of the way to allow me to come in.

Don't overthink this, Rosie, I say to try to settle myself. It's years of familiarity and nothing more, and then all thoughts dissipate as I take in the beauty that is his home.

"Wow, this place is incredible," I say in an awed whisper.

"Thank you," he says back, his voice oddly rough.

And it is. It looks like it's straight out of an architectural design magazine. It's a huge urban loft with an open floor plan for the kitchen, dining, and living room, and then on each end of the space is a hallway. The majority of the walls are brick, the floors are a light distressed wood, the ceiling has exposed pipes and beams, the kitchen is state of the art, and the far wall is lined with windows, framing a perfect view of downtown.

I turn to look at him, and his hands are in his pockets as he watches me take in the details of his home.

"How did you find this place?" I turn away to keep looking at his beautiful dwelling and not him and how those jeans perfectly fit and stretch across his thighs.

"Realtor," he says, now moving toward the kitchen. "Do you remember Mike Casey from high school? He started his own agency, and I reached out. This building had just been refurbished, and with one look, I was sold."

"I do remember that guy." I slip off my shoes and drop them by the front door.

"Beer, wine, or water?" he asks, offering me the same as I did for him at my place.

"You know what, I'll have a glass of wine."

I hear him open a cabinet door, but I'm too busy walking into the middle of the room to pay any attention to him. I stop next to the couch and do a three-sixty turn. This place is exactly what I would picture for Stokes. It's then that I realize I've never seen the inside of his house at the farm either. Is it urban or country? Both styles fit him, so I'm not sure what I'd expect.

Taking in the details, I drag my feet through the plush rug the couch sits on while trailing my fingers across the back of it. He has a huge television mounted on the wall over a fireplace. There are shelves that hold enough books to make a small library, and along the wall that goes to the left hallway, I spot large black and white framed photos of the farm and his family. They're beautiful, and as I move closer, I'm stunned to find one is of the three of us: Stokes, Molly, and me. I'm in one of the photos in his home.

Me.

I remember when this picture was taken, too. It was Thanksgiving weekend my senior year of college. Stokes was heading back to law school, and his mother asked that we pose together. We were standing next to his car, but the way the photo is taken, all you see in the background is one of the fields with a horse's head popped over the fence. He's standing in the middle, and at the time I thought he'd wrapped his arms around both of us, but it turns out it was just me. His arm is draped across my shoulders, mine is around his waist, and Molly is leaning up against him on the other side. We look close, affectionate toward each other, and poor Molly looks like a third wheel.

I turn to look at him and find he's watching me almost

warily. I point to the photo without saying a word, and he just shrugs one shoulder before popping the cork.

A strange feeling courses through me. Part of me thinks I should ask him why in the world he would have a picture of me on his walls—after all, he's always hated me—but the other part doesn't want to know the answer. I might like his response, but it also might force me to take a deeper look at myself and the role I played in our never-ending feud.

Not touching that subject with a ten-foot pole, I steer the questions in a different direction.

"I always thought you lived more downtown—I had no idea you were here in NuLu. Why haven't you ever come into the shop?"

"Would you have wanted me to?" he asks as he walks over and hands me a glass of red.

He's got a point.

"Hmm," I mumble as I walk over to the wall of windows and look out while he walks back to the kitchen and begins pulling things out of the refrigerator and placing them on the island.

There's music playing throughout the loft. I didn't notice it at first, but it fills the quiet space that's grown between us. There's also the deliciousness of barbecue floating in the air, and my stomach growls.

"It smells amazing in here. Where did you get the barbecue from?" I make my way to the island and sit down on a stool across from him.

"I made it myself." He turns and points toward a crockpot on the counter.

My jaw drops, and he smirks at my reaction.

"You have a crockpot?" I hold up my hand. "No, wait—better question: you know how to use a crockpot?"

He gives me a flat look, even though I can see the humor in his eyes.

"Yes, Thorney, I do know how to read a manual and follow a recipe."

"But . . . a crockpot is so domestic. This changes my view of you entirely."

He chuckles, and the sound plus the image in front of me does strange things to my heart.

"I work late, I don't want to eat out all the time, and it's an easy way to have dinner ready when I get home." He grabs our plates, pulls some Texas toast out of the oven, and moves them to the kitchen table. I follow, noting the large salad, roasted broccoli, and pie that are already set out.

That's right, a pie.

I try hard not to smile but fail.

He sees me looking at the dessert. "I didn't make that, but I know you like peach pie. It's from that bakery a few blocks over."

The bakery I love and get my scones from.

A blush burns through my cheeks. I don't like peach pie—I love it, and he remembered. I take a longer look at him as he moves back into the kitchen, and it hits me: his favorite is apple. I kind of love that I know this detail about him too.

"I do, thank you." I take a seat and set the wine down. "How often do you cook like this?"

"At least three or four days a week," he says over his shoulder as he scoops out the barbecue and puts it in a bowl.

"Well then, make enough for two, because I'm officially inviting myself over."

"Okay," he says quietly as he puts the bowl in front of me and sits down. "I know you also like toast, so I was thinking you could stack the barbecue if you wanted."

As I put my napkin in my lap, I take a look at the food and then at him. This entire situation feels surreal to me, and his overt kindness these past few weeks has my heart rate increasing.

He lifts his gaze to mine, and we stare at each other. His usual broody, stiff self is gone, and in its place is a guy who, if I'm not careful, I could fall for.

"The me prior to our little agreement wants to blurt out some type of snarky comment, only, I can't come up with anything, nor do I want to."

One side of his mouth tips up, and he seems to relax even more into his chair. "Well, look at that. We're making progress."

"I guess we are." I smile back.

Dinner, of course, is perfect, and once I've transitioned into a food coma state, we clean up the dishes and make our way over to the couch. Neither one of us sits on an end, both kind of landing in the middle, and we prop our feet up on the large rectangular ottoman that sits before us. This is such foreign territory for me, to be just casually sitting here with him, but at the same time, because I really have known him for so long, it again feels normal. We feel normal. My disdain for him is definitely gone and has shifted to something new. I can't help but wonder what will happen when our time comes to an end.

"You look tired," he says after finding us an old movie and tossing the remote to the side.

"I am, but it's worth it—it really is. Only three weeks left and then it will all come to a sudden halt."

"What will you do once the Derby is over?"

"There are other events later in the year like the Breeders' Cup, the Kentucky Fall Classic, and the steeplechase races, but aside from that and the weddings, mainly I will just be rebuilding my inventory for next year. I'd like to have twenty-five percent more stock."

He grabs a blanket and tosses it over both of us, and all I can think is that this fake relationship is feeling less and less fake by the day.

"So, just to clear the air here . . ." He shifts so he's facing me a little and puts one arm across the back of the couch. "I've been meaning to ask you: why do you think I'm mean, cunning, and two-faced?" He runs his hand over the back of his head. He's uncomfortable asking me this, and now I feel bad for saying it.

I shift a little so I'm facing him too. He asked, so I'm going to give it to him. "Well, we both know you haven't exactly been a pillar of kindness to me over the years." I let out a deep, exhausted sigh. "I don't know why either, but at this point I just want it to be water under the bridge. I also may have taken it a step too far. I don't think you are two-faced, Stokes—you've never had a problem telling me what you think. I just sometimes felt you were different with me than you were with others."

The hand that's on the back of the couch finds my braid, and he looks at it as he picks it up, runs his fingers down it, and thinks about what I said.

I don't mind the quiet. I do wish I knew what's going on in his head, what he is thinking, but I also know in order for us to ever move to a place of friendship where there is no animosity or doubt about one another, these conversations have to be had—that is, if he does truly want to be my friend.

I find I'm nervous waiting for his response.

Eventually his eyes make their way back to mine. "And you've never had a problem leaving realistic little rubber snakes lying around for me to find."

A laugh bursts out of me. Stokes hates snakes. Hates them, fears them, you name it, and pranking him with them over the years has been the best. His expression softens as he's pleased he made me laugh.

"Let's talk about you for a minute. What's up with that boss of yours, and why do you still work there?"

He lets out a heavy sigh and runs the hand sitting in his lap over his face. "Honestly, I don't know anymore. My mother has worked with this firm for years. Her attorney was Mr. Richardson, who I interned under and who ulti-mately offered me the job. Six months later, he retired."

"So the last two and a half years, you've been reporting to this Collier guy?"

"Yes, and I do try to give him the benefit of the doubt, but things there have changed."

I tilt my head. "How so?"

His fingers pick up my braid again. "It's been subtle, but the morale across the firm is different, and the clients we've taken on in the last eighteen months or so are not our usual. I don't know . . ." He shakes his head and frowns. "And now that Suzy is there all day every day . . ." He stops talking, but I understand.

"So why do you stay?"

We all know he doesn't need to work there, and he's certainly put in enough time to learn what he needs to learn from a practical application standpoint. I know he's never been one to quit things, but this is different, and ulti-mately the goal was never for him to stay long term.

His eyes find mine. Instead of uncertainty, there's disappointment mixed with resoluteness, and that's when he says, "Lately, I've been asking myself that same thing."

16

———

Stokes has become an enigma to me.

When this charade first started, I was confused by him and his sudden friendly behavior, but over the past two weeks, I've now found him to be more of a mystery.

At some point during the movie, I fell asleep. I didn't mean to, but I did, and what woke me was his hand. With his arm across the back of the couch, I'd somehow drifted his way and landed with his thigh as my personal pillow. I don't remember this, but what I'm certain I'll never forget was his arm resting on me with his fingers massaging my scalp. I could have lain there all night and enjoyed the feeling of him doing something so simple and sweet, but that wouldn't have been fair as he too had to work on Monday, and I'm not quite fully comfortable with this newfound kindness from him. It goes against the grain—all of it.

The Stokes I've known for so long is closed off and rigid. I never in a million years would have pegged him as someone who is lovey-dovey and touchy. Yet every time we are together, he's getting more bold and touching me somehow, some way, including this morning when he popped in with coffee.

Previously, he would place the items on the counter, smile, and be on his way. But today, he came behind the counter, wrapped me in a hug, and kissed my temple as he wished me a good day.

Of course, with his fresh scent surrounding me and his hard body pressed against mine, I wanted to dissolve into him so he could take me with him, but it was the look on Molly's face as I thought she might pass out from shock that had me releasing him and pondering all my life choices.

"You like him," she whispers to me just as he reaches the door and turns to give us one last smile.

"Maybe. I don't know. I don't know what to think of any of this," I tell her, and she waits until the door closes before she squeals.

He's not messing with me, is he? I wonder. I mean, of all our pranks and torturing each other over the years, messing with my emotions like this would be taking it one step too far, right? I know he has the ability to be a complete dick when he wants to be, but I wouldn't have thought him to be at this level of cruelty.

"Well knowing you, you are definitely doing just that— overthinking it. Stop. Have a good time with him. Stokes is amazing when you take the time to know him versus drive him mad and bring out his worst. You should know this at least." She takes her coffee and moans at the taste.

I do.

I think.

Gah, there I go again.

It's the doubt. I can't help it, because if I fully give in to this new sparkly version of Stokes and all of this just turns out to be one big joke on me, I'm not sure I would survive it.

Have I always disliked him? Yes, but as we all know, there's a fine line between love and hate, and I'm honest enough with myself to know that deep down I do love him. I've always loved him in a way that's due to our family connections, the years spent together, and his presence in so many of my memories. I've learned how to have thick skin against his superficial jabs and spars, but to purposefully take over my heart and then break it . . . there's not enough glue in this world that would put it back together.

"I'm not overthinking it, I'm just still wary and am trying to ease into this new version of him." I pick up my coffee and pop off the lid so it can cool.

"This is the same version Stokes has always been—you just refused to see it."

Is that true?

I'm not too proud to second-guess myself. After all, I pegged him wrong all these years and missed that he was quiet and introverted because he's shy, but I think she's wrong. He was a willing and equal contender in our life-long battle, and up until that Sunday dinner in March, he had never touched me before.

I turn to look at her. "Maybe, but sometimes what you see is what you get, and you know firsthand how he's made me feel over the years."

She lets out a sigh. "I do, but he only behaved that way around you, no one else. That's not who he is."

"I hope not," I tell her, and I mean it.

"I'm meeting a client at the bakery at two, so you've got me all morning and through lunch. Would you like me to bring down more hats?"

"I think so, and the fascinators too. We're down to the last of the inventory, so may as well put it out. I mean really there's only two weeks or so left. Most people won't be shopping for a hat the day or two before. We can line them on the counters and then, as some are sold, move them to the vacant spots on the wall."

"Right-oh, boss. Sounds like a great plan to me."

Over the next couple of hours, we empty out the second bedroom in my apartment. It's such a surreal sight to see it vacant, but I feel so grateful and blessed at the same time. It's after Molly finally leaves that my ears pick up on a familiar word I've already heard once this season.

"All I'm saying is horses don't just get laminitis, not horses of this caliber who are under such intense supervision."

My eyes immediately shoot to the woman, and it's Mrs. Neal, wife to the owner of Bluegrass Fields Farm.

"I agree with you completely," says the woman

standing next to her in a tone that is as completely dumb-founded as Mrs. Neal's.

"They don't even let the horses out in the afternoon for fear of them eating too much grass. Sugar content is highest in the afternoon, so they are always let out to graze first thing in the morning," she says, all exasperated.

"Is it just Smooth Jazz?" the friend asks. That's the name of their qualifying three-year-old.

"Yes, I just don't understand. We're devastated that he won't be able to run in the Derby this year."

There's something about all this that I don't understand either. My stomach turns as I think about all the gossip, the disappointment, and the coincidence of it.

It is a coincidence, right?

That ache in my stomach grows, and as the two women continue to talk and try on hats, I pull out my calendar. I look to see what day Mrs. Rupp from Sterling Bells Farm was here: March 16th. Her friend made the comment that she couldn't believe she waited three weeks to tell them. If I back up three weeks, that makes it Wednesday, February 23rd. Flipping to the back of my calendar, I retrieve my printout of this year's race schedule. A gasp slips through as I see this was three days before the Rebel Stakes race where the purse was one million dollars.

The second incident I heard about was with my mother the day of Mrs. Whitlock's party. Grabbing my phone, I google *barn fire at Shaded Oaks Farm, Louisville*. Immediately, articles pop up. The date of the fire was Wednesday, March 23rd. Looking at the race schedule again, I see this was just before the Louisiana Derby, where the purse was also one million dollars.

I heard about the third incident the day before I went to Stokes's work function, which makes that April 7th. This time a horse from Blanton Farm was hijacked on the side of the road while heading to a farm in Florida to get ready for the Florida Derby, another million-dollar purse.

And now with the fourth incident, another case of laminitis, something definitely isn't sitting right with me. The last race of the series two championships to qualify for the Derby is Lexington. Grabbing my phone, I pull up the race to see what horses ran in it. Sure enough, I don't find Smooth Jazz, which means this must have happened last week. Granted, that purse is only 400,000, but still. While the points earned are lower at twenty, eight, four, and two, if a horse is on the fence to qualify for the Derby, placing high in this race would be a must.

Sterling Bells Farm, Shaded Oaks Farm, Blanton Farm, and Bluegrass Fields Farm—these are four of the top farms in Louisville. Each consistently has a horse to run in the Oaks and the Derby, and if I'm being honest with myself, all signs point to sabotage, not coincidence.

If those farms were targeted, Whitlock Farm has to be next.

Chills race down my arms and fear nearly steals the breath from me. Moving toward the back office with my phone, I hit Stokes's name while my blood races through my veins.

He picks up on the second ring. "Hey. You okay?" His

voice is deep and familiar. It instantly begins to calm the uneasy energy coursing through me.

"Why wouldn't I be?" I ask him, pacing around with my heart in my throat.

He chuckles. "Because you've never called me, and I'd just assumed pigs would fly before you ever would."

I hesitate and think about this because he's not wrong. I've never called him.

"Well, maybe something is wrong." I start chewing on the skin on the end of my thumb.

"What do you mean?" There are a few clicks on a keyboard and then some papers being shuffled in the background.

"Can you come over tonight?" I'm certain he's also thinking I've never truly invited him over before either.

He pauses, and silence fills the line.

"I'll be there as soon as I can wrap this contract up."

Instantly the anxiety in my chest lightens. Stokes is a good critical thinker. He'll be able to hear what I'm saying and stay as objective as possible. He'll be able to tell if I've put way too much thought into this or if I'm possibly onto something.

"Okay, great. Are you hungry?" I ask, peeking out to the shop to see if I'm needed. The two women are still trying on hats, and on the other side of the store, two younger girls are trying on fascinators while snapping pictures in front of the rose wall.

"I will be by the time I get there." He chuckles again.

That sound . . . why do I love that sound? For so long, it

would grate on my nerves. It meant he was in some way making fun of me, laughing at me, but lately, it's felt more like he's laughing with me, like together we somehow share an inside joke against the world, a joke that makes me feel special.

"Okay, once these people leave, I'm going to close up, and order food."

"Sounds good. You sure you're okay?" he asks one last time.

"I am. I just need to talk something through with you to see what you think."

"All right. Then I'll see you in a bit."

Warmth and elation trickle through my veins. Who would have thought I'd ever get this excited to see Stokes Whitlock? Not me.

"Thank you, Stokes."

"Hey, Rosie?" he says just before I hang up.

"Yeah?"

"I'm glad you called me."

17

I make it upstairs five minutes before Stokes will arrive. My place is a mess, and I let out a deep sigh as I glare at the dishes in the sink and some shipping boxes with new supplies that I just stacked up against the wall. I wasn't expecting company, but it is what it is, and I don't have time to pick up. I'm ordering dinner from the Italian place down the street when I hear Stokes's voice through the wall. My neighbor must have let him in, and now he's heading up the stairs. Those toddler butterflies start jittering, but I'm not sure if it's because I'm going to see him or if I'm just nervous about the crazy conspiracy theory I've concocted in my mind. I stare at the door, waiting, and then there's the knock.

Either way, their tiny wings tickle my insides as I open the door and Stokes smiles at me. It's a real smile too, one that reaches his beautiful eyes and says his day just got infinitely better and there's nowhere else he'd rather be.

My stomach swirls and dips, and if I didn't know any better, I'd say right at this moment, he's giving me weak knees.

Stepping close, he runs his fingers down my arm to my wrist as his greeting and then bends to give me a kiss, only this one isn't on my forehead—it's lower and on my cheek. I suddenly have a whole new appreciation for the five o'clock shadow as his lips are so soft, but the scratch just around them marks my skin.

He strides in, and heat flashes through me. I grip the door and watch as he tosses his charcoal gray jacket over the back of the couch, pulls on his tie so it loosens, and undoes the top button on his shirt. Pushing his hair off his forehead, he turns to face me, and a sharp jab of longing hits me.

Longing for Stokes.

What is happening to me?

He's so tall and handsome. His broad shoulders, imposing stature, and overall serious air have him filling the space and sending out magnetic waves. Those waves .. . they're trying to pull me toward him, not push me away. I'm not sure when the flip occurred, but it did.

Sure, I've always thought Stokes is attractive—most of the female population does—but what I'm feeling right this second about wanting to be stuck to him, lost under his hands with his mouth fully enraptured with mine, has my lower stomach tightening and makes me almost panicky. Molly was right, I do like him, and after this reaction I just had to him, once this little fake relationship is over, I already know things are not going to end well for me.

Slowly, one corner of his mouth tips up, and reflex has me doing the same. I smile at him until he chuckles, and his hands land on his waist, his waist that has zero fat on it and I'm certain sports that V that is so sexy on a man, sexy and pointing straight to the promised land.

"I don't know why your outfits continue to surprise me, but they do," he says as his eyes trail down the length of me.

I look at the dress I wore today. It's royal blue and has a short full skirt made of ruffles.

"It's the same dress you saw me in this morning," I tell him, looking back up and pushing the door shut.

"Yeah, but . . ." He twirls his finger over his head.

"Oh." I'd forgotten I was still wearing a matching fascinator. This one has black netting that's shaped into a disk, and adorning it is a large black and white feather flower with royal blue and teal filler feathers surrounding the back half of it to give it height.

"I should be used to them by now, but I'm guessing I never will be." His expression softens, and I might even say he's looking at me affectionately. "It looks good on you."

This time the heat crawls up my neck to my cheeks.

I start fidgeting with the skirt and eventually clear my throat. "Right. Thanks. Well, food is ordered, and I'm going to run and change real quick," I say as I start walking toward my bedroom.

"Okay." He makes his way into my kitchen, lays his cell

phone on the counter, and opens the refrigerator like this is an everyday thing and not something he's doing for the first time.

Pull it together, Rosie, I tell myself as I slip into a pair of yoga pants and a tank top and pull my hair up into a bun. I realize this is an overly casual outfit, but this is what I wear at the end of a long day, and I'm not trying to impress him. Wait, am I? No. That's ridiculous. This is Stokes. Besides, he's seen me every which way to Sunday and doesn't care.

"So, not that I mind rushing over, because I'm happy to see you, but I'm wondering how much longer you're going to keep me in suspense," he says as I walk back into the living room. He's lounging on my couch and drinking a beer he found. He's rolled up his shirtsleeves and looks so delicious I wonder what he would do if I went and sat on his lap.

I almost laugh out loud at the reaction I think I would get, but then again, his behavior lately has been so starkly different. Only a month ago I'm certain he would have pushed me onto the floor, but now, who knows.

I sit next to him, facing him with one foot tucked underneath me, and I breathe slowly to calm myself. He watches me, and at whatever expression he sees on my face, the playful look vanishes and the familiar little lines drop between his brows.

Nope, this won't do. Buzzing with energy, I decide it's best to stand and end up walking back and forth in front of him. He sits up and leans forward so his elbows are on his knees, his eyes never leaving me, tracking me around the room.

"Spit it out, Thorney," he says gently as I make my way to the kitchen where my planner lies. I wrote out the timeline so I could keep everything in order, and I hand it to him.

He's looking up at me with full concern, the muscles locking in his face.

"Okay." I let out a deep breath. "You may think I'm crazy, and I might be, but hear me out. I'd rather give you all the details so you can formulate your own conclusion."

"Conclusion about what?" He sets his beer on the floor and now stands too. His voice has changed a bit; he knows I'm about to tell him something he isn't going to like to hear, and he's gone into lawyer mode.

"A couple of weeks ago, Mrs. Rupp came into the shop."

"Mrs. Rupp from Sterling Bells Farm?" He's completely confused now. The sun is just barely out, and the sky has shifted from orange to a nighttime purple. The hue bounces off the side of his face and enhances his features: sharp cheekbone, defined jaw, skin that looks smooth and rough at the same time. I want to run my hand over it.

"Yes. She was with her friends. They had an appointment so no one else was there."

"Okay . . ." He draws the word out, his tone telling me to get to the point.

"They're drinking tea, I'm minding my own business, and she starts talking about downsizing her hat to a fascinator since they don't have a Derby contender this year and she doesn't feel the need to be large and flashy."

"What do you mean? What happened to Big Red?" he asks, frowning.

"Laminitis."

Stokes's face pales.

"Right!" I throw out my hands. "I felt so bad for her, but then, while I'm getting ready for your mom's party, my mother tells me about the fire at Shaded Oaks Farm and how poor Black Bandit has smoke inhalation and won't be running the rest of the season."

His lips press together. I'm certain just from hearing about those two incidents he's now following my train of thought.

"But then it gets worse." My heart starts pounding as this is the part where he will think I'm crazy or onto something.

"How so?" His hands are back on his waist, and his eyes have switched to laser beam mode. I feel like they are boring into me, not in a bad way, just that he's hyper-focused on what he's hearing.

I then tell him how people come in and gossip, how I heard about the stolen horse from Blanton Farm, and then about today with Smooth Jazz from Bluegrass Fields Farm.

"Look here." I hand him the paper. "I've done my best to get the timeline correct. You'll see the date of the incident with each farm, what race it was before, the points awarded, and the purse attached to it. All four of these farms are now out of the Derby, and something in my gut says that's too much of a coincidence, too many of the best farms in Louisville, and I'm afraid your farm is next."

His eyes snap to mine from looking at the timeline. There's no wariness or uncertainty in them, just shock and anger. He's processing what I've told him, as he should.

Sabotage in the horseracing community is as old as the sport. People go crazy over the money and have done the dumbest things. There's obviously doping the horses, but there's also bribing jockeys and swapping horses, and one time someone even painted a horse to look like another, not considering that when it sweat from running the race, the color would drip off.

A loud knock on the door startles me, and I jump. Stokes lets out a deep sigh, and the hand holding the paper drops to his side while I go to answer the door for our dinner. He begins pacing in front of the windows, the evening light making him even more gorgeous than he already is.

Back and forth.

Back and forth.

Pacing means he's thinking, and where before this tic of his would annoy me, now I find it somewhat endearing.

I can't really blame him. The more I've thought about all of this, the more I'm convinced there is foul play happening. If one or two things happen, sure, that's coincidental, but four, and right here in Louisville at the end leading into the Derby—it's too much.

He turns to look at me and tilts his head. "Two cases of laminitis?"

"Right?" I've set the food on the table, I grabbed dishes and silverware, and I'm now scooping out some salad into two bowls for us.

"And neither one said what caused it?" He starts rubbing his forehead.

"Nope." I grab a bottle of wine and two glasses and pour myself a hefty amount.

"It's insane how I really haven't heard about any of this. I mean news of the fire spread around, but the others have been really quiet." He grabs his beer off the floor, walks to the table, and sits down.

"Do you think I'm crazy? Do you think there's reason to be concerned here?" I take the seat next to him. Garlic wafts up between us, and my stomach growls. I know Stokes likes sausage, so I ordered a sausage rigatoni for him and a pasta carbonara for me.

"No, I don't think you're crazy, and honestly, I'm not sure. For all of these things to have happened in the last month, and to elite farms and horses . . . it is suspicious. I understand why your brain went where it did. At this point, I can't see how we shouldn't be worried about it."

Relief washes through me.

"What are you going to do?" I take a bite and almost moan at how good it tastes.

He rubs a hand over his face. "I need to tell my mother, and I need to have a conversation with security. Maybe we need to amp up a bit for these next two weeks." He picks up his fork and takes a bite, although I'm not sure if he's actually tasting the food or just consuming it.

"At least nothing happened during the party."

He looks at me, and his brows pull down. "Grayson called last minute before the party and told me he was taking Ace and a few others off the property. He said he had this strange feeling buzzing on his skin, and he didn't like it. Said with all the people coming to the house, he felt we needed to be a little more cautious."

"Do you think he knows something we don't?" I hate to think the worst of Grayson, but people have done much worse for less, and these horses stand to gain people millions.

He tilts his head as he thinks this through and then shakes it. "No, I don't think he has anything to do with those other situations. He and my mother . . ." He trails off, looking at me.

"I was wondering." I smile at him. The idea of Birdie and Grayson really does make me happy. It's been so long. Maybe he can introduce my mother to someone too.

"Tomorrow after work, I'm going to head out to talk to them." He picks up his fork to resume eating.

"Wish I could go," I tell him, and I mean it.

His eyes find mine and then reverently paint a path down to my lips. Stillness surrounds us as a new tension builds between us. My tongue slips out to wet them, and he lets out an almost audible groan as he exhales. My stomach bottoms out, because I do know what it feels like to kiss him, and I'm starting to think there isn't anything I wouldn't give for him to kiss me again.

He shakes his head, and his eyes reconnect with mine.

"If this turns out to be a legitimate thing that's happening, I don't know how to thank you."

"Are you kidding? Whitlock Farm is my home—you don't need to thank me." I pick up my wine glass and take a large sip.

The reverence returns. "You're right. It is your home."

For so long, Stokes made me feel like I was passing time at the farm, like my being there was temporary and he couldn't wait to get rid of me. But with these words, I have to fight the burning behind my eyes. Everyone wants a place to call home, and his confirmation of what I already knew in my heart means more than he knows.

For a few minutes, we eat in silence. I forgot to turn on music, but he doesn't seem to mind, and the quietness isn't awkward. Then again, being with him stopped being awkward sometime over the last couple of weeks. It just fizzled away.

"So, I know we agreed on three outings and a dinner out, which I still owe you, but my firm is hosting another party in two nights on the rooftop of our building down-town for the Thunder Over Louisville. Would you like to go with me?" he asks with a wariness he never needs to feel when it comes to me.

I can't help but think back to the last event which he all but demanded I attend per our arrangement, whereas this time it feels like he is genuinely asking me if I would like to be his date.

"Is this something you want to go to? I didn't get the

feeling you particularly liked being around your work people that much."

He lets out a sigh. "It's not that I dislike them." He looks away as he collects his thoughts then turns back to me. "I guess it's just with the way things have changed, I've begun to want something different. I hear the view of the fireworks will be good."

Something different. Am I allowed to include myself in this scenario? After all, we are different now, and I like this new version of us.

"Wanting something different isn't a bad thing," I tell him hesitantly, and I know he understands what I'm saying as his lips curve up into a small smile.

"No, it's not," he says, his voice a little deeper, rougher, his gaze a little darker.

And just like that, my toddler butterflies stretch and grow to kid size.

"I'd love to watch the fireworks with you."

LUVU TEA
A RACE FOR LOVE

Well, well, well, what do we have here?
Spotted on the streets of downtown Louisville was none other
than our bachelor of the season, Stokes Whitlock, but he
wasn't with Ms. May. Our sources tell us this is Suzy Collier, a
colleague and longtime city socialite. The two were seen
having lunch together and strolling back to the office arm in
arm. The way she was glancing up at him leaves us
wondering if we have a competition developing. Has another
filly taken the lead in the race for our bachelor's love?

18

"I'm sorry I'm late," Stokes says as he jumps out of his SUV and rounds the front to open my door.

"It's okay," I tell him as I take in his frazzled state. It's clear he's been in these clothes for a while, as they aren't in their normal pressed-smooth state but are wrinkled from sitting. His shirtsleeves are rolled up, his hair looks like his hands have made it their mission to create an all-new style, and despite all that, he still looks insanely good.

"I should have anticipated the traffic coming into the city for the fireworks, and I just didn't." He lets out an exhale. Poor Stokes. With his stringent personality, he can't handle being late anywhere. He's one of those people who isn't prompt, but instead always early.

"It's fine. No worries at all." I smile at him, and he visibly relaxes. "I was working on Avery's dress—I always have something to do." I shrug like *No big deal.*

As I brush past him to slide in, he stops me by pulling me into his arms. His lips land on my temple, where he holds them and just breathes me in. My heart thumps hard against my chest at his nearness. He's warm, smells deliciously like him, and I take the unexpected moment to lean in closer.

"Missed me did you," I tease as his head drops a little, his hair falling forward and tickling my skin.

He lets out a single chuckle, and I feel it straight to my bones. "I did."

Letting out another exhale, he releases me and takes a step back so I can climb in. As we pull away from the curb, he reaches over and takes my hand.

Always touching me.

I like it.

A lot.

"How was your day?" he asks, quickly glancing at me so he can keep his eyes on the road. "How is Avery's dress coming along?"

"My day was good. We were busy all day. I was starting to worry that people would not be happy with the inventory I have left since it is kind of picked over, but people are still buying and they're still happy. Avery's dress is pretty much done. At this point I'm just tinkering with it."

With Stokes at the farm last night and Molly out with Austin, I had a quiet evening where I ate leftover Italian and worked for hours on Avery's dress. I'm so proud of this garment, and I can't imagine that she won't love it.

"That's great. I can't wait to see it." He rubs his thumb

across the back of my hand, and for some reason, a blush warms my skin. Avery seeing the dress and liking it is one thing, but Stokes is another. I want him to like it. I want him to be proud of me, too. Stupid? Yes, but I still do.

"How's the farm? Did you talk to Grayson?" The streetlights kick on as the sun is about to set. The fluorescent lights flash throughout the car as we make our way downtown.

"The farm is good, and I did. We sat down with Rick, the head of security, and my mother. Grayson had heard about the Blantons' horse, but not Bluegrass Fields. They are in agreement that it is one too many incidents to ignore, but we're going to keep this quiet to not alert anyone that we might be onto something—if there is even something to be onto." He shrugs his shoulder and shakes his head. "But we would hate to entice anyone to do something more severe. For the next two weeks, the only people who will have access to Ace are the family, Grayson, Jody, his handler, and the veterinarian. Even then, Jody and the vet will be searched out of precaution, and we are adding more security cameras to the barn."

"That sounds like a good idea, and I'm glad they didn't think I was crazy either."

"Never." He cracks a smile, and then it fades as we come to a stop at a red light. The double lines have dropped into place as he looks at me, and instantly I'm uneasy.

"What is it?" I ask, squeezing his hand.

"The Tea." He says it like it pains him.

My eyes shift down to my lap, and I look at our hands. "Yeah, I saw it. Molly showed me."

"Rosie, you and me, we're in this together. You know I would never, right?" he asks, worry laced between his words.

Do I know this? Relationship Stokes is someone completely different from my-enemy-number-one Stokes. That is, unless he's ultimately doing all this as one big prank to mess with my emotions. But even then, I'm pretty certain his code of honor to always do the right thing would win out. Plus, he hates change and messy situations. Inserting one person into his daily routine is probably hard enough on him; he could never add two. Also, unless he lied—and deep down in my gut I don't think he did— he's made it clear how he feels about Suzy Collier.

My eyes rise to find his. Whiskey and mossy green, my two favorites of the ever-changing colors, are present and swirled together. "I do," I tell him, and he briefly closes his eyes. His shoulders relax as he lets out a long sigh.

Mostly, I think Stokes couldn't care less about what people think of him. He knows who he is and he's worked so hard to be the man that he is, but that simple movement tells me what I think does matter to him. Maybe his feelings aren't so different from mine.

Maybe this isn't as fake as it was meant to be.

Then again, I care about what Molly thinks, and I don't want to be in a relationship with her.

"Good," he says as the light changes and we're on our way. "She's just so . . . awful." He scowls. "I had Christopher revising something for me, so I offered to run out and grab us a couple of sandwiches. On the sidewalk, she ambushed me out of nowhere and followed me to the deli across the street. To be polite, I offered to buy her lunch, but that's it. We didn't eat together, I certainly didn't touch her, and that picture looked so bad. You've seen her—you know how she is."

"I know her type. I'm not worried about the picture, and you shouldn't be either." I pat the top of his hand with my free one.

"It's not me I'm worried about . . . it's you." He looks over at me, concern stamped across his gorgeous features.

I want to ask him why. I should ask him why, but for some reason I don't. While my revelations about him have made me see things clearer and my feelings toward him have shifted, there's the possibility that his haven't. I'd rather live in this fake relationship bubble with him for a little bit longer than have him tell me otherwise.

"Well, you don't need to. I'm good." I plaster on a smile I hope he doesn't see is somewhat fake.

Besides, it wasn't that this photo was of him and Suzy that ultimately bothered me; it was the photo in general. One day there will be a photo, lots of photos, of him with someone who will not be me. That's what I saw when I looked at the picture. That's what got to me.

The rest of the ride to his building is quick and mostly quiet. We park in his underground designated parking spot for the firm, and he slips on a black sweater over his shirt. He pulls out the collar and lines up the cuffs of his sleeves, and then he takes my hand as we enter the elevator and head to the roof.

"I've never been to your office," I tell him as the doors open and we step outside, the cool spring air instantly wrapping around us.

"No, you haven't. Once the Derby has passed, you should come and meet me for lunch one day. I can show you how small and boring it is."

"Do you at least have a window?" I tease, and one corner of his mouth tips up.

"I do have that."

"Stokes!" Mr. Collier, the man who hosted the party at his house, shouts when he spots him.

Instantly, Stokes tenses, straightening so he's taller, and his hand becomes viselike around mine. A thought occurs to me: maybe it isn't so much what he's doing that he wants to be different, but who it is he's working for that is really the problem.

"So glad you decided to come," he says with a big toothy grin—that is until he spots me and his expression briefly falls. "And I see you brought your friend again."

"Why wouldn't I?" Stokes asks with a slight edge to his tone. "Rosie, you remember my boss, Dean Collier." He steps closer to me. "Dean, my girlfriend, Rosie."

Girlfriend.

My heart flutters. I'm getting way too used to how this sounds.

"I do. Thank you again for inviting us." I release Stokes's hand and wrap my arm around his waist. He follows suit, wrapping his around my shoulders. "It was a lovely party, and we had a wonderful time," I tell him, making sure he understands that there is no Stokes and his friend, that we are an us.

Suzy flounces up beside her father and basically sneers when she sees me then turns it on when she looks at Stokes. I mean do these two even realize how obvious they are? It's awful.

"Stokes! You made it. Oh my God, you have to try this drink, it's delicious." She's holding two glasses and shoves one in his direction. Both of us recoil—there on the edge of the glass is a slice of orange.

His fingers dig into me, and I reach out and take the glass from her. She frowns but relinquishes it to not be rude in front of her father.

"Ah, thanks for bringing this to us. It looks delicious, but Stokes and I aren't drinking tonight. We both have an early morning tomorrow." I release Stokes to set the glass down on a nearby cocktail table then return to him. Suzy watches me and glowers as we've snubbed her offering.

"Really? On a Sunday?" Mr. Collier asks, eyeing us both. "Do tell." Why our personal life is any of his business, I have no idea, but to keep the peace, Stokes indulges the question while running his hand up and down my back. Does he realize he's doing this? I have no idea, but it feels amazing.

"Obviously, Rosie will be working in her shop, and the

television crew is coming out to get some film of Ace, the farm, and the family."

Every year, a crew comes out to make a short bio of the farm and whatever horse is racing in the Derby. They do this for the top five horses based on points earned over the preseason to qualify for the race.

"Oh, it's too bad you won't be there," Suzy says to me in an overdramatic tone. "I'd love to be there to watch." She smiles up at Stokes.

He squeezes me closer to him. "The farm is closed to visitors until after the Derby," Stokes says, his annoyed scowl dropping into place.

This is news to me, though I understand limiting Ace's contact with people, and this must be something else they decided on last night while he was meeting with the farm management team and security. The petty part of me is smiling on the inside. I'm also very pleased to know they will be stopping the tours.

"Oh!" I turn a little toward him to place my hand on his chest. Hazel eyes lock with mine, and my stomach swirls at his nearness. "Your mother wanted me to remind you that we are all wearing shades of blue tomorrow, not green."

"But he just said you wouldn't be there," Suzy interjects, annoyance laced throughout her tone.

"In the morning," I state as if she's the dumbest person ever. "I'll be there for the family filming."

At this, Suzy gives off a slight pout, and Mr. Collier frowns. The shine that was in his eyes dulls as he takes in the two of us, like really takes us in. He's a smart man; in his mind, he's conceding and realizing his dreams of Stokes and Suzy will never happen. Unfortunately, his daughter has not gotten the memo.

Mr. Collier claps Stokes on the arm and says, "Sounds exciting, my boy. We look forward to watching that horse of yours run."

Stokes's fingers dig into my arm. "Thank you. So do we."

"Enjoy the fireworks," he says before he wanders off to speak to another member of their firm. Too bad he didn't drag his daughter along with him.

"Stokes, did you see us in the Tea today?" she asks, all excited.

"Unfortunately," he deadpans.

She startles but quickly covers it up. "So many of my friends have reached out and asked about us."

"Suzy, there is no us, and there never will be," he tells her in a tone that leaves no questions. "That picture was a lie, most likely orchestrated by you, and quite frankly, I'm disgusted by your enthusiasm over it."

She starts to say something, but I cut her off. "If you'll excuse us, we're famished, and I see snacks over there. Can't have poor Stokes getting hangry, now can I?" I laugh, and without another glance in her direction, we walk off hand in hand.

"Hangry," he whispers against my ear.

Looking up at him, I see his face is amused, and I again decide it's way too pretty for him. "Just keepin' it real," I whisper back as we stop next to a table near the food. "You were all tense and super growly back there—not that she didn't deserve it, but you're much more pleasant after you've eaten." I grin.

He just shakes his head and pulls me close.

Why is it so easy for us to be affectionate like this?

"You look great tonight," he says, his lips pressed into my hair.

I'm wearing a burgundy sweater dress with black leggings underneath and black ankle boots. Right now, I want to go out and buy three more of this dress in different colors so he'll compliment me again.

"You don't look so bad yourself," I tell him, when really I think he's the best-looking person here, perhaps in all of Louisville.

He hugs me tighter and then releases me.

"Food," he says, and I giggle. Maybe he is a bit hangry.

Over and over people come over to say hello to us. This time I don't feel so out of place as people are becoming familiar, and I love watching him with Christopher, who is once again alone.

Stokes laughs with him. Well, it's more of a chuckle, but coming from him, it is a laugh, and I soak up the sound. The sound, the smile—all of it has my children butterflies turning into teenagers. They keep growing and stretching, and I know before long, if I'm not careful, they will be fully grown.

As the fireworks start, the lights on the roof dim, and we head to the railing of the building, where Stokes moves behind me. There are people everywhere—on other rooftops, all along the riverfront, even here, next to us—but as the large sparkly explosions light up the night sky in varying colors, I feel like we are the only two people on the planet.

Gold. Red. Silver. Green.

Flares. Shapes. Bursts. Falling stars.

Booms that rattle my chest and send tingles straight down to my toes.

Beautiful.

Or maybe it's Stokes.

As we watch, his hands slowly run down my arms to find mine, and our fingers lock together. Using the backs of his hands, he softly pushes on my hips to bring us flush against one another, my back to his front, and while I'm being surrounded by his heat, his muscles, and his smell, I lean my head against him.

I'm standing here, like this, with Stokes. It's still a little hard for me to wrap my head around this, us. With the feeling of being pressed against him, him against me, my emotions vary from suspicious and surreal to DNA-altering.

At some point, although I'm looking out at the fireworks, I no longer see them. I'm lost in my head and lost in him. Every breath he takes, every shift of his muscles . . . I'm so in tune with him that I just want more. Raising our hands, I cross them over my stomach and let out a contented sigh as his arms wrap around me.

His head drops down so his forehead rests on my shoulder, and his arms tighten. His soft hair tickles the side of my neck, and my eyes slip shut. I'm completely enveloped by him, and it's the most incredible feeling. He breathes in and out, and the air wafts against my skin, giving me goose bumps and a yearning so deep in my bones I'm certain only he has the ability to ease the weight of this feeling.

Eventually the fireworks end, but neither of us move as the people around us begin murmuring about the show and walking away from the edge. We, however, stay frozen together. I'm afraid to move, afraid to pop the bubble he's encased us in, and I'm afraid that once we drift away, I'll never get this again.

"Rosie," he whispers, his lips brushing against my ear. I shiver, and he tucks his face into my neck.

I close my eyes to memorize this moment. I want to relive it once the night is over, but as he says my name again, I know it's time. Turning, I slide around in his arms and look up at his face. Even though it is still dark, I can see and feel his gaze. It's deliciously potent with his eyes halfway closed and his stare imprinting on my soul. He's so familiar and so handsome I find it hard to breathe.

"Thank you for bringing me," I tell him, wishing we could stop time and this night could be stretched longer.

"Thank you for saying yes," he says as he tucks a piece of loose hair behind my ear then wraps his hand around the side of my face.

Are people watching us? Maybe, but at this moment, I don't care, and I don't think he does either. After all these weeks, all this time, maybe even all these years, it's all come down to this.

He dips his head slowly, and the air from our lungs mingles as he gives me time to say no if I don't want this, but I do. Yes, Stokes and I have kissed twice, but standing here with him now, in many ways, this is our first, the first for just us.

His thumb gently swipes across my cheek, he licks his bottom lip, and then his mouth settles against mine. My eyes close, shutting out the world and every single distraction in the background. I could stand in this spot forever, just like this with nothing more, and be completely content, just him and me.

Gently, his lips move over mine while keeping things PG. His hand on my lower back pulls me tighter against him, and it feels like he's relinquishing the self-control he exercised to stay away from me, but at the same time embracing how he so perilously wants this. Does he want it as much as I do? It feels impossible to think that he does, yet here we are, almost as close as two people can be.

Sliding my hand up his chest, I settle it over his heart, which is beating wildly. But instead of deepening the kiss and giving us what we both so desperately want, his lower lip drags between mine before he pulls back, studies my face, and then with a rough voice says, "Let's get out of here."

That's when I realize they've turned the lights back on.

He takes my hand, and we walk to the elevator. There

are others leaving just as we are, but we barely acknowledge them as we can't stop staring at each other.

At his car, he opens the door for me, and as I watch him walk around to his side, I feel like I'm about to burst. The door shuts behind him, and he turns my way. He looks at me like there's nowhere else in this entire world he wants to be, and he looks at me as if he is starving. There's the intense way his jaw is clenching, how his nostrils are flaring as he breathes in the scent of me in his space, and the way he bites his bottom lip as it begs to continue that kiss we started. The silence is nearly deafening, and my ears ring. Without any words said, each of us leans toward the other, surrendering to the pull.

Here it's just him and me, in a dark vehicle with tinted windows, in a poorly lit parking garage. For sure no one is watching. His hand slides around to the back of my neck, and as his fingers tangle in my hair, our mouths collide.

On the roof, his kiss was sweet and reserved, but this one is not. This one is more like the kiss on the night of Birdie's party. There's concession, passion, and new flavors.

His lips are warm, full, and so soft. They fit against mine perfectly, and the way they move, it's like he knew before he ever even touched me what we would be like together and how this was going to go. There's no fumbling, no learning phase, just perfection.

I'm in awe of the way he knows how to tilt my head to the perfect angle so he can deepen this kiss like no other. I'm in awe of the way his tongue so expertly strokes against mine, and I'm in awe of the way he gives as much as he takes, making this the best kiss of my entire life. It surpasses the party kiss. It's what fairy tales are written about.

In our story, I am being kissed by the prince, only I never want to wake up.

I'm pretty sure I could kiss him for a lifetime and then some.

19

———

As I pull onto the driveway at Whitlock Farm and wait for the gates to open, I roll down the windows and take in a deep breath. The air is cool and fresh, the grass smells sweet and inviting, and in the distance I can hear horses neighing to each other. The feel, the smell, the sound—all of it envelops me, sending my senses into a state of relaxed bliss, and then I realize I now have a taste and a feeling to include. While this farm is my home, the farm is Stokes too. After last night, I know I need to tread carefully to not blur one with the other.

At the main house, there are four cars parked out front, one being Stokes's, and I assume the others belong to the film crew. Part of me wonders why I agreed to come out tonight. After all, I'm really not family, but the other part of me is happy to be included. I love watching the Whitlocks shine. They've worked so hard to make this farm what it is.

But that doesn't change the fact that I feel bone tired.

All in all, Stokes didn't keep me out too late last night. After he walked me to my door and gave me another kiss that left me breathless, I still made it to bed at a reasonable time. Unfortunately, I was restless reliving those kisses and what they might mean for us going forward, if they really mean anything at all. Then, I still got up early to nitpick over a few details on Avery's dress. Add in that the store was off the charts crowded today, and I'm just peopled out.

But I'm here, for him, because he asked me to come.

Lowering the mirror, I check my makeup and fascinator then hop out of the car. There are voices coming from the left, I see people walking from behind the house to the front porch, and that's when I spot Stokes.

Anxiousness engulfs me.

He's wearing a blue suit with a white shirt, no tie, and the top button is undone. He has on a brown belt with brown shoes, and if I had to come up with words to describe the way he looks, they would be polished, exquisite, and in a league of his own. He's simply confidence personified.

I've never not really considered us equals. In my mind we always were, but watching him with these people surrounding him, the way he carries and presents himself, I suddenly feel like the daughter of the help that I am.

What have I got myself into?

Stokes hears the sound of the car door as I close it, and although I'm looking down to gather my composure, I can feel the moment he sees me. Goose bumps run down my arms and the hair on the back of my neck rises. Lifting my gaze to his, I see he's rerouted to come greet me, and he breaks out in the largest smile.

My smile.

Cartwheels—that's what it feels like is happening in my stomach. My teenage butterflies are officially all grown, and I'm not prepared for the havoc they are wreaking on my insides.

Not wanting to embarrass him or myself in front of these people, I smile back and make my way toward him.

He's the same guy, I tell myself. *Same guy. Same guy. We are the same.* Only, after his kiss last night and with the way my heart is currently pounding in my chest, I know I am not the same.

"Hi," he says as we meet in the middle. He bends down and kisses me right next to my mouth, and my breath catches. I'm not sure how I will ever get used to this or how I will get over it when our arrangement ends.

"Hi," I whisper back, grabbing his arm to steady us. "How's it going?" I ask as his moss green gaze shines down at me. The color of this suit completely changes the look of his eyes.

"It's been great. We're almost done. I told them you were dropping in after work, and they want to get a few clips of us together if that's all right."

I wasn't kidding when I told him everyone was to wear blue. Birdie really did pass that along, and just to be on the safe side, I did as well.

"Are you sure you want me in your film about the farm? About Ace? Everyone will see it." I look down at the pale blue dress I chose, and my hand drifts to the fascinator I paired with it. Do I look okay? Am I presentable enough to stand next to him?

"Yes," he says, with zero hesitation.

Taking me by the hand, he walks us over to the three people waiting quietly off to the side. Each is holding some sort of filming equipment, and all three smile.

"Hello," I say to them collectively, and they return the greeting.

"This is Cameron." Stokes points to the guy holding an iPad. "He's the director for today."

I smile at him and reach out to shake his hand.

"It's nice to meet you, Rosie," he says, and a blush hits my cheeks. They talked about me, and I can only wonder what was said. "We did a lot of interviews earlier with the family, Grayson, and a few of the staff members, so I think we're good with talking points. What we'd like from the two of you is just a few shots of normal interactions. Maybe walking, leaning over the fence, laughing, things like that. The clips won't be long, but their intention is to show a little of the day-to-day life of the Whitlocks. Viewers like the glimpses into the families. The more connected they feel, the more they will be rooting for Ace to win."

"Okay. Speaking of Ace, will we be with him or any of the other horses?" I ask nervously. I can't imagine Stokes would put me in a situation where I was uncomfortable, but who knows.

"No, we've filmed enough of him. This is the human

interest side of the farm. We also filmed Birdie with Molly while they baked Kentucky bourbon bars and drank mint juleps while rocking on the front porch."

"Okay, I understand." I glance at Stokes. He's looking at me so fondly he makes me feel like this fake relationship is becoming real. Then again, maybe this is for show; maybe he's looking at me this way for the film crew. "Should I take the fascinator off?" I ask him, and the double lines draw down.

"Why would you do that?" he asks.

I shrug one shoulder. "I don't know, just thought I'd ask."

"Rosie, you always have something on your head. It's who you are, and I love that about you. I would be sad if you took it off. Besides, it's like free publicity for your shop, right?" He winks at me.

Love.

He said the word love, and my insides have a visceral reaction to it in the best way.

Does he love that about me? Does he love the hats and fascinators, or is he just saying it in front of these people? And free publicity—is that him subtly reminding me of our deal? I help him and he helps me?

Everything is just so confusing.

I don't know what to believe or what has a double meaning. I want to believe it all, I really do, but there is this little voice in the back of my head reminding me that this is Stokes, the same Stokes who's made it his life's mission to make me miserable.

"Okay," I tell him, and then we spend the next hour feeling as if we are being filmed for a reality television show. I'm not sure how those people do it with the cameras always following them around and recording everything they say and do. It's kind of unnerving.

Stokes and I walk hand in hand, and he quietly asks, "Are you okay?"

I look up at him as he looks down at me and rubs his thumb over the back of my hand. "Yes, I'm just tired."

He gives me a sympathetic smile. "I understand, but we're nearing the end. This will all be over soon, and then you can relax. I appreciate you coming out to be here with me."

Nearing the end of us, or nearing the end of the season? I just don't know. I'm overthinking this, but I'm at a point with him now where I don't want this to be over in two weeks.

"Of course, whatever you need," I tell him.

He pulls me close, wraps his arm around my shoulders, and kisses the side of my head.

He pushes me on an old swing, and I laugh as I try to hang on, hold my skirt down, and keep the fascinator from falling off. He leans up against one of the barns while twirling a piece of hay as we chat about our day. And to end our little film session, he calls for his mother to meet us out front, where she comes with big smiles and huge hugs.

It's quite possible if we didn't have an audience, I would have broken down and cried in her arms. I need to pull it together, remember what this is, and just live in the moment. Eventually the two weeks will come to an end. I just need to forget about that and leave the worrying for when I actually have something to worry about.

"Let's check on Ace one last time before we leave," he says as we watch the film crew drive away.

"Okay," I tell him, wanting to spend just a few more minutes with him. He links his fingers through mine and then redirects us toward his barn. It isn't the closest to the house, but it isn't the furthest either. At this point I'll take as much time with him as I can get.

As we walk in, a few of the horses pop their heads out of their stall to see who is coming. They are such pretty animals and all vary in their markings and coloring. If I wasn't so afraid of them, it would be easy to love them.

"Ace was on his best behavior today," Stokes says as we come to a stop in front of him, and he smiles fondly at him. Ace is currently occupied with a fresh hanging kabob treat that's loaded with apples, vegetables, and a salt lick. Ace has dark espresso coloring with nearly black hair for his mane and tail, and right on his forehead is a white patch that looks like an upside down heart or a spade.

"Are you surprised? Because I'm not. Of all the horses you've had over the years, he is definitely the friendliest. He loves people. In fact, it's quite possible he thinks he is one." I chuckle as Ace looks over at us. If I didn't know any better, I'd think he understood what I said.

"I can definitely see that," Stokes says affectionately as

he wraps his arm around me again. Mine slips under his jacket and around his waist.

"Do you think he's going to win this year?" I ask, looking up at Stokes.

He tilts his head a tiny bit as he watches Ace and thinks about my question. "It's possible. He has a good chance. This morning, Grayson and I reviewed the others who qualified to run, and although some of the top contender farms have been removed, there are a few who will still make it a great race. He could do it, but we'll see."

That's what I love about watching the historic race at Churchill Downs—you just never know. It usually isn't who they predict it's going to be. While oftentimes it does end up being one of the featured farms, every now and then it's a longshot underdog, a low-dollar-claims horse who surprises the world and wins it all.

"Well, I'd bet on him."

Stokes looks back down at me. "Would you now?" One corner of his mouth rises as his eyes lock onto mine.

"Every time," I tell him, just barely over a whisper.

Does he understand what I'm saying? Does he realize I'm talking about him?

His smile grows, and with his hands moving to my hips, he turns us, backs me up against the wall next to Ace's stall, and steps directly in front of me. My palms flatten to his chest, the warmth from his skin pushing its way out from under the suit jacket and his shirt.

"I'd bet on you, too," he says as he leans down, leaving his lips only about an inch from mine.

Oh my.

Any hope I had of being able to keep him at arm's distance from my heart just vanished. Poof, gone.

Bending, he grabs both of my thighs and picks me right up off the ground. My skirt slides up, and my legs wrap around his very muscular waist. He leans further into me, using the wall to help anchor my weight, and my arms drape over his shoulders.

"There, that's better," he says, his gaze, which is now almost level with mine, narrowing in on my lips.

Involuntarily, my tongue slips out to wet them, and he groans. The vibration from his chest seeps into mine and causes my stomach to tighten. This guy, this man . . . he turns my insides upside down. Feelings, cravings, wants, things I've never known—he's bringing them all out in me, and I am completely on board with wherever he wants to take us.

"Pandora's box," he says, his lips now brushing against mine.

"What?" I ask, sharing his breath.

"You . . . you are the box to me. You're curiosity and temptation, and now that I've experienced a peek inside, it's not enough."

"Tell me," I state, taking his bottom lip between my teeth and gently biting. His body pushes into me a little more.

"Oh, sweetheart, if I told you all the things I've been curious about, I'm certain you'd cut off my balls and feed them to me," he teases.

At the mention of his balls, my legs tighten around him even more, and he settles right where we both want him.

"Quite frankly, you're lucky you've made it this long with them." I play along, running my fingers along the inside of his shirt collar and around his neck.

He smirks. "Long being the correct word here." He pushes against me again, his hardest parts pushing against my softest.

A small gasp escapes as heat climbs up my neck and into my cheeks. He notices the blush and runs his thumb over my skin, from my cheek down to my neck, over my collarbone and to the swell of my breast.

I watch his gaze as he watches his thumb. With each second, his eyes are getting darker, and my heart beats faster in my chest.

"So pretty," he whispers, and that heat shoots straight south.

"That's the first time you've ever called me that," I tell him as I cup the side of his face. He's been here all day, and an evening stubble has made itself known. It's slightly rough, but in a way that would feel so good being dragged across my skin.

"No, it's not," he says, his mood turning more serious.

"Yes, it is," I tell him a little more sternly, my thumb moving to trace the edge of his bottom lip. I would have remembered if he'd ever paid me a compliment like this. For years, I wished for something from him, anything, only to realize it was never going to happen.

"No. It's just the first time I've allowed you to hear," he says earnestly as his tongue slips out to tease my thumb.

I pull back just a little, and my eyes find his. "But why?"

"You know why." He leans forward and takes my bottom lip between his then runs his tongue along it. But the truth is, I don't know why. I don't know what I ever did to make him hate me so much.

"I don't," I whisper, but he's done talking, his tongue moving past my lips and caressing mine. My stomach swirls, my heart feels like it's seizing, and my fingers grip him tightly.

Apparently that kiss last night was introductory, because tonight it's on fire. We go from zero to sixty in literally sixty seconds.

"All I've thought about since last night is kissing you again," he whispers. His mouth moves across my cheek to my neck, where he drags his teeth up my skin and sucks on the spot just under my ear. "I just can't get enough," he says, sounding tortured.

With no one around and no one watching, Stokes loosens his hold on the public armor he constantly wears and surrenders to himself, to me, and to this moment. His full lips are on mine, and his body is warm and solid against my chest and under my hands. There are no thoughts, and for several long heartbeats, he and I need the exact same thing. His hands are under my skirt, his fingers are under the edge of my underwear, and along with squeezing me, he moves me over him. It feels so good, and he was right—long is definitely the right word. I breathe him in as he does me, and a pang of disappoint-ment hits me hard as I think we could have been doing this together for years.

"Why do you kiss like this?" I ask him, wondering how many others he's kissed, who taught him, and how he became so good at it.

"Why do you taste so fucking good?" he growls against my lips before again claiming them and deepening the kiss enough to have my fingers slip underneath the suit jacket and push it off. For an instant his hands are off of me, and it falls to the ground. Right at this moment, I want all of our other clothes to join it.

While one of his hands dives back under my skirt, the other pulls the fascinator off and drops it on top of his jacket. With his lips on mine, his hand in my hair, and his body flush against mine, I pull on his shirt and untuck it from his pants. I want to feel his skin—no, I need to feel his skin, so I slip my hand up the back and around over his rib cage. My fingertips worship the hard ridges and warmth.

His hand slides to the back of my thigh, where his fingers wrap around my leg and just barely graze against my center. He has to feel what he's doing to me. After all, I can definitely feel what I'm doing to him.

And I want more.

In the pocket of his pants, his cell phone buzzes, and we freeze. He pulls back from me, startled at how lost in the moment we were, and stares down at my mouth. I lick my bottom lip, and he blinks out of the trance. Grabbing his phone, he glances at the caller ID then answers it.

"Mr. Whitlock," I hear come through the line.

"Yes," he mumbles.

"Sir, just thought I would remind you real quick that there are now cameras in Ace's barn."

I suck in air, and Stokes closes his eyes.

"Sorry about that," he tells whoever called from the security booth.

"No worries. Have a great night." And the line goes dead.

Letting out a sigh, he shoves his phone back in his pocket, and his forehead drops to mine.

"I forgot about the cameras," he says, frustration and embarrassment laced through his words.

"We can go to your place," I suggest. He does have a house here on the property.

He lifts his head so his eyes find mine. "Rosie . . ." He lets out a disgruntled sigh. "If I take you there, we won't be leaving. I know you're tired, and I know you have a long week ahead of you."

We won't be leaving.

Oh, how I want him to take me there. I don't want to leave; I want him to show me all the things he's curious about, but his clear stare lets me know he will not be swayed. He's right, I do have a busy week coming up and there are a thousand things I need to be doing, but right this second, I can't think of one of them.

"Okay," I tell him, my hopes tumbling down. He's right. I know he is.

It's then that Ace pops his head out of the stall to see what we are doing and bumps me with his nose.

"AHHH!" I let out a high-pitched scream.

Simultaneously, Ace jumps, Stokes jumps, and I jerk us hard to get away from him, so hard my weight throws Stokes off balance, and we both freefall with him trying to twist while holding on to me so he doesn't drop me or land on me, and me—well, I'm just clinging to him out of sheer terror.

With a loud *oof*, we hit the ground, and hay and dust from outside Ace's stall fly up around us. I'm sprawled on top of Stokes, he groans in pain, and very quickly I realize Ace and several of the other horses are staring at us.

"Oh my God. I'm so sorry. Are you okay?" I prop myself up and look down at him.

"What the hell? What was that?" he asks, looking up at me as I'm hovering over him.

"He scared me," I tell him, his dark eyes connecting with mine.

"Clearly," he grumbles as he reaches up to remove some hay that is stuck in my hair.

"I'm sorry." I bend down and kiss him to try to make this better.

His arms come up around me and pull me to him. He's hugging me, and I let go of my weight, snuggling into him.

"Forgiven." He chuckles as his hand sweeps down my back and pulls on my dress to make sure I'm completely covered. "Although, we should get up, or security is going to think we've decided to give them a show after all."

I giggle as I take us in, lying on the barn floor. He's so handsome with his cheeks full of color and his lips a little swollen from being worked over by me. I did this to him, to me, and I love how it makes me feel.

20

Today is the day.

The day Avery comes to pick up her dress.

I've barely slept at all this week, and I'm not sure if it's from nerves or excitement. I can't imagine she won't like the finished product. It's not too different from what she saw when she was here last month, but assembled and completed with its matching hat, it is by far the most beautiful dress I have ever created.

It is a vision, and I can't imagine she won't be one in it.

"So, I just got a text from Stokes," Molly says as she walks out of the office in the back of the shop with a grin splitting her face.

"Oh yeah?" I reply while reaching over to tap the top of my phone to wake it up and see if I got one too. I didn't, but then again, I did see him this morning when he dropped off coffees for us, and he's been texting me off and on all morning. If I didn't know any better, I would think he's just as excited about today as we are.

Just thinking of him, that swirly feeling in my stomach returns.

"Yep, he's asking if Austin and I want to join the two of you for dinner tomorrow night." She comes to stand next to me, and as I look at her twinkling eyes, I know the wheels in her brain are turning. She's watched us closely over the last month—well, she's watched me. My claws have retracted when it comes to him, and I can't help but wonder what she notices, what she thinks.

Although I have seen Stokes the last four days in a row, we haven't really had an opportunity to spend any time together. Each morning he's brought me coffee, and last night he dropped off some Thai food to make sure I stopped for dinner. He didn't stay, saying he knew how important today was for me and he just wanted to make sure I was taking care of myself. I might have stared at him with hearts in my eyes for a little too long, because he just chuckled, kissed my forehead, and then popped open our boxes.

He and Christopher have also been working on a project together that has kept him as busy as I am, but that hasn't stopped him from making time for me or giving me a searing kiss each time he sees me. I swear this man loves to leave me breathless and wanting more and more.

"He mentioned he was going to ask you. David's Distillery on Main is hosting their annual Bourbon and Bowties pairing dinner, and he has four tickets."

"Bourbon and Bowties!" Her jaw drops. "He so did not mention that's where dinner is. How on earth did he get these tickets? They're like impossible to come by."

Every year, David's hosts a large charity tasting dinner. They bring in some swanky chef from somewhere, the dinner seats seventy-five, there's a silent auction, and the tickets are some of the most sought-after of the Derby season. This year, the chef's name is Sebastian, and he's a celebrity chef from the *Food Network* channel.

"I didn't ask him, and well, he's Stokes Whitlock— people just give him things." I walk to the front of the store.

"This is true," Molly replies as she wipes down the tables one more time then moves to the counter. "I've never really understood it. Mostly he gets products and things for the horses. He has social media, but he doesn't use the accounts for any real purpose. Once or twice I've mentioned a few of these things on the farm's pages, but it's not like he's going to be personally endorsing them."

"Can you imagine if he did post on social media? Pigs would fly." I grin.

"What I can't believe is that we are finally going on a double date." She squeals as she moves back to the counter to store the cleaner.

Heat fuses into my cheeks as I smile back at her. She sees the blush and lights up even more.

"Maybe we should get a nice photo of the two of you tomorrow. It would look great on your pages, and maybe some of his adoring fans will see it and come in this week."

All of my pages now are focused on the shop. From

its conception to where it is today, Molly has documented everything in video or photo form: moving in, creating the rose wall, opening day, and many, many different items from the shop. She's also been very adamant that we need to keep the human interest side there as well. It's the same thing the film crew told us at the farm. People like to see what you are doing in your everyday life. It makes them feel connected, helps them become more invested, and in return they want to see me succeed.

"Okay," I tell her, thinking I'd love a picture of the two of us together. Other than the upcoming ball and Derby, I don't have many opportunities or a need to take one of us, but it'll be nice to have them once this thing with us is over. My heart frowns at the thought.

Is it going to be over? Will we finally be friends, or will he want something more? My already anxious heart squeezes more, and my chest tightens even further. I am not good with uncertainty. I'm a planner. I'm responsible and, overall, a great troubleshooter. I've always had this ability to foresee problems and react swiftly and confidently. However, when it comes to him, I have no idea where he's really at, and it's starting to leave me unbalanced. I feel like I'm staring into a black hole.

Sliding the curtains across the shop windows, I hang a chalkboard sign on the door that says, "Closed for an appointment. Will reopen after 2pm." It's while I'm standing there that the familiar black SUV pulls up.

Letting out a deep breath, I push the thoughts of

Stokes away, pull my shoulders back, and tell myself, *It's go time.*

"They're here," I call over to Molly, whose eyes are now large with elation. I open the door as Blair slides out of the front seat, and she begins surveying the surroundings. She nods to me in greeting, peeks her head into the shop, and then goes to open the back door for Avery. Out she pops in athleisure wear, her long blonde curls going wild and a smile stretched from ear to ear, and behind her follows Emma White. Emma is a member of her three-piece group who sings and plays the violin. Molly is going to die.

"I hope y'all are hungry because I brought cupcakes." She holds out a large sealed plastic container that holds chocolate cupcakes with light pink icing on them then dances by me into the shop, the scent of sugar trailing her and Emma. She turns to face me. "Ash told me I had to take them with me because he didn't feel like adding another twenty minutes to his workout." She giggles. "I love to bake, and well, unfortunately for him, he is the recipient of it all."

"Not just him!" Emma chimes in. "Cora and I also suffer."

"What do you mean, suffer?" Avery laughs out loud. "Y'all love when I bake."

Emma turns around and points to her butt. "It's bigger, Avery, and you know it."

"What I know is last weekend you were all, 'Can you make us some banana bread?'"

"That's different!" Emma declares.

"Why is that different?" Avery asks her.

Watching these two bicker is fantastic.

"That was brunch. It was for a meal, not a snack."

"Tuh-may-toe, tuh-mah-toe," Avery fires back.

Beside me, Molly lets out a tiny noise. Just like the first time Avery was here, she's fangirling and trying hard to hold it in. I think she mentally prepared for Avery, but with two superstars here, she can't help herself.

"Lucky guy and lucky friends," I tell her, inserting myself as I take the container from her and place it on one of the tables in the middle of the shop. Blair comes in behind us and locks the door, and when I glance back at Avery, that's when I see her freeze. She's spotted the dress on the mannequin behind me, and her eyes are wide in awe.

"Rosie," she whispers. "It's just stunning." Slowly she walks around me. I've set the mannequin up next to the platform with the mirrors. It's close to the fitting room and placed centrally so it is the star of the show.

No one in the store moves except for Molly; she's pulled out her phone and is recording Avery's reaction. Meanwhile, Emma, Blair, and I are just staring as she makes her way to the dress then walks around it to get a full three-sixty view. I made the train eight feet. It's longer than the one she originally looked at, but I figured if she's not going to wear it the whole night, she may as well make a grand entrance. My heart is pounding so hard in my chest it's hard to breathe, and my eyes prickle. I wasn't expecting these wild emotions, but here I am. Here we are.

Avery Layne. Global music star. In awe of something I made.

Someone shake me.

"I can't believe you made this for me." She looks back at me, and I have to swallow hard. The lump in my throat keeps getting larger and larger, and I can't speak to her, only stare.

I'm not going to cry. I'm not going to cry. I'm not going to cry.

Stress, excitement, and anxiety are funny things. I've done such a great job this season compartmentalizing the different stress factors in my life and not letting them bleed and blend together, but here with her, at this moment, all the hours of work, the heart and soul I poured into this dress, the few grains of sand left in the hourglass of the season, and my emotional uncertainty about Stokes have me so overwhelmed I feel like a shaken soda ready to burst.

Oh, God. I'm about to lose it right here.

What is happening to me?

I breathe in through my nose, trying to hold it all in while giving her a small smile. My eyes are burning more fiercely, and I'm blinking over and over in an attempt to stop what is so desperately trying to come out. What is it that is doing this to me? Is it relief that she loves the dress? Is it the anxiety of her walking out the door with it for the world to see? I don't know. I don't know why I'm suddenly bordering on an emotional meltdown of epic proportions.

Molly, having known me for almost half my life, sees

that I need a little saving—well, maybe a lot—and steps in.

"Isn't it just beautiful? I've loved watching her build this dress. Every day it came together a little bit more, and I'm not going to lie, I'm jealous you get to wear it and I don't." She grins at Avery.

"It's almost too pretty to wear," Avery says as she runs her fingers over the feathers of the hat and then picks up the crystal-covered sash.

"Nonsense," Molly declares as she walks to Avery and stands next to her. "The world needs to see you in this. It was made just for you." She grins proudly. "How about we go ahead and show you how each part connects, how to put it on and take it off, and how the detachable skirt works. We'll also see if it needs to be tightened or loosened anywhere."

"Maybe Ash is right about the cupcakes." Avery glances at Emma and then my way, her eyes wide. "I probably should lay off them until after the gala."

"You'll be fine," I tell her, my voice squeaking out as my heart rate starts to come down. "With the corset tie in the back, we can make it as tight or as loose as you need."

She looks back at the dress and lets out a deep sigh. "Well, that's a relief."

"All right, let's get started," Molly says, clapping her hands together. "Can I get you some tea?" she asks Avery and Emma. She carefully lifts the matching hat off of the mannequin and moves it to the other one I have set off to the side. I know we didn't discuss this, but I went ahead and made Ash a black and silver feather vest and bowtie.

The hat, along with the dress, is to me a complete work of art. I worried a bit that it might be a little too avant-garde with the way it sits on her head and the shape, but then again, part of the roaring twenties was known for glitz and glamour. I designed this hat to enhance the natural beauty and lines of Avery's face, not cover part of it, and it flows seamlessly over one shoulder and her back, down to the dress. It's as if the dress doesn't stop at her breast line; it just keeps on going and going, wrapping her in decadence. Silver feathers, Swarovski jewels, and an iridescent fabric shaped like the bubbled waves of the skirt—this is me being a true milliner, a true creator.

"I'd love some iced tea if you have that," she replies as she watches Molly closely.

"Of course. Today we have orange blossom, and it's divine. I'll grab glasses for you, Emma, and Blair, and I'll be right back." She scurries off, leaving Avery, Emma, and me standing together.

"You know, it's quite possible you become my new dressmaker." She smiles broadly. I smile back and think how crazy it is that dreams do come true.

"Mine too," Emma says with wonder.

My cheeks flood with heat, and I'm certain they aren't just pink, they are beet red.

As I begin to break down the dress and how each part connects, Avery pulls Emma in a little closer to watch.

"Are you going to the gala too?" I ask her.

"Oh, no. I've been appointed as her official lady's maid. I'm going to be helping her get ready." She laughs.

"Whatever," Avery fires back. "It's not like going to Nashville is a burden for you," she teases, and this time it's Emma who turns pink.

Interesting. I haven't heard about any love connections with her, but that doesn't mean she doesn't have one.

"Here we go," Molly says, bringing a tray of drinks to the table with the cupcakes. I see she's included glasses for the two of us also. "These are unsweetened, but we have all kinds of sweeteners here for your choosing."

"Perfect and thank you," Emma says.

Both of us move to the table. I pick up my glass and take a long pull on the cool drink.

Get a grip, Rosie, I tell myself, and then I take a deep breath.

Smiling at Avery, I remove the skirt from the mannequin and send her off to change. Surprisingly, it doesn't take us very long to teach her how to don the pieces. The fit is perfect, and as she stands up on the pedestal in front of the three-way mirror, I almost forget to breathe. It's one thing to make something; it's another thing entirely to see it on someone else, and this is so much more than just a hat.

Be still my heart.

Whipping around, Avery looks at the four of us, her eyes finally landing on Blair. "What do you think?" she asks.

Blair steps away from the door and moves more toward

the center of the store to get a better look. It's so easy to see the friendship between them, and Blair gives her a breathtaking smile. "What do *you* think?" she asks instead of answering.

Avery's eyes drift back to mine. "I think it's perfect."

My eyes burn again, and this time I let them. I feel no shame in being proud of what I created.

A moment of silence passes over our group, and then quietly from the door, Blair says, "I think jaws are going to drop."

$\mathcal{L}$ooking down at my calendar, I cross off today's date and count. There are eight days remaining until the Derby. Eight days left with my dwindling inventory. Eight days left with my fake boyfriend. Eight days left until it's all over.

As much as I've enjoyed my first season, it's not lost on me that I did in fact bite off more than I can chew. I will be relieved to have this behind me, and it's also quite possible I will sleep for two weeks straight. I'm reaching the point of no return on my anxiety levels.

I had originally planned on closing the shop for a week, but now I might make that a little bit longer. I also think I'm going to cut back on the shop hours. I won't need to be open as much, and it will give me time to start working on my stock for next year.

A stock that, as I look around at the walls and racks, I see is wearing thin. Tomorrow will be my last remaining busy day. I'll have some business on Sunday, but as for next week, I predict it will be mostly last-minute attendees looking for something, anything to wear. Hopefully, shoppers won't be too disappointed and will buy what I have left.

Right at six on the dot, the door to the shop opens, the bell rings, and in walks Stokes with his long legs and a broody vibe. My heart rate picks up at just the sight of him. He hasn't gone home to change from his day at work, still wearing the same dark gray suit from this morning, only he's swapped out his navy plaid tie for a burgundy bowtie with white polka dots. He's so handsome, and right this second, it hurts to look at him.

His eyes find mine. I'm still behind the counter, and I've just closed the sales from the day. The perma-scowl on his face instantly relaxes, and I automatically know it's been one of those kinds of days at work.

"Hi," I say to him, just barely over a whisper.

He returns the greeting with a closed-mouth smile, and it's the color of his eyes that I notice first as he approaches. Tonight they are more muddy than bright.

He comes around the counter and pulls me into a hug. His face drops to my hair, and he lets out the longest, slowest exhale.

Oh, man.

"Wanna talk about it?" I ask, wrapping my arms around him and pulling him closer, not even skirting the elephant in the room.

He pauses as his head moves lower into the crook of

my neck and shoulder, and he thinks about my question. Eventually he pulls back a bit and says, "No. I just needed a minute like this." He brushes his lips against mine.

There's that word from him again . . . need.

"Or maybe two," he says as he settles into me again.

Warmth, sage, body wash . . . all of it surrounds me, and I breathe him in. Since Avery came yesterday, I've been off, and I don't know why. I'm thinking I need this hug too as I close my eyes and just stand here in his arms.

"How long until you're done here?" He lifts his head and looks down at me, green and gold painting my skin.

"I'm pretty much done. If you'll give me maybe five to ten minutes, I just want to run up and change real quick."

He releases me a little then looks down to see what I'm wearing. It's a day outfit, not a night ensemble, and he nods his head in understanding. "I'll be outside."

Together we walk out the front door. He watches as I lock up, and then I sprint up the stairs to change. I grab an olive green dress that reminds me of his eyes. It's long-sleeved, tight, and short. Paired with a few long necklaces, some high black boots, and no headpiece, this is the perfect outfit for a bourbon tasting.

A car is idling at the curb, Stokes is standing next to it on his phone, and he opens the door for me as I approach. I can't help but notice the way his fingers curl into his hands as he drinks me in from head to toe.

"Car service tonight?" I ask as I slip into the back seat and he follows.

"Yeah, I figured it's just better this way. There's no

telling how much bourbon we'll end up tasting, and I'd rather be prepared than not."

"Smart."

As the vehicle pulls away from the curb, I angle a little so I can look at him and lean my head against the headrest. He does the same and then reaches over to wrap his warm hand around my thigh. He pushes the edge of the dress up a tiny bit and slips his fingers underneath. I cover his hand with mine. Neither one of us says anything, we just stare at each other and let our muscles relax. His presence is comforting, and just being near him, I feel better than I have all day. Maybe he does too.

"How was work?" he asks.

"Long," I tell him, and I mean it. These days have felt endless. "How about you?"

His fingertips press into my skin a bit as he thinks about his answer, but in the end he just says, "Also long. The whole week has been long."

"Well, it's the weekend now, and I'm happy to be here with you." I give him a small smile, which he doesn't return; he just continues to stare at me with something that looks a lot like adoration in his eyes—or is that just me seeing what I'm so desperately craving to see from him? Overthinking things is not helping with my already-off-balance mental state.

Eventually, the car turns on Main and lines up behind a few others who are also dropping guests off at the large historic brick building. Other than the two work outings, this is really the first time Stokes and I are stepping out together in public. I didn't think anything of it when he asked if I wanted to go tonight, but now that we're here, things just got a whole lot crazier.

Outside the distillery, a pathway is roped off to the door and is lined with a red carpet. There is security standing there ready and waiting, but there are also a ton of cameramen. It looks more like a scene you would expect in Hollywood than Louisville. My already anxious chest tightens even more as Stokes swears under his breath.

"You good?" he asks me just before it's our turn.

"Yep."

An attendant opens his door, he slides out, and then he holds out his hand for me. I take it, and together we make our way to the door. There are a few flashes, but mostly it's just a lot of clicking with random people yelling at us.

"Stokes! Rosie! Look this way," one reporter yells.

It's crazy to me that these people know my name. His, not so crazy. After all, he is a Whitlock, but me—I'm no one.

"Rosie, how does it feel to be chosen by the bachelor of the season?" another asks.

"Stokes, should we be placing our bets on Ace of Spades this year?"

Stokes's ever-present scowl drops into place as his hand tightens around mine and we cross the short distance from the curb to the door.

"I'm sorry," he says as the door is opened for us. "I didn't think about that."

"No need to apologize. It's not your fault." I give him a small smile.

"Still . . . those pictures will be posted somewhere."

"It's okay. Besides, didn't you once tell me it would be good for business for me to be seen with you?" I bump his shoulder with mine, teasing him.

He exhales, releasing his irritation, and then he wraps his arm around me, pulling me into a side hug.

"Mr. Whitlock," the greeter says, smiling at us as we approach him. "If you and your guest will follow me, I'll show you to your seat."

Looking around, my eyes are greedy as I take in the details. Obviously, being from Louisville, I've tasted bourbon, but I wasn't living here when I turned twenty-one, and since I've been back, I've yet to visit any of the distilleries. I've passed this one on Main Street what feels like hundreds of times, but I've never seen the inside. More brick walls, lots of windows, vintage industrial lighting, rustic wooden high top tables, and a grand sweeping bar that is backed and lined with lit full bourbon bottles.

"Downstairs, you will find the silent auction, and through that hallway"—the greeter points—"is where the tours are being offered. If you haven't had the chance to discover us here at David's, I highly suggest you explore or come back soon and let us tell you our history. Upstairs is where the dinner is being served."

We continue to follow him up the stairs, and the chatter becomes significantly louder. This room is decked out like you would expect a rustic wedding reception, and it is gorgeous. Molly and Austin are already at the table, and they've unintentionally cocooned themselves into a bubble. They are so into talking to each other it's as if no one else is here, and they don't even see us approach.

"Molly," Stokes says, loud enough to grab her attention. Her head shoots up and a smile splits her face.

"You're here!"

Both of them stand. Molly rushes me for a hug while Austin reaches out to shake Stokes's hand.

Pulling back, she keeps a hold of my shoulders and asks, "Oh my, were the cameras still out there just now? Wasn't that crazy?"

"Yeah, they're still out there. They called me by my name."

"That's so fun!" She's grinning from ear to ear.

"If you say so."

"Thanks, man, for inviting us. As you can see, we are excited to be here tonight," Austin says, tipping his head Molly's way.

"Of course. I'm glad it worked out," he tells him, pulling me away from Molly so he can link his fingers through mine. "Let's head to the bar and get a drink before they get started," Stokes says, looking down at me. His gaze is tender, intimate for me, and as much as I love it, it adds another layer of heaviness to my chest. Is he feeling this way right now because we're in the moment or because I mean more to him, like he does to me?

"Sounds good." I barely get the words out.

"Can we get anything for either of you?" he asks.

Austin looks at Molly, and she shakes her head. "Nope. I think we're all good for now. Thanks for asking, though," he answers for both of them.

Together, Stokes and I weave our way past other guests, making our way to the bar to stand in line.

"Do you know what you want?" he asks.

"Not really. I mean obviously I know a few of the standard drinks like a whiskey sour and an old fashioned, but after that, not too much. I actually don't know a lot about bourbon or what makes it different from whiskey. I just know that for it to be called Kentucky bourbon, it has to be made in Kentucky."

"That is correct."

Stokes unlinks our hands and wraps his arm over my shoulders to bring us closer. Mine slips under his jacket and around his waist. He smells so good, feels so warm and solid, and I can't help but lean into him as he drops his head a little so I can hear him better.

"Can it be made somewhere else, yes, and it is, but mostly bourbon is made in Kentucky so it can have the name. It's kind of like champagne. Unless it comes from the Champagne region of France, it's not really called champagne. It's a sparkling wine. The difference between bourbon and whiskey is also that in order for it to be classified as bourbon, it needs to be distilled from a mixture of grains, or mash, that's at least fifty-one percent corn. That corn gives bourbon its distinctive sweet flavor. Also, it must be aged in new charred oak barrels for at least two years. That is not the case with whiskey. Whiskey can be aged in barrels that were previously used to make other spirits such as port, sherry, and rum."

"Gotcha." Well that seems easy enough.

Reaching around the guest in front of us, Stokes grabs a drink menu that was designed for the event. He hands it to me so I can select a cocktail.

"Oh, look at this one, it's called Strawberry Soiree." I grin at him. It's made with one ounce of David's bourbon, one ounce of strawberry puree, sparkling brut wine, and mint. It sounds delicious.

"Are you trying to tell me something?" His lips tilt just a little while his hand runs up and down my back a few times.

"No, just that I like the name." My grin widens as his smile grows too. Gah, he is so handsome.

"Sounds perfect for you then, especially if you're intent on causing me misery."

I laugh as I remember his sensitivity to citrus. There would be no kissing if I chose this one, so I pick out another instead.

After we grab our drinks, we attempt to make it back to our table, but it seems the entire room wants to say hello to Stokes. Whereas I know a few of these people here, like Mr. Evans, the owner of Thunder Alley Farm, and Dr. Miller, Stokes's veterinarian, the rest of them are just strangers to me. To him they are other business associates he knows from around town and acquaintances from the horse community. He includes me in each new conversation, but so far, this is not the night with Molly I had been hoping for.

"Dr. Miller, it's nice to see you this evening," Stokes says as they shake hands in greeting.

"Likewise," the older gentleman says in return, smiling at both of us. I've always liked Dr. Miller. His clinic mainly focuses on thoroughbreds, and for years he has been sought after for his expertise and care. "How's Ace doing these days?"

"Oh, he's well. Demanding attention and eating snacks as if he's worried we're going to forget to give him his next meal, even though we never have."

Dr. Miller chuckles. "Better him eating than refusing to."

"This is true."

"I'll be by next week to see him as we get closer to the race."

"Sounds good. Don't forget to schedule it with Grayson so we know you're coming."

"Will do." Then he shifts his attention to me. I'm sure he's done this to not be rude, but still, I'm not surprised when he asks, "So, Rosie, how's the shop coming along?"

It's funny, all I've ever wanted is my shop, but this question is asked so often by so many, it's officially become my most hated question.

"It's amazing. I couldn't be happier." I smile, but I can feel it getting faker with each new person who asks, and I know Stokes sees this. His hand reaches out and rubs across my lower back.

"That's great. And Stokes, how's the firm treating you these days?" His gaze shifts from me to Stokes, and I look at him as well. Stokes really doesn't talk about work all that much. I don't know if it's a confidentiality thing or if he's just one of those who, when he leaves work, he leaves it and doesn't want to drag it home.

I glance up at his face, and it seems this just might be his most hated question too. He's trying hard not to scowl, but his jaw is clenched tight behind a closed-mouth smile, and he's fighting those two little lines.

"The same as always," he replies, leaving it at that.

"Good. Did you know, a good lawyer knows the law, but a clever one takes the judge to lunch." He slaps Stokes hard on the arm and laughs at his terrible joke.

Stokes nods his head like he thinks this is funny too. As much as we love Dr. Miller, both of us are ready to be done socializing.

Eventually, we make it back to the table, and I sit down next to Molly just as the celebrity chef cooking for us tonight picks up the microphone to greet the room. Stokes sits on my other side and lays his arm across the back of my chair. Everyone cheers and then gives the chef their undivided attention.

Leaning over, I whisper to Molly. "I'm sorry we aren't really getting the double date you were wanting. I had no idea so many people would stop us."

She gives me a warm, friendly smile. "It's okay. It's always like this with Stokes. I should have remembered that."

I frown. Maybe I should have remembered that too. I've been in enough social settings with him over the years to know he's always being approached or talking to someone. For some reason, I always kind of thought that was his choice, but maybe it's not.

"If it's any consolation, you know he hates it. Next time, we'll go somewhere a little more quiet, maybe Stokes's house at the farm. Austin and I will invade and cook while y'all drive out."

"That sounds great," I tell her, my heart sinking just a bit. Why didn't I recognize sooner that he hated it? Why did it take these last couple of weeks for me to really see him? I also don't know if there will be a next time, but I'm hoping there will be. I've never been to Stokes's house on the farm. Sure, I've been past it a thousand times, but I've never been inside it. He's never invited me.

"You doing okay?" Molly asks, concern laced in her voice at whatever expression she finds on my face.

"Yes," I tell her, but she sees the lie. She knows me better than anyone. Her hand reaches over and squeezes my leg just as Stokes leans in close to us and asks the same thing.

"Everything okay?"

His voice . . . it soothes my spirit and makes my heart beat faster at the same time. I don't think there is one thing about him that I dislike. When this is over, it's going to hurt. Just thinking about it has my eyes stinging and turning glassy. Molly sees this and answers for me.

"Of course." She grins at him and then shushes him so we can hear the chef.

I make it through most of the meal and decide just before the dessert to make a small escape to the bathroom. While the dinner and the pairings were delicious, and I was sitting with my two favorite people in the world, I just needed some space to drop the face and allow this anxiety in me to run freely. Thank God it's a single-user bathroom and not a large shared one. In and out I breathe while telling myself I can do just another hour or two. I can.

Coming out of the bathroom, I open the door, and as I do, Stokes steps in. Gently pushing me backward, he shuts us in and locks the door.

My eyes widen as I stare up at him. "What are you doing? Someone will see us."

One side of his mouth tips up. "So?"

"What do you mean, so?" I feel slightly panicky at the idea of being caught in here together.

Reaching for my elbows, he spins us around so I'm leaning against the door and he's towering over me. He tips my chin up so our eyes are locked on each other. "You needed a minute, and so did I, only I want mine with you."

"Stokes," I whisper.

"What's going on?" he asks, his fingertips gently pushing a few loose strands of hair behind my ear. He runs those same fingertips over the outer shell of my ear and down my neck, where he lightly clamps onto my shoulder.

"I don't know," I tell him. It's not that I don't trust him, because I do. It's just . . . he's Stokes and I'm me. Maybe there is still a little distrust lingering, but it's there for a good reason. I've felt the damage he leaves in his wake.

"Yes, you do. Talk to me."

Talk to me.

His voice is like truth serum to my soul, and I can feel the longing and sincerity in his words. He wants me to talk to him. He wants me to trust him, wants to be the person I go to when things feel off, and even though it exposes the vulnerable pieces of me that I like to keep hidden, I do want him to be my person too.

"I just feel off." I shake my head, and he frowns. "Everything has been happening so fast. I feel like I've been living life at warp speed for the last two months, and next weekend it's all coming to a stop. Avery's dress is finished and picked up, the Met Gala will be aired, the season will be over, the Derby will have come and gone, and so will have we."

His expression shifts to one that is unreadable, and instead of talking, he lets dead air hang between us. The silence makes me fidgety, so I drop my gaze and keep talking instead.

"It's just jarring, that's all. I'm certain this has been building for a while, but this level of anxiety started yesterday when Avery was in the shop and had her dress on. I can't seem to shake it. I don't know, for months—no, for years, this shop has been all I've thought about. The excitement, the buildup and the anticipation, the worry, the stress, the workload . . ." I look down at the ground, pausing, and then back up at him. "And now you … my mind is trying to shift gears as things are coming to an end, and it's just a lot. Plus, I'm over-tired, which makes this a thousand times worse."

Tears fill my eyes, and slowly they tip over the edge. Stokes continues to remain silent as he watches and listens to me. Tilting his head just a little, he reaches his other hand up to wipe the tears away and tuck a few more strands of hair behind my other ear. His fingertips graze down my cheek, and my heart stutters at the contact. Can he see what he does to me?

"Do you know how proud of you I am?" he asks softly, wrapping his hands around my face. His thumbs swipe both sides dry.

"What?" My eyes find his, and they are more green than hazel. They are soft and understanding. They are kind and sturdy. They shine with an intimacy that's just for me, and it makes my breath shaky.

"I am so proud of all you have done. I know this has been your dream, and watching you work for it, reach for it, and achieve it—it's inspiring. I know you've had a lot on your plate, and I know I added to it, but I'm not sorry. I've loved being on this journey with you. Things may feel like they are coming to an end, but they aren't. This is just the beginning for you."

But is this just the beginning for us too?

I want to ask him. Actually, I'm pretty sure I want to beg, but there's this tiny part of me that's still holding on to myself. As much as he's seemed to enjoy this, enjoy me these last couple of weeks, I can't dismiss the twelve years prior.

"Also . . ." One side of his mouth tips up. "I'm not going anywhere. I'm here for you. You know this. On your long list of things to fret over, I should be the least of your worries."

My racing heart slows.

Does he mean that?

I sure hope so. I want to believe he does.

"You're here for me?" I whisper, more tears tipping over.

"Very much so," he answers, swiping his thumbs back and forth.

Bending down, he places his lips on mine and just holds us together. We breathe in sync, and my eyes close. Seconds, minutes, hours could pass—who knows how long we stand there, but eventually someone knocks on the door, and I let out a deep sigh. He knew exactly what I needed, and he knew exactly how to calm me down.

He hugs me tight before asking, "You ready?" His clear gaze bores into mine to see if he can seek out any wariness. He won't find any, because with him by my side, I feel like I can take on the world.

"Almost." I push up on my toes and kiss him, like really kiss him.

He groans at the contact and pulls my body flush with his. He tastes so good, and he feels so good, but knowing our time is up, he drops his head to my shoulder and again hugs me so tight he picks me right up off the ground.

"All right, let's go." He spins me around, opens the door, and pats me on the butt.

"Wait." I stop the door from opening all the way. "What about you? You said you needed a minute too."

He pauses as if he's trying to think of what to say, or maybe he just forgot he needed this moment too. Then he says, "You. I needed alone time with you. There hasn't been much of it this week."

"No, there hasn't," I tell him with a sad smile.

"That will change soon enough, and then you'll be sick of me," he teases.

"I highly doubt it."

Wide eyes stare at us as we exit, but we just ignore them. Stokes takes me by the hand, and instead of leading us back to the table, he guides us downstairs to the silent auction, where it is in fact silent. A few more minutes, for us—it's just what I needed.

I'm pretty sure he could lead me anywhere, and I would follow.

LUVU TEA
BOURBON, BOWTIES, AND OUR BACHELOR

Dear readers, while you may have seen our coverage of the annual Bourbon and Bowties charity dinner last night, we felt it apt today for us to also report on our beloved bachelor of the season, Mr. Stokes Whitlock. If there were any question of who he might attend with, rumors here at the Tea were immediately squashed by the two very different expressions that could be found on his face. One was adoration aimed at his date, Ms. Rosie May, and the other was vengeance directed toward anyone who might attempt to disrupt their night. Grab a hand fan, ladies and gentlemen, because that look alone left us all feeling a little hot and needing some cooling off.
When he stepped out of the town car, our jaws dropped at the stylish cut of his Hugo Boss suit and at Rosie with her perfectly fitted dress and striking over-the-knee boots. The pair walked in sync across the red carpet as if they had done this a thousand times.
Inside David's Distillery, they were seen socializing with the

upper echelon of the city, laughing and drinking the specialty cocktails prepared by David himself, bidding on silent auction items, and dining with Stokes's sister and her date. It also wasn't lost on those in attendance how captivated our bachelor was. It seems never once was he seen without having his hand on Ms. May somewhere, somehow. A little bird even told us that at one point during the dinner, they slipped away together and locked themselves in the bathroom. My, my, Mr. Whitlock, hearts are aflutter as a girl can't help but ask, wonder, and imagine—what were you doing to Rosie behind that door?

22

———

*I*t's amazing how unloading my brain on Stokes and getting a good night's sleep could make such a difference. When I woke up this morning, the sun streaming through my window felt brighter, and I just knew there were birds chirping a lovely song somewhere. The weight I've been carrying over the last couple of weeks doesn't feel as heavy, I'm excited for this last weekend before the Derby, and I can't wait to see Stokes later today.

Last night, he calmed my nerves in a way I didn't know he could, and after we left the bathroom, he held my hand for the remainder of the evening. It's like he knew I just needed some support, and he stood there strong as I emotionally leaned all over him. I shouldn't have waited so long to share how I've been feeling. It isn't a mark on my character or on how I run my business to feel overwhelmed and to share that with him. If anything, it makes me better. I am grateful for him, and at the end of the day, what he said is true. Deep down, I know he's not going anywhere. He's still here with me, and he will be even after next weekend. I've finally dropped that one last wall of insecurity, and today I've decided to fully allow myself to fall.

I trust him.

Who knows, I might even tell him.

I've just flipped the sign on the door to open, and I'm walking back to the counter when it opens and the bell chimes. Glancing over my shoulder, I'm about to call out hello, but my words get stuck in my throat. Stokes smiles at me as our eyes connect, and I swear this man just made my day and he doesn't even know it.

"What are you doing here?" I ask, feeling way more excited than I should be to see my fake boyfriend, who I'm certain isn't fake anymore.

"I thought I'd work in the shop with you today." He grins and then walks past me to set three coffees and a to-go bag on the counter.

"Really?" My jaw drops. I've never considered asking him if he might want to help out. I didn't really think this environment would make him very comfortable, yet here he is.

Of course he's wearing his typical work attire, but this time the suit jacket is left behind, leaving him in tailored black pants, a white shirt with the sleeves rolled up, and a pale pink tie that I already know is going to make his eyes pop more than they normally do.

"Why not? How hard can it be?" He faces me and grins, giving me one of my smiles.

And then it hits me: he wore pink and black because it's my colors.

Be still my heart.

"It's not that hard, but you worked all week, too. Aren't you tired?" I walk over to him and place my hand on his arm. One of his hands falls to my hip.

"Yes, I'm tired, but I didn't realize just how tired you are until last night. I know I've added to your stress level this last month, and well, we're in this together, right? I have to spend the day at the farm tomorrow, but I can be here with you today."

My heart thumps hard in my chest. "I don't know what to say."

His hands wrap around my face. "What kind of boyfriend would I be if I just sat around all day and then forced you to spend time with me at night? Seems a little unfair to me."

"First off, you aren't a slouch—you work hard too. And second, I don't feel forced to spend time with you, at least not anymore." I giggle as he frowns, and then I rise up on my toes and close the distance between us. His lips are soft this morning, while his face is just a tad prickly from not shaving. He tastes like toothpaste and happiness and every color of the rainbow.

The bell rings over the door, and I try to jump away from him, but with his arms banded tightly around me, he holds me close.

"Gross. Do you really need to be kissing out here like this?" Molly asks, turning her nose up at us.

"There's coffee for you on the counter. Your favorite kind," Stokes replies, and her face lights up.

"By all means, carry on then." She walks right past us to the counter and grabs her coffee. She breathes it in, just like I am Stokes, and my insides dance with happiness. Does my face look like hers, full of complete euphoria? If so, I'm not mad about it. I find it hilarious given that just a few weeks ago, I'd have rather cut off my nose than press it into him. "I might have to eat this toast too," she says, eyeing the bag.

"Don't you dare," I warn, and she laughs.

Grabbing the bag, I peek inside to see today's toast is covered with peanut butter, bananas, honey, and granola. My stomach growls, and my mouth waters.

"This looks amazing." I glance up at Stokes; he's just watching me. "Do I have to share?" I ask playfully.

His eyes crinkle in the corners. "Not if you don't want to."

"Good. Mine," I declare, and Molly just shakes her head as I dive in.

"I'm on the register." She waves her hand back and forth between us. "You two can work the counters together."

Excitement bubbles inside of me at the thought of working with him all day, and I can't help the grin that takes over my face. He smirks at my reaction, but it's in a loving way and not sarcastic.

"Any advice or anything you specifically want to direct me on?" He picks up his coffee and takes a sip.

"Nope." I grab mine and pop the lid so it can cool down just a bit. "Mostly, people just want to try things on. They'll ask you your opinion and you give it, good, bad, or indifferent. I want them to feel confident and beautiful. I don't want them to walk out of here looking like an idiot in something that isn't right for them."

He rubs the back of his neck with his free hand. "I'm not sure how good I'll be at telling someone the hat they picked out doesn't look good."

"Well, if you're not sure, just grab one of us and we'll tell them." I bring the cup to my mouth and blow on the coffee.

"Deal," he says, his gaze shifting lower on my face. Wanting to get under his skin a little, I lick my bottom lip and then bite it. His eyes flash back to mine, and he narrows them.

I giggle just as the bell over the door rings and a young woman walks in. I turn to Stokes. "Okay, you're up, superstar. I'm too busy eating to have to be polite and social." I give him a wink as I cut into the toast and take a big bite. We both watch completely amused as Stokes faces toward the woman.

"Good morning, welcome to Rosie May," he calls out to her. My heart thumps hard listening to him say my name that way. Who would have ever thought he would be here, like this, voluntarily? Certainly not me, and by the look on Molly's face, not her either.

The woman pulls her eyes off the fascinator wall and looks at him. Her eyes widen as she clearly recognizes him, and Molly snickers next to me.

"Ah, let me know if I can help you with anything," he tells her, and then he turns to us and scowls at how much humor we are finding at his expense. Oh, I've missed that scowl. I haven't really seen it in a while.

I give him a thumbs-up and mouth, "Way to go!"

He rolls his eyes.

Over the next hour, business picks up significantly. Now I'm not sure if word spread that he was in the store today or if the Saturday before the Derby is always going to be this busy, but whatever the case, we are packed. Thankfully it's busy in a way that means people aren't super stressed but instead are having a good time. We crank up the music and proceed to have the best day. Stokes remains at the hat wall and is surrounded most of the day, while Molly and I work fluidly side by side helping people with the fascinators, wrapping up purchased items, and serving tea.

"Do you think he's having fun, or do you think he's miserable?" I ask Molly as we both stare at him.

"Who cares?" She laughs. "I'm having fun watching him squirm while trying to politely charm these women into buying things."

"This is true."

Feeling that we must be talking about him, he looks our way and his eyes find mine. They go from curious to heated in point two seconds flat. Whereas his laser beams used to want to incinerate me to dust, now they are burning me up in an entirely different way. My stomach clenches, and next to me, Molly gags.

Whatever. I should remind her that it wasn't too long ago when she was championing her brother and wanting us to happen, but I don't. Instead, I give him a wink and mouth, "Thank you."

For lunch, Austin saves the day. He picks up sandwiches then sticks around for an hour to help out while we each eat. He takes photos of people at the photo wall, makes Molly laugh, and adds to the vibe of the store. Molly takes a ton of photos for social media and several videos of Stokes, Austin, and me, and all the while, my cup isn't just running over—it isn't even big enough to hold all the feels I have, feelings that are topped off with grateful and blessed.

At one point a young woman asks if Stokes would take a picture with her, and he frowns and says no. I can't help but laugh at his discomfort and offer to be in the photo with them. The woman immediately agrees, and he just stands there grimacing the whole time. She leans on him and he leans on me. If it wasn't so comical, I would feel bad for him.

Stokes also gets to witness firsthand how strong the gossip can be, from who's dating who to drama in the workplace and family matters. He even heard two women talking about a horse named Dream Catcher that would no longer be running in the Oaks. He didn't specifically hear what was wrong with her, but another horse suddenly falling out of the race left both of us feeling suspicious.

To my knowledge, nothing has happened out at the farm. Then again, Stokes and Grayson have had it on a strict lockdown.

"Today was fun," he tells me as he leans against the counter and I finish closing out the sales for the day. It was by far the shop's biggest day to date. I've never been one of those people who wait until the last minute to buy things, and I'm shocked by the number of people who flooded into the store to buy a hat one week out from the Derby. It's also left me so barren on inventory it's funny. The wedding counter is full, but the rest of the store looks like I am going out of business. Maybe tomorrow while Stokes is at the farm, I can make a few more items just in case.

"It really was. Thank you again for being here." I glance over at him and watch as he loosens the tie around his neck and undoes the top button.

Molly left about two hours ago. She wanted to spend the rest of the day with Austin, and with Stokes here, she really didn't need to be.

"Can I repay you with dinner tonight? I can cook something or we can order in," I ask as I admire his throat. He's running his fingers underneath his collar to pull it away from his skin.

"I say we order in and get you off your feet. Also, I'm buying," he states like there's no discussion about it.

"What? No way. I want to say thank you for helping me." I power down the computer and face him.

"You already have. Besides, I told you earlier, today is about me being there for you." He moves to stand in front of me, and I lean back against the counter and look up at him.

How does a girl get used to this? Get used to him? Every speck of my being is aware of how close he is, how overly masculine he is with long limbs and layers of muscle, and how just his presence makes me giddy.

"I really like the way you dress," I tell him as I run my hand up his chest, the warmth of his skin pressing back against his shirt to greet me.

"What?" he asks with a chuckle.

Heat climbs into my cheeks as I move my hands and run them down his arms. The fabric is soft, and it fits him perfectly.

I shrug. "You just always look so nice." And he does, so nice he's like a pretty package, and I'd like to peel these clothes off of him one piece at a time.

Picking me up, he places me on the counter next to my computer and steps between my legs. Today I'm wearing a cute little denim dress with brown cowgirl boots.

"Thank you," he says, tipping my chin up then running his thumb over my bottom lip. "You are so beautiful." My heart stutters at his words.

Stokes's eyes trail across my face and then to my hair. They pause on my head, and subconsciously my hand drifts to the fascinator I'm wearing to see if it's in place, or maybe just to pull it off. He reaches for my wrist to stop me.

"Don't do that," he says gently.

"Do what?"

"Make that face. I know I've teased you about your hats, headbands, whatever, but I meant what I said the other night—I love them all. I love that you put so much thought into them when you are making them, and I love that you wear them. They are you and you are you. If I saw you here and you weren't wearing something, I'd be worried about your belief in your own products." He gives me a small smile.

"Careful, Whitlock. That sounded an awful lot like another compliment."

"That's because it was," he says, looking down at his hands, which are resting on my calves just above the boots.

Slowly, he slides them up my legs and over my knees until they fall just under my dress. This reminds me of the dinner at his mother's house almost two months ago, only then he didn't look affected at all, and now he does. Then we were surrounded by other people. Now we are not.

"I like the way you dress too," he says, his voice a little huskier than before. His thumbs swipe back and forth across my skin. My stomach and my core both clench.

"Stokes," I whisper.

His eyes rise to find mine, and there's an intensity to them I haven't seen before. A sudden longing threads its way through my chest and lower. It has every muscle tightening and my feet hooking around his legs to hold him in place. Slowly, without breaking eye contact, he slides his hands all the way under my skirt until they wrap around my hips, and he pulls me forward so we are pressed together. Even though I'm sitting up higher, he's still taller than me, and I have to lean back on my hands so I can continue to see him.

My breath catches as long dark lashes hover over his heavy-lidded eyes, and no words need to be said as he leans forward and our lips catch lightly once, draw apart, and then slip together again. He sucks my bottom lip into his mouth, and a whimper escapes me. I bite his top lip, and he growls. The vibration is like the rev of an engine that urges us on and drives me wild.

Stokes kisses me with abandon.

Deeper.

Longer.

Hungrier.

Kiss after kiss and touch after touch, he memorizes every sound, every gasp, and every movement, like when I arch my spine and when my fingertips grip his shoulders to steady myself. He bends over and places his wet mouth on my neck. Dragging his teeth across my skin, he stops at the hollow of my throat and sucks as his fingers dip into the crease of my legs and hips with his thumbs pressing so close in my inner thighs to where I'm desperately aching for him. A whimper escapes, and my legs wrap tighter around his to hold him closer. He in turn rocks my hips against him, and I'm rewarded with a hardness that makes me moan.

"How much of you can I have tonight?" he asks,

moving his mouth lower to where the edge of my dress lies over my breast.

Without hesitation, I tell him, "All of me."

He groans as he lifts his head, and his lips crash down on mine. His tongue moves against mine, and I know without a doubt tonight is about to be the best night of my life.

Stokes. Me. Us.

"If we do this, things will forever be different," I say softly.

He pulls back to look at me, those two little lines slipping in. His lips are full, and his cheeks are high with color. "Aren't they already?"

He's right, things are different, at least they are for me.

And I guess they are for him too.

I nod, and what looks like relief washes over his features.

Sliding his hands underneath me, he lifts me so easily, and I wrap around him, just like in the barn. He walks us to the door, and with each step, my heart rate increases. The anticipation of what's to come is almost too much, but I am here for it, here for him . . . all of him.

Somehow we make it up the stairs and into my apartment. I should be asking him if he is hungry. After all, we did talk about dinner, but something tells me if he is hungry, it's not for food, and the feeling is mutual.

The door closes behind us, and he spins so my back is against it, and I'm hoisted back up in his arms with my legs now locked around his waist. This position has become familiar for us, and it's quite possibly my favorite as I get to climb him like a tree and wrap around him like a koala bear, only this time no one will be calling and interrupting —or at least if they try, they will be ignored. His hands make themselves at home beneath my underwear as he holds me up, and I just can't get close enough to him.

My hands cradle his head, and my fingers thread through his hair as his mouth takes mine. His tongue is exploring every part, even dipping to the insides of my lips, where he licks from one side to the other. I can't help the noise that escapes me or how my thighs pull him even closer.

"I look forward to peeling these clothes off of you, one by one," he says, his voice rough against my skin.

"So do it already." I wiggle a bit, wanting him to move this show along.

He pulls back just a little to look at me. His lips are wet and look utterly delicious. His eyes are dark and dilated, letting me know he's in complete control. It doesn't matter what I say to him or how I try to entice him—he's running this, and he won't have it any other way.

A small smile tips one side of his mouth. "I haven't spent this many years undressing you in my mind just to rush through this." He leans forward, bites my bottom lip, and then releases it with a pop. "We're going nice and slow, and you will enjoy it. In fact, I'm certain I'll have you begging for more."

Two things stick in my mind. The first is him saying he's mentally undressed me for years—years!—and the second is that I'll be begging for more. Does that mean there will be more? Oh, how I hope so. Just imagining it sends electricity racing across my skin, my blood heating to near boiling, and my mind turning to a state of delirium. To know someone for so long, and to know so many sides of them . . . though I had no idea of this side: dirty, sexy, intimate.

"Begging for more, huh?" I tease.

"Much more," he mumbles underneath my ear as he

hoists me a little higher and runs his wet mouth down my neck to the swell of my breasts where he sucks on my skin.

The back of my head hits the door, and my eyes slip shut. He takes advantage of my exposed throat and licks his way up it. Meanwhile, my hands find their way to his tie; I pull it back and forth until it comes undone and can be pulled free. I drop it to the floor and move on to the buttons of his shirt. He drags his face across mine, the stubble rough and sensual, until his lips latch onto mine and he lowers my feet to the ground.

When he takes a small step back from me, a rush of cold air replaces his warmth. Stokes is always so put together, and seeing his hair all disheveled, the top of his cheeks flushed, and his shirt partly undone makes me feel like I'm entering a secret club only he and I belong to. No one but me gets to see him this way, and I want to be so close I can crawl inside of him.

He puts his hands on my waist then slides them up my rib cage until he reaches the underside of my breasts. I'm still leaning against the door, and I arch my back as he cups me with both hands and squeezes.

"Perfect," he murmurs as his thumbs glide back and forth across the tips.

Reaching for him, my fingers tuck under the edge of the waistband of his pants. I pull a little so he comes a step closer and then make quick work of unfastening his belt. There's something so erotic about removing a man's belt. It slips through the loops, it joins the tie on the floor, and I watch as his pants slide down a little to settle on his hips.

He toes off his shoes then takes me by the hand and leads me to my bedroom.

"I've never been in here," he says as he looks around. The sun is setting so its rays are muted, but neither of us reaches for a light. There isn't much to my bedroom. I keep it clean, and the shabby furniture is a set. I've always loved it. The bed is queen sized, and it has a royal blue velvet pin cushion headboard. It's a statement piece, and right now it's telling us both this is where we belong.

"I know. If you had, I probably would have dreamed about it frequently." I feel a little naughty confessing this to him. After all, we were enemies for years and never meant to be lovers.

His eyes flash to mine. "Did you dream of me, Thorney?" he teases, a pleased wicked grin on his face.

I don't answer him. Instead, I bend down to remove my boots, dropping each one with a hard *thunk*.

"I've dreamed of you," he says as he pulls off his socks then stands to his full height and begins to unbutton his shirt. "You can't even begin to imagine how many nights I've dreamed of you." He pauses and then resumes working on the buttons. "Or mornings, as I took a shower."

Mentally I take what I know of him, put him in my shower, and make him wet. It's almost too much for me. I swallow hard and continue to watch him and the buttons. With each one, more of his skin makes an appearance, and I'm not oblivious to the fact that I'm breathing hard. Stokes is getting undressed in my room. He's going to be naked, and I feel like I'm having an out-of-body experience.

His shirt lands on the floor, leaving him in just his slacks with the band of his black boxer briefs peeking over the top, briefs that are hugging his narrow waist and all the parts of him I've never seen but will have after tonight.

Taking a step closer to me, he eyes me like I'm something he cherishes and also something he wants to devour. He pulls the fascinator from my head, slides the denim fabric belt from around my waist, and then moves to the buttons. There are only three, but as his fingertips brush against my skin, I can't help but tremble. It's not because I'm nervous, but because I feel like a live wire that's about to electrically charge the entire room.

Once the buttons are undone, he reaches down, grabs the bottom of the dress, and lifts. It slips over my head, and a few pieces of hair fall loose from the rubber band holding it back. He turns me a little and pulls the band free. My brown hair falls around my shoulders and down to the top of my breasts, breasts that are barely covered with nude lace.

"R-Rosie," he verbally stumbles. "I have no words for what you do to me. Beautiful."

A full-body flush starts somewhere in my legs and then climbs higher, ending in my cheeks. I'm so hot for him that I instinctively reach for his pants, undo the button, slide down the zipper, and push on the fabric until it puddles around his feet. He steps out of them and toward me, his mouth descending at the same time his arms wrap around me and pull me closer.

His skin is as hot as mine, and my hands become

greedy as they touch as much of him as they can. His strong arms, his back, bump after bump of his ribs and his abs, even the trail of hair that drops beneath the last remaining waistband to what I crave most. I can't get enough, and apparently neither can he.

Stokes's hands run over my butt, over my breasts, and around to my back, where he undoes the clasp and watches as my bra drops away. He cups the weight of one breast and lowers his mouth to suck it tenderly then hard. I can't help the groan that escapes as his hand travels south and runs between my legs. I want him, desperately, and he can feel just how much.

"I want these off," he says as he gently bites me and pulls on the fabric over my hips.

"You first." I'm on the verge of panting.

He releases me, and without so much as a smile, just a hunger I know matches mine, he drops his briefs, and I swear my mouth goes dry. There isn't one part of him that isn't beautiful. From head to toe, he is perfection.

Clasping the edge of my underwear, I wiggle them down, moving toward him as I step out of them. Should I feel vulnerable being naked with him? Maybe, but I don't. There is no one in this world who knows me like he does. I trust him implicitly, and given the energy that's wafting off of him, he does me as well. Without hesitancy, we reach for each other.

Time passes. Minutes, hours, days, months—who knows, who cares. It's lost meaning as it takes everything in me to stay present in this moment and not float away as he gives me an orgasm with his fingers, with his tongue, and then he's hovering over me. His weight comes over me and presses me down onto the bed in the most enticing way, and his gorgeous hazel eyes pour gallons of want and desire into my brown ones.

"Birth control?" he whispers, his breath brushing against my lips.

"Yes." A thousand times, yes.

Our eyes stay locked on each other. I understand the question he's asking, and he understands how I'm answering. He mumbles something else against my lips, but with my heartbeat pounding in my ears, I can't understand him.

Guiding himself to my entrance, he pulls his hand free so his forearm settles next to my head, and with his cheek pressed against mine, he pushes in.

I have never wanted anything as much as I want this with him. My heart is pounding so hard it feels like it's going to burst out of my chest.

"Stokes," I whisper, voice almost pained, not physically, but this is ruining me emotionally.

"I know, sweetheart. Me too." He rocks out then pushes in again, filling me completely.

How did we get here?

How did we go from hating each other with a passion to literally being in the throes of passion?

Pausing to let both of us adjust, he shifts his head and kisses me so tenderly I feel my eyes prick with unwanted tears.

And then he moves.

At first it's slower so we can adjust to the enormity of what's happening, and then it's faster as he finally gives in to what he wants, what we both want.

Words tumble from his lips. Some are incoherent, others I understand perfectly.

"So tight."

"So perfect."

"Mine."

And I am his, for as long as he wants.

Stokes has his way with me. Stokes makes love to me. Stokes does it all. I should be more of a participant, but he's owning me so completely that I know he needs it to be this way, and so do I. I'm letting him tell me without words what this is doing to him, how unhinged he feels but also how devoted, and I am here for every sound, every move, every moment.

Sitting back on his heels, he pulls my hips with him to keep us connected. His gaze finds mine through the darkness of the room, and he reaches forward to trace my collarbones. He lightly palms my breasts before he drags his hands down the center of my body to my thighs, and his thumbs slowly explore where we are connected. He's mesmerized. He's worshiping my body and rubbing me in a way that has me shaking. All the while he is still rocking back and forth inside me.

There's no way I'm going to be able to hold out, and there's no way I'll be able to wait for him. It feels too good. He feels too good.

"Just let go," he whispers, and with my eyes clamped

shut, I do. Bright white heat flashes behind my eyelids, a feeling close to adrenaline but more rapturous races through my bloodstream, and as my breath leaves me, I know without a doubt I am in love with him. This isn't just the aftereffect of endorphins and what we are doing; it is soul-deep. It is stitched into my very being.

Falling forward, he pushes my hands up over my head and stretches me out as his chest lays against mine. His face suspends over me, his cheeks are flushed, and his hair is slightly damp, loose pieces falling over his forehead. He slides his hands up my forearms until we are palm to palm, and he threads his fingers in between mine. Holding tight and squeezing with a force meant to anchor him, I wrap my legs around his waist and hang on as he loses himself inside of me. His expression, his sounds, his smell, his warmth—I want to bottle it and keep it forever.

No, I want to keep him forever.

Period.

Is it cliche to say I am floating on cloud nine?

Because I am. There's no other way to describe this lightness in my head, my chest, my limbs, my heart.

Just a few days ago, everything felt so heavy, but not today. Stokes has one hundred percent removed all the pressure and anxiety that was darkening my door. He was there for me, literally and figuratively, and I can still smell his presence in my room. Just the memory has me blushing and feeling giddy.

Along with that, the tough part of the season is officially behind me, and now, as I head into this final week, it's smooth sailing.

Stokes stayed the night on Saturday. I'd like to say we got some sleep in, but we really didn't. Sure, there were a few power naps here and there, but inevitably, his hands or mine would reach out, and we would start all over again. Fingertips brushing over my hip, my foot rubbing against his calf—that was all it took to create the spark and send the fire blazing. Stokes teased that we had years of wasted time to make up for, but I don't want to look backward, only forward to what the future ahead of us will look like.

I never thought this would be me.

I never thought this would be us.

But now that we're here, I can't see it any other way. It was always meant to be.

Him.

Us.

Soon we'll have to have a talk, just to close the door on any uncertainties either of us might still have lingering, but not today. Today, I just want to bask in the glow.

Like Stokes mentioned, he spent Sunday at the farm. His plan had been to come back that evening, but he was held up working on something with his mother and ended up staying the night there. Of course he called, and we did something else we'd never done before: we talked on the phone. We talked for more than just a few passing minutes; we talked for hours, hours where I was smiling, laughing, and having my eyes filled with little dancing stars. Even now, with the two nights combined and almost forty-eight hours later, I'm still glowing. I can feel it radiating from the inside out.

Does he see how he's changing me? Does he know what he's doing?

I'd like to believe I'm a confident person. I've worked

hard to get to where I am and to feel strong enough in myself to do things like open my shop and run this business, but it's amazing how I feel knowing I have him by my side. Yes, I have my mother and Molly, but Stokes just takes this underlying fear that lingers and squashes it. He doesn't even realize he's doing it, but he is. With him, I feel invincible, and I'm so appreciative. It's funny how one unexpected kiss and a gossip article have changed my life.

"Do you think they'll show her?" Molly asks as she carries a large bowl of pad thai from the kitchen and sits next to me on the couch. I know I should be eating too, but I'm nervous, and the thought of having a full stomach makes it ache even more than it already is.

"I don't know. There are so many people there, there's no telling." Whenever the camera pans to the crowd, it's as if they are endless. There are overflowing parade bleachers lined up and down Fifth Avenue with metal street barricades to keep the spectators off, members of the media are stacked up and down the museum stairs, and there is security everywhere.

To watch the Met Gala, we set up the television to show the live stream from *Vogue*'s digital platform. I closed the shop early, Stokes surprised me by also leaving work early and bringing dinner, and there was no way Molly was going to miss this.

"Of course they will—this is live," Stokes reminds us. "I imagine they'll show everyone who walks up the steps, even if it's just for a split second."

The three of us are on my couch with our eyes glued to

the television. There's a star-studded lineup of hosts, and *Entertainment Tonight* is there on the steps to cover the biggest moments, along with the magazine's global editor. We watch the hosts talk and speculate about who is attending and what and who they will be wearing. In theory, the arrivals are scheduled. It's set to begin around six, and it will end around eight. They'll commentate on the behind-the-scenes details of fashion's biggest night and slip in little tidbits about how the magic is made. It's all just so exciting, and as the first limo arrives, I hold my breath.

One celebrity after another makes their way up the famous red carpet steps of the Metropolitan Museum of Art, and I'm enthralled with the clothes, the designs, the glitz, the glamour, and the people.

"I don't understand some of the clothes these women wear," Stokes says.

"A lot of them are there by invitation from different designers, and they don't really get to choose—it's chosen for them."

"Still," he mumbles, and I can't disagree. The person walking in now looks like they are dressed as a lamp shade, while the person before them looked like they should be on the set of *Alice and Wonderland*. Neither look like the theme of the roaring twenties, but then again, what do I know? It's just that this is a night when you're meant to shine. I guess I agree with him—why people would choose attire that isn't flattering or dazzling is beside me.

"Some of the men, too," Molly chimes in. "Did you see that guy with the butler-looking outfit with pants cut at the knees? His shoes looked like black patent leather go-go boots. It was awful."

Stokes chuckles.

"You laugh, big brother, but if Rosie asked you to wear that, you so would," Molly teases.

He glances at me, his gaze warm and affectionate. I'm certain mine is the same.

"Don't worry, I'll never ask you to wear that." I pat him on the leg. His hand covers mine, and he holds it.

And then, a little over an hour and a half into the show, there they are, Avery Layne and Will Ashton. The camera pans to him as he steps out of the car and holds his hand out for Avery. He opted not to wear the vest, but he is wearing the feathered bowtie. My heart gallops, and there she is. She's so stunning, and my heart pounds hard in my chest as pride overflows.

At this point, I'm not sure I even care what people think. She loved the dress, I love this dress, and it just looks to die for on her. Even the hat. No one else could ever wear this the way she is, and when she smiles for the camera and winks, I know that little shoutout was for me; she told me to look for it. I can't believe something I designed and made is making its way up the red-carpet-covered steps.

Flashes are going off around her, the train of the skirt flows perfectly, and when she stops to be interviewed, I don't hear one word because I'm too in my head. Feathers, sparkles, and the gorgeous person Avery is—at this moment, I've accomplished enough.

Next to me, Stokes intertwines his fingers with mine and squeezes. I don't need to look at him to know he is proud of me; it's gleaming off of him in waves. On my other side, Molly has taken out her phone and is recording the whole thing. She's recording the television, me, Stokes, all of it. I'm certain she's snapped a few pictures too, and knowing her, her mind has gone wild with how she plans to ultimately post this with the others she took when Avery was in the shop and weave it into the brand's story.

Just as quick as Avery was there, she's gone, and they're on to the next person.

"That was amazing," Molly says, jumping up, but I barely hear her. I'm in a trance, staring at the television and too lost in the surreal moment I'm having with myself.

Behind me, I hear the telltale sound of a cork popping and Molly laughing. Turning, I find her in the kitchen with a bottle of pink Moet champagne and three glasses.

"You didn't think I'd let this night pass without some bubbly, did you? We're celebrating!" She holds up the bottle and does a little dance before she pours it. "Here's one for you." I stand as she hands me a glass. "One for you." She holds it out for Stokes to take. "And one for me."

The three of us hold up our glasses while Molly takes a few photos then forces us to do a short video of us clinking them together. She's so crazy, but she's so good at what she does. My love tank is overflowing with appreciation for her.

"Okay, cheers to you. Cheers to the most amazing dress that's ever been created. Cheers to the best first season the shop could have asked for, and cheers to many more nights where we're all together and celebrating our successes," she says.

My eyes blur.

"Cheers to celebrating all our successes." I look at each of them, smiling and so happy for me. I can't think of one more thing that could make this night more perfect. "Thank you, to both of you. This . . . the two of you . . . it means the world to me."

We clink our glasses again and drain them.

"Okay, I'm off to Austin's, but I'll see you in the morning," Molly says as she collects her things. Picking up her phone, she laughs and then looks at me. "Your name is blowing up right now. Notifications are coming in left and right. I'll be up all night looking at them and responding. Well, maybe not the whole night." She wiggles her eyebrows, and Stokes groans beside me.

"Thank you, Molly." She's so happy, and she should be. She's been there with me for every step of this. This is not just my moment, but hers too.

Rushing over, she throws her arms around me one more time and hugs me tight. "Congratulations, babe. You deserve this."

Deserving something is such a strange concept. I'd like to think I am a humble person and am just giving back to the world the talents that have been gifted to me, but I do feel like I deserve this moment. I created something that is worthy of being recognized, and it's okay if I allow myself to stand in the spotlight for a few minutes. Even if that spotlight is just here between the three of us, it's enough.

Molly leaves, and I find myself back on the couch, watching more of the show as Stokes locks the door and cleans up the kitchen. Eventually, the couch dips next to me. He's back, sitting on the edge facing me, and he's watching me.

"I'm proud of you," he says, and the tears that were unshed and lingering in my eyes break free. "Why?" he asks as his thumb comes up to wipe them away.

"I don't know," I whisper, and then I lean over and into him. "It's all just so overwhelming."

His arms wrap around me, and I bury my face in his chest and breathe him in. Melons, sage, and smooth leather . . . the most complete and wonderful smell in the world.

"Is it crazy to say this doesn't feel real? Like I know that's my dress—I spent so much time working on it—but seeing it there on the television . . . it kind of doesn't feel like mine."

"No, I don't think it's crazy to feel like that, but it is real, so real, and you should still be celebrating."

I pull back and look up into his face. There are little happy wrinkles in the corners of his eyes as he smiles down at me.

"How should we be celebrating?" I ask in a sultry tone, and I enjoy the surprise as it flits across his features. His eyes widen slightly, and one side of his smile tips up higher than the other. Maybe he's enjoying learning this side of me as well.

I grab the remote to turn off the television and silence descends upon us, but that doesn't matter. The quiet doesn't bother him, nor does it me. Standing, I slide over his lap so I'm straddling him as he settles back into the couch. His large hands wrap around my hips and then run up and down my thighs. Like always, he's warm underneath his clothes, which he wears so well. Tonight it's a pair of worn jeans and a black T-shirt. Stokes wears a lot more black than I thought he did. I like it. I like it a lot.

"I think I like the way you celebrate," he says as I lean forward and brush my lips over his.

"I thought you might." I gently suck on his bottom lip.

Sliding his hand up my back, he pulls me closer so I'm basically leaning on him chest to chest. My arms drape over his shoulders as his fingers tangle in my hair, and he cradles my head.

Dragging his mouth across my cheek to my ear, he asks, "Am I staying tonight?"

I want to tell him to stay indefinitely, but something holds me back. Instead, I tuck my face against his neck and answer, "Yes."

His acknowledgment and approval of this plan come to me in the form of a rumble in his chest and a kiss so thorough a rush floods my veins like a sugar high, and my toes curl inside my fuzzy socks.

We might need to find something to celebrate every night.

LUVU TEA
ROSES FOR ROSIE

To our dear beloved readers, I have two words for you . . . Met Gala. While of course we had our eyes glued to the fabulous event coverage for any and all of our beloved Louisvillians who made an appearance at fashion's biggest night out, it turns out the star of our night ended up not being a person, but rather a dress—a dress and hat ensemble so divine we here at LuVu Tea collectively experienced a spiritual awakening.

For several months now, we have been reporting on the activities of our handsome and dashing bachelor of the season, Stokes Whitlock. As most of you know, he has been seen smitten with none other than our newest NuLu hat girl, Rosie May. But what you might not know, and neither did we, is that her talents extend beyond just hats and headwear. She is a fashion designer extraordinaire.

Stepping onto the red carpet last night were music legends Avery Layne and Will Ashton. We had heard whispers recently that Avery was seen in town, but other than a post at

Rosie's shop, her reasons and whereabouts were left unknown.
That is no longer the case.
Avery's ensemble sparkled, shimmered, and blew us all away.
Heads turned. Astonishment, wonder, and a hush swept over the crowd, leaving even the hosts speechless and everyone wondering, "Who is she wearing?" It wasn't until she was interviewed that her mysterious designer was revealed. Color us wildly shocked and delighted, because who knew we had such incredible expertise in our town? Well, apparently Avery Layne did.
We bow to you, Rosie May.
Just exquisite.

25

Today feels like the last day.

All day it has. I'm not sure if it's because business is slowing down, or if it's the fact that I know, for me, the season is officially over.

Tomorrow the shop will be closed as I have fifteen delivery orders to take to various hotels around Louisville for travelers coming into town, and then after that I have to get ready for the Bourbon Ball. It's a ball I've never gone to but have long dreamed of.

It's two minutes to four, almost closing time, and as I cross off the second-to-last day on my calendar, the bell over the door rings.

Looking up, I find Stokes walking directly toward me. Excitement bursts through my veins at just the sight of him, but then suddenly I'm doused with alarm at the murderous scowl stamped on his face.

"What's wrong?" I ask as I move out from behind the

counter to greet him. Like usual, he wraps his arms around me and hugs me tight while dropping his head and breathing me in. He's still in his work clothes, so he must have come straight here. The fabric of his suit is cool from the air outside.

"Do you think you could close a little early today?" he asks.

I pull back. "Of course, but why?" I scan his expression, looking for any tell.

Stokes runs his hand over his face and then looks at me; I'm lasered with hazel.

"I got a call from the security team and then Grayson."

A gasp slips past my lips. "No. Way."

"Yes, way." He reaches up, tucks a loose piece of hair behind my ear, and then walks away. He walks from me to the tables with his hands on his hips and then comes back. He's full of energy and can't help the pacing. Stokes is angry, and his brain is running twenty-five miles an hour.

"Is Ace okay?" I'm suddenly sick with worry; this must have to do with him.

"Yes, but I'm headed to the farm, and I wanted to know if you'd like to go." His tone is almost pleading.

"Absolutely. Just give me five minutes to close up and run up to change."

His gaze sweeps over me once before he nods, retraces his steps, and takes my chin between his fingers as he bends down to press his lips to the corner of my mouth. It's sweet and not urgent, even though I know he's ready to go and get there as fast as we can.

The ride to the farm is silent. He's stewing as he drives, those two little lines are present, and I know Stokes well enough to just let him be. He's ditched his suit jacket and tie, having left them lying across the seats in the back. Today he's wearing a navy pinstripe suit with a white shirt. He's rolled up his sleeves, and more than once, I find myself staring. At one point he does reach over and take my hand, but I don't ask him any questions, even though I have a million of them.

Ace is fine, I repeat to myself to attempt to settle my nerves. I'll find out the details soon enough.

We pull onto the farm, and it's eerily quiet as the guards wave us through. Stokes drives us straight to the security team's house, where they keep their headquarters, and outside are several golf carts, three trucks, an unknown vehicle, and two police cars. My stomach dips, and I try to sneak a peek into the back of the cop car. I can make out the shape of someone, but I can't see who it is.

Oh my God—did they catch the saboteur?

Stokes takes my elbow as we walk into the house, and the room goes silent.

My anxiety skyrockets.

I've never been in the security house, but it's about what I would expect: function over aesthetics with an open floor plan. There's the standard kitchen with a table and there are couches in the living room, but the dining room has three long tables set up in a horseshoe shape, complete with twelve flat-screen monitors. Images rotate on them from various locations around the farm.

"Mother." Stokes greets her first, walking over and kissing her on the cheek.

"I'm glad you both were able to come." She glances from him to me, and I just return her greeting with a friendly smile.

In the room, there are four members of the security team, two police officers, Grayson, his mother, and now the two of us. All eyes are on Stokes, and the mood is mainly somber.

Weird.

"Stokes. Rosie," Grayson says matter-of-factly.

"Did he do it? Is it him?" Stokes asks Grayson. I want to shout, *Who is he???*

"I think so," Grayson says. His words are not harsh, but there is an edge to them I've rarely heard from him.

Stokes again rubs his hand over his face and then moves us to the couch. We sit down, and everyone in the room follows. I take his hand and hold it tight to reassure him that I'm here for him. He glances at me appreciatively before he turns to the room and says, "Start from the beginning."

The tallest of the security guards begins speaking. I don't know him; I really don't know any of them. The only contact I have with security is when I come through the front gate.

"When he pulled up to the gate, he said he was here to see Roughhouse."

Roughhouse is a stallion that has to be close to eight years old. He won the Derby a few years back, the last time the Whitlocks won it, and now lives his days being spoiled and studded. He's also not kept in the same barn as Ace; he's further back on the property.

"We asked him if he had an appointment to meet with the horse or Grayson, and he said it was fine, said he had spoken with you last week and you said to just come on over. Of course we instantly knew something was off. Per protocol, we called Grayson, who then called you."

"He is a liar." Stokes shakes his head then looks at me. "Rosie was there, she heard me tell him to call you"—he glances at Grayson—"to make the appointment."

A gasp slips out, and Stokes looks at me.

"You're talking about Dr. Miller?" I ask incredulously.

"Yes." He frowns.

My jaw drops. This older man has worked with Whitlock Farm for probably thirty years. Stokes has known him his whole life.

"You did tell him that last Friday," I confirm, wanting everyone to hear me say this, and Stokes rubs his thumb over the back of my hand.

He looks back at Grayson, wanting him to continue.

"We let him in and kept watch. He didn't know. He did first stop by Roughhouse's barn and was with him for about fifteen minutes. I don't know exactly what he was doing, but once he left, the cameras picked him up heading not toward the exit, but toward Ace's barn. I had already made my way there and was in Eternal Dust's stall, hiding. Security alerted me when he was in Ace's stall, so I walked out and over to check it out. He had a syringe loaded and ready to go, and when I asked him what he was doing, he jumped, clearly startled, and squirted the liquid out."

"What was in it?" Stokes asks.

Yes! What was in it? I want to ask too. I can't believe this. Did this really almost happen? Was Ace almost compromised? I mean . . . why?

"I'm not sure, but he became very agitated and yelled at me that I was not allowing him to do his job, said you had sent him in and because I scared him, Ace wouldn't be getting the vitamins he needs."

"Vitamins for what?" Stokes asks, the anger rising in him like the ocean's tide. Waves of it are now lapping around us.

"That's what I asked. He became even more flustered and said, 'For the inflammation.'"

"What inflammation?" Stokes asks, gritting his teeth while tilting his head a little.

"Exactly. There's nothing wrong with Ace at all, not one tender or enlarged spot. He's as healthy and happy as he always is," Grayson states emphatically. "About this time, the security team arrived, and Dr. Miller started getting very vocal. I've never once in all these years heard him yell, but he became someone different. He accused us of interfering with a routine procedure, said you personally spoke to him and knew he was coming, and he refused to hand over his bag. He completely refused to cooperate with us, so for precaution's sake, they handcuffed him while we called for the police."

"It just doesn't make any sense," Stokes murmurs to the room. "Why?"

No one has an answer for him. Eventually his gaze lands on his mother, and they have a silent conversation.

"So what happens now?" Stokes asks, looking at the two police officers who've been observing the conversation between Stokes and his trainer.

"We'll take him in and detain him until a judge announces bail. In Kentucky, there are several different types of trespassing misdemeanors. He can argue that he was let onto the property, but he lied about his reasons for being here. The question now is, was his intent criminal?"

"Cruelty to animals—tampering or drugging livestock," Stokes mutters, letting out a sigh and letting go of my hand. With his elbows now resting on his knees, he leans forward and drops his head.

"Exactly," Grayson confirms.

Eventually, Stokes lets out a deep sigh and stands. I follow suit as he turns to face the two cops. "Is there anything you need from me or my team?"

"Not at the moment. We'll just have to wait for that syringe to be run through drug testing. At the end of the day, he wasn't supposed to be here, he knew he needed an appointment, and whatever he was about to inject into your horse, he was not given consent. Once we speak with our people, we'll let you know. Keep your phone near you in case we have questions. We'll be in touch soon."

Stokes lets out another sigh and glances over at the monitors. No one says anything as we all watch him. Birdie hasn't spoken at all; I guess they informed her of all of this before we got here, but everyone is acting as if Stokes is the one in charge. I suppose, in a way, he is. After all, he's the second-in-command, but I've never seen this side of him here at the farm, and I like it.

"We're sure there's something going wrong here, right? Is it possible all of this is a miscommunication?" he asks one more time.

The tall security guard answers him. "Sir, I don't think so. We've looked at the security footage. His behavior was suspicious, and combined with the fact that he broke the farm's visiting rules and was caught in the wrong barn with an unapproved medication, it's definitely better to be safe than sorry."

"I suppose you're right. Keep me updated, okay?" He looks around the room. Heads nod, and then all but two of the security guards begin shuffling for the door.

"Do you two want to come to the main house for dinner?" Birdie asks. Bless her, she looks hopeful, but even I can tell Stokes is done peopling. He needs to decompress and ruminate on all of this.

"Thanks, but I think we'll head to my house. I still have some work to do, and I need to call Christopher," he tells her, letting her down gently.

"All right, darling. I'll see you later." She smiles at both of us, her eyes lingering on me for a second longer, and then she's gone, whipping away in one of the golf carts.

Climbing back into Stokes's SUV, we drive the short distance to his house and walk in together hand in hand.

His grip is a little tight, but considering his mood, I don't even think he realizes.

"Can I get you something to drink?" he asks, flipping on the kitchen light.

Like his condo in the city, this is also the first time I'm entering this home. It definitely has Birdie's touch, but it is all Stokes and looks straight out of a Restoration Hardware catalog: warm brown leather, a farm table in the kitchen, and white cabinets and walls. There are pops of color here and there, and his personal items are casually found all over, from shoes by the door and mail on the counter to a book open and upside down on the coffee table to hold its place, a cell phone charger stuck in the wall, and a sweater thrown over one of the island chairs. This home looks comfortable, almost more lived in than the condo, and my heart squeezes that it's been here all along, but I haven't.

"Maybe a glass of water," I tell him. There's a pinch in my chest at the thought that there are things about him I really don't know. Granted, I do feel like I know more than most, but when it comes to his daily life, I'm still learning. Like the book—I wander over to see the cover: a biography about Roosevelt. Although I've never given it much thought, considering Stokes is a lawyer, he probably does like to read, but biographies? Is it that he loves history or politics? Does he enjoy nonfiction more than fiction? I have no idea.

He pulls two glasses from the cabinet and fills them with ice and water from the refrigerator. We're standing in the middle of the large room next to the island, and we stare at each other as we each take a drink.

"I've never been here," I tell him, almost whispering.

His brows pull down. "What do you mean?"

"I've never been in your house."

His face smooths out with understanding. He looks around—I imagine he's trying to see what it is that I see—and then he looks thoughtfully back at me. "You know today wouldn't have happened if not for you."

"You don't know that. Your security here has always been very good." I smile sheepishly.

"I do know that, because we wouldn't have been on alert like we have been otherwise. Also, Ace's barn only had cameras that showed the outside, not the inside. We installed cameras throughout the building so we could see what happens inside as well, specifically Ace's stall. The vet's strange behavior and catching him on tape holding the needle—it just adds to the case."

"Oh." I take another sip, my mind reeling a little bit. I had been hesitant to tell him about my crazy theory, but maybe it really wasn't so crazy.

"Oh is right." He moves a step closer. "Are you hungry? I didn't even think about dinner." He runs his hand down my arm. It's so sweet, him and his constant need to touch me. I love it.

"I probably could eat something," I say, just as my stomach growls.

One side of his mouth tweaks up, and he sets his glass on the island. While moving toward the smart television to turn on some music, he informs me, "You have your choice of steak and fries or spaghetti."

"Which is easier?"

"Both are easy, but let's go pasta." He walks back to the kitchen and to the freezer. He pulls out a package of ground mild Italian sausage, opens it, and puts it on a plate to defrost in the microwave. I move to the pantry and retrieve noodles and a jar of sauce. Simple, easy, and it'll be delicious.

Side by side, we work together to make this dinner, and I can't help but wonder if this is how life would be if I was with him every night, if we lived together. I know I'm getting way ahead of myself, but being with him, imagining a future with him, it's not hard to do. Would we live here or in the city? Would it be at one of our current places or somewhere new? My heart lights up like a sparkler with excitement. Together would be so good.

We're quiet as we sit down to eat. It's an easy quiet where we don't feel forced to fill the silence, but we talk about our day, speculate over Dr. Miller, and laugh at stupid things. For the most part, I think he's calmed down a bit, but the reason we're here lingers in the background.

Just as we're finished, his phone rings in his back pocket, and we both jump at the sound. Pulling it out, he flashes me the screen so we both see on the caller ID that it's his security team. His eyes connect with mine and hold as he takes the call.

"Whitlock," he murmurs as I lean back in my chair and watch him. His back has gone straight, and his face has turned to stone. At this moment, he's the other Stokes I know, the prince of the castle, the one who dutifully knows his role. "Right. Okay. I'll meet him at the station, and thanks for all you're doing. We appreciate it."

"Duty calls?" I ask after he hangs up, trying to lighten the mood.

"Seems so. A detective has been assigned to the case, and he wants to go over everything with me." He lets out another sigh, slouching in his chair. "It shouldn't take too long, but do you mind if we stay here tonight? Feel free to borrow any clothes. What's mine is yours." He gives me a small smile. "I'll take you home in the morning whenever you want, or I can call you a car if you want to go back now."

"I'll stay," I tell him, and relief washes over his handsome face. Standing, I take both of our plates and place them in the kitchen sink. Dinner is done, and I know he needs to go. Following, he pulls me into a hug and lays his lips against my forehead. "I'm glad."

He wouldn't do and say these things if this relationship were still fake, would he? It's real to me; does it feel real to him, too? He said he wasn't going anywhere, said I don't need to worry, but I still do. I'm certain we won't go back to being enemies, but I want to be more. More than fake, more than casual, and definitely more than friends. I want to tell him this. I should have told him the other night; I just have to figure out a way to gather the courage to do so.

"Don't forget to call Christopher," I remind him.

He nods but then says, "He can wait. I'll see him at some point this weekend."

"Are you going to the office tomorrow?"

"No. I previously scheduled it off so I could be here to help my mother and Grayson."

I should have known this; he's always helped the days leading up to the Oaks and the day of the Derby. In fact, everyone helps. It's all hands on deck. There are fourteen races slotted the day of the Kentucky Derby, and Ace is not the only Whitlock horse who will be running.

"Of course, I knew that. You always help."

"More like I help by doing my best to not get in their way." He grins. "I'll be back, okay?"

"Yep. I'm all set here." And I am. I plan to fully snoop through all his things while he's gone.

"Good. I like you here," he says against my lips as he bends down to kiss me.

Sometime later, after I've gone to bed, I feel cool air slide over me and the mattress dips as Stokes slips in. I'm met with his warm skin as he curls around me, and his hand runs over my hip and up under the edge of my shirt. It settles on my stomach, and he lets out a sigh that tells me just how exhausted he is. It isn't long before his breathing evens out, and I dangerously allow myself to not wonder but imagine that this is my life and my future.

26

Heat.

That's what wakes me.

Heat, sunlight, and a spicy smell that is so good and familiar. A relaxed exhale escapes me.

Heaven.

That's what this is.

Did I date a little in college? Yes. Since then, though, I've been so busy, and intertwining my life with someone else's was never the goal. But now, here I am, and I can't imagine it any differently. Waking up next to Stokes is quite possibly my new favorite thing in the world. It feels like home. He feels like home.

And I can't decide if that is scary or exciting.

"Morning." His hand finds my back and rubs up and down. We shifted during the night, and my head is lying on his shoulder, my arm is draped across his stomach, and my leg is wrapped over his.

I stretch and push my body up closer to his, snuggling in.

He chuckles.

"What time is it?" I run my hand up his very flat stomach and over his chest. His hand catches mine, and he holds it over his heart.

"A little after eight." His voice is different in the mornings when he wakes up. I noticed it the other morning, and I definitely notice it today. It's rougher, deeper, and one hundred percent sexy.

I pull back to look at him. His face is covered with stubble, his hair is all over the place, and his eyes are a little sleepy. "How did it go last night?"

"Okay. I brought the paper where you wrote everything out and gave it to him. I also told him what I heard on Saturday. He didn't seem surprised, but what do I know? Detectives have a way of always keeping their face neutral. He wanted to know why we didn't mention this to someone sooner. I didn't really have an answer for him."

"Um, maybe because when someone thinks they've come up with a multimillion dollar conspiracy theory, they tend to keep it to themselves versus telling the world they might be a little kooky."

His lips tip up just a little. "Yeah, you are a little kooky, aren't you?" He's teasing me, so I wrap my leg around his just a little more so his is between mine, and I squeeze. Thigh clamp! He laughs while releasing my hand and moving his to my leg. He palms my butt, and my brain short-circuits as his thumb traces the edge of my underwear.

"Mmm," I murmur. "Anything on Dr. Miller?" I'm trying to appear calm and collected.

"Not yet. He was denied bail until the drug test comes back. With the Derby being days away, everyone is on notice for shady activities."

"Well, hopefully they'll figure it out," I tell him, and mean it. Part of me wants Dr. Miller to be the guilty party, because then that means this is over, but the other part of me doesn't due to the long relationship they've had with him.

"Hopefully." He lets out a sigh then pulls me closer and presses his lips against mine. Should I worry about morning breath? Maybe, but right now I just don't care. Stokes is kissing me.

Shifting, I move so I'm lying on top of him, and I smile down at him.

"You have too many clothes on," he says, pulling on his T-shirt, which I put on last night.

"You should take it off me," I tease, and he does. He slides it up over my chest and head so we are skin to skin. He flings it somewhere as I prop my chin up on my hands, my elbows resting on him.

"How did you sleep last night?" he asks, smoothing the hair back off of my forehead.

"Perfectly."

He smiles. It's one of my smiles, and it spears me in the heart just like one of Cupid's arrows.

"What time do you need to leave this morning?" He's now running his hands up and down my shoulders, back, and sides.

"Not until later. I gave myself this afternoon and tomorrow to deliver hats."

Surprisingly, I had quite a few people call the shop and ask if I would deliver to their hotel the weekend of the event. It didn't occur to me that this would be something I would need to do, but as order after order came in from out-of-towners, I ended up with a list of fifteen different hotels I need to drop by.

"Are they all packed up?" he asks.

"Yes, I packed them when they were ordered. They're sitting in the second bedroom at my place."

"Smart." He pushes a piece of loose hair off my face then runs a finger down my cheek. It's sweet, and the way he's looking at me sends off cherished vibes. My poor fallen heart doesn't know whether to stumble around love drunk or strap on its running shoes with the adrenaline pumping through it.

Pushing up a little bit, I decide to do the same and run my hand through his messy hair. His head tilts a little to push into my hand; he wants my hands on him.

"What do you think about letting me borrow your car? It's bigger and will hold the boxes better."

"Fine with me. I don't need it today, and you can either come back and get me tomorrow, or I'll catch a ride back into town."

I trace his eyebrows, press my finger between his eyes

where those two little lines have almost permanently left their mark, and then drag my finger down the bridge of his nose to his lips, which I outline softly. Stokes has the softest lips. Needing to feel them, I lean up and kiss him chastely. His eyes crinkle in the corners; this made him happy.

"Tell me something about you that I don't know." I move to kiss the corner of his mouth.

"Like what?" he asks, the grumble of his voice vibrating into my chest. His hands have moved to my back, where his fingertips are inching down my spine, one bump at a time.

"I don't know. I just want to know you."

The warmth of his gaze shines on the details of my face. The room is a little brighter than it was a few minutes ago, and being this close to him, I can see the tiny details on his face as well. There are small freckles on the bridge of his nose from years of being in the sun, there's a tiny scar on his forehead near his hairline, and his eyes really are a mixture of three colors: green, chestnut brown, and splashes of amber. They remind me of a paint palette with the way the colors are spread around.

"You do," he tells me, and I'm certain he believes that.

"I want to know the little things. I saw you have a book you're reading in the living room—I didn't even realize you like to read. Do you always read nonfiction?"

"I do like to read. I always have. I'm not a very social person, as you know. I do nonfiction mostly, but I like it all."

"What else?" I ask curiously.

"Does this little game go both ways? Do I get to ask you questions?" He grins.

"You can ask me anything you want." And he can. I can't think of one thing I wouldn't tell him—well, maybe one, only because I'm still coming to terms with those three little words associated with Stokes.

"Let's see . . . I know your favorite food is toast. Mine is frozen fruit." He slides his large hands up my rib cage until his thumbs reach the side of my boobs. They brush back and forth in a way that's so normal it's like he's done this every day for years.

"Frozen fruit?"

"Yes." His grin stretches. "Strawberries, peaches, blueberries—you name it, I love them. So much better for you than candy, and I prefer a bowl of frozen strawberries over ice cream any day."

"That's so . . . healthy of you," I mock.

"Are you teasing me?" he grumbles. "I'll show you tease." There's a mischievous glint in his eyes as he grips me tight and then slides me down his body until I'm dragged over his lap.

"Oh." My eyes widen as they find his, and every muscle in me clenches.

"Oh is right. You have no idea what you do to me." And just like that, our very short get-to-know-you session is changing direction.

"What do I do to you?" I roll my hips over his and his hardness, and he groans.

"You drive me crazy," he all but growls.

"Ha, I already knew that," I taunt. "My sworn life's mission."

"I have a mission, too. Let me show you."

Stokes sits up, taking me with him. My hair tumbles around my shoulders as he pulls my hips snug over his. The impressive length of him presses against me, and more than anything, I want to incinerate my underwear and his boxer briefs so I can sink down on him. Wrapping his hands around my face, he claims my lips with his in a kiss that beats out all other morning kisses to ever exist.

Time is lost as we make out with no hurry, just the desire to taste and consume each other in a way I once only dreamt of. Our hands are greedy and insatiable as they roam and explore, and I'm so turned on I'm certain he can feel the evidence through his boxers and on his skin. Eventually he twists so he's placed me on my back. He strips us bare and shows me what our mornings together would truly look like. Underneath the soft sunbeams and him, after he's fed my body and soul twice, I can't help but think this is the most perfect way to start a day. I didn't realize this level of contentment was possible.

He decides we need coffee, and I watch as Stokes slips on a pair of navy athletic shorts then makes his way out of the room. If I could drool on cue, I would. Satisfied eyes, lazy gait, muscles for days—he looks so good. He looks like mine.

While the pot is brewing, he comes back to the bedroom and leans against the doorframe. The sunlight is bathing his skin golden, and, almost timidly, he asks, "Go for a ride with me this morning?"

My brain goes blank, and white noise rushes through my ears. I know it's stupid, but I'm having a hard time comprehending what he just asked. Ride? Like on a horse?

My brows pull down, and my lip curls as I realize that is exactly what he's asking me. In fact, I can't believe he's asking me this, and my heart starts to race.

"Um, I don't think so," I tell him as I let out an unbelieving laugh. There's an edge to my tone, and he hears it.

His eyes narrow, and if I didn't know any better, with the way he just stiffened, I'd say it's like he's thrown up invisible armor, cloaking himself behind it. It's something that hasn't been present for weeks, maybe even months. What is happening right now?

"What do you mean?" he asks quietly, returning my tone, and that sends up red flags.

"I don't want to go for a ride," I tell him as I break out in a sweat.

Standing up straight, he drops his gaze to the ground, and his hands clench in fists before they find his waist.

"Why not?" he asks without looking at me. The color on his skin deepens, the tops of his cheeks, his chest, the top of his arms—I'm not sure what is happening right now.

"You can go, but I don't want to go with you," I tell him, giving him an out. I know he likes to ride, he always has, but you won't catch me anywhere near a horse.

He lets out a chuckle and shakes his head, looking disappointed and angry at the same time.

"Why are you mad? What difference does it make?" I sit up and wrap the sheet around me.

He takes a deep breath as he thinks about how to answer me. I don't understand. "I asked you once before to ride with me, and you said no then too."

"When?" My brows pull down in confusion.

His eyes rise from the ground to find mine. What am I seeing right now? They're stormy, completely walled off, and accusatory.

"Right after we met. You'd lived here for maybe two weeks, three at the most, I don't remember. Things were hard for me then after my dad passed, but I wanted to be friends with you like you were with Molly. Riding horses is my escape and one of my favorite things, as you know. I wanted to share that with you. I spent all morning getting the horses ready. I washed them, brushed them, saddled them, and packed a picnic. I was so excited to take you out, but when I asked you, you stood on your porch and laughed just like you did now and shot me down—hard. I was completely embarrassed. I guess you could say I didn't take it very well."

I scoot to the edge of the bed, moving closer to him. His feelings are hurt, like really hurt. This is an old wound, and if I'm hearing him correctly, it's the reason we were not friends all these years. This right here, this is the reason, the beginning of it all. A lump forms in my throat.

"Stokes." I say his name gently to get his attention and

to diffuse some of the emotions coursing through him. "I do remember that. I remember you coming to my house and being so excited that you were there and had asked me. Trust me when I say I was crushing on you hard, but when have you ever seen me on a horse?"

The two little lines strike between his eyes, and his lips flatten as he thinks about my question. He thinks about it but doesn't answer.

"All these years, you hated me because you thought I was somehow snubbing you that day?" I shake my head in disbelief, my eyes flooding with tears.

As much as I don't want to get emotional over this conversation, my heart is breaking into a thousand pieces. Years—years he hated me, and all this time I had no idea what I had done to earn his perpetual scorn. Slowly the tears spill over.

"I mean . . ." he stutters, shaking his head too. "I thought it was me you didn't want to be with. At fifteen, my feelings were crushed, and I just . . . I thought it was me you didn't want. Why don't you ride horses?" He's completely dumbfounded by this revelation.

"Because I'm afraid of them," I say bluntly.

Shock and confusion flit across his face. "Why?"

I pull on the sheet around me to see if I can tighten it a bit, even though it's already pretty secure. It's as if I'm using it to hold me together when I feel like I'm about to blow apart. "Stokes, do you know how my dad died?" My voice is unsteady. Even after all these years, it's still hard to talk about.

He runs his hand over his face then back through his hair before he drops it to his side. His wary eyes find mine. "Yes, he had a heart attack like mine."

Does he really not know?

"He did, but he went into cardiac arrest after being kicked in the chest by a h-horse."

His jaw drops then snaps back up. The scowl I know so well shifts his expression and replaces his shock. "How have I not ever heard this story?"

"I don't know." I shake my head in perplexed confusion. "My dad was an electrician. He was out at the Kingsleys' farm working on some wiring in one of their barns for something, I don't even know. He was walking toward Mr. Kingsley, who was standing next to a groomer who was holding a horse, and the horse got bit by a horse fly. It was a complete freak accident."

"Horse fly," he states and questions at the same time, dread laced in his tone.

"Yes." I can feel my chin quivering, and I see the moment he sees this too. The anger and turmoil he was shrouded in just moments ago have evaporated and, with them, my resolve. I start crying, for so many different reasons.

I've learned a lot since his accident. Most horses don't like horse flies. They are large insects, about the size of a thumbnail or bigger, and almost all horses kick out and try to run when one lands on them and bites. Talk about the wrong place at the wrong time. Ten seconds, five paces—

so many variables that could have been different and given us a different outcome.

The emergency room doctor told us being kicked by a horse is the equivalent of getting hit by a car going twenty miles an hour. It's enough to shatter bones and inflict massive trauma to soft tissues, and it is common for someone to go into cardiac arrest afterward. They tried to save him, but the damage was too much.

"The horse kicked him?" Moving forward to sit on the bed beside me, he places his hand on my leg.

"Yes." I'm watching him, and tears are now falling rapidly. I wasn't the one kicked in the chest, but mine feels so tight and so sad right now. I just close my eyes and drop my head.

Oh, Stokes.

All these years. This one thing, and all it's done is snowball into something bigger and bigger until it was bigger than us. Why have we never talked about this? How did he not know I'm afraid of horses? Why hasn't he ever mentioned that day, even in passing as a passive aggressive comment?

"I didn't know," he says as he pulls me into his arms and against his chest. "I'm so sorry, Rosie. I don't know what to say right now. I'm just sorry for all of it, for what happened to you, for what I didn't know . . . how I perceived that moment, how I've treated you . . ." He groans into my hair. "I'm so sorry."

And I am too. I'm sorry. I'm sorry I never asked him once why he didn't like me. Would he have told me?

Maybe, maybe not, but I could have tried harder. I cling to him with utter sadness for a lifetime that could have been different for us. I didn't know I had hurt his feelings so much that day. That was the last thing I ever intended—I wanted that friendship with him so badly.

At least now we know. It's out there, in the open, and, hopefully, forever over.

27

*D*riving Stokes's big SUV is a dream. I thought I would be nervous to navigate it due to its size, but surprisingly, over the last two days, I did all right. The boxes fit perfectly into the back, and both yesterday and today, I only needed to load it up once, which saved on time. I donned a Rosie May T-shirt and a matching fascinator and headed out to each of the hotels. The valets let me double park to unload, the concierges were more than accommodating and took the boxes from me, and I was even stopped a few times to take a picture. I'm certain Molly will be over the moon when she sees me out and about and tagged in photos.

Once I was finished, I refilled his tank with gas and headed back to the farm to pick him up. He was waiting for me outside his house when I pulled up, and my insides fluttered. Repeatedly, I've thought of our conversation from yesterday morning, him opening up to me and his confession as to why he hated me all of these years, and having an answer has made me feel lighter, freer. For the first time since I realized I want more, want him, I feel like it's a real possibility.

A smile splits his face, and I can't help but marvel at the change in him over the last couple of weeks. He's not as rigid and stiff as I've always known him to be, and although I still think he's an old man in a young guy's body, I can appreciate how he has classic tastes and values simplicity.

Opening the driver's side door, he leans in and kisses me. "You might look adorable driving my car, but when I'm here, you sit over there." He points to the passenger side.

I roll my eyes, just to harass him a little, but he won't find me arguing, so I scoot over and buckle up. Stokes climbs in and off we go, making a quick pit stop at Parksdale Farm on the way home. Parksdale has a large roadside produce stand that also serves up barbecue, charcuterie boards, fruit platters, milkshakes, and cider.

"I've always loved this place," I tell him as we sit down at a picnic table in the shade. There are a few under a tent and then a few outside of it. This one is outside and under a large oak tree. Those who might have stopped in for lunch have all gone, leaving just us and a few random shoppers.

"Me too," he says, and then he drops his gaze. He's pulled into himself as he thinks of something, and then he says, "I've imagined asking you if you would like to come here with me a thousand times."

"Really?" I'm so surprised my shoulders jerk back just a bit.

He nods. "You and Molly have mentioned repeatedly over the years how much you like it here." He shrugs. "I wanted to come here with you too."

"I do like it here, but I hate to say it—if you had asked, I would have said no for fear of your ulterior motives."

He frowns but nods his head in understanding. "No ulterior motives today." He picks up the glass of dry cider he chose and holds it out.

"None." I smile back and return the toast with my strawberry mimosa cider. "So how did you get out of having to attend the Oaks?"

"I had some work to do at the farm today, and my mother gave me a free pass." He chuckles.

"Work, shmerk. So boring," I tease, picking up a candied pecan and eating it.

He flashes me one of my smiles. "It is, but unfortunately today's work was a necessary evil."

"Is it all done?"

"Almost," he says, looking like he wants to say more, something else, but he doesn't. Instead, he changes the subject. "What color is your dress tonight? I plan on wearing a black tux, so anything will match." He plops an almond into his mouth. We chose a large charcuterie board that's covered with different types of cheeses, meats, berries, and nuts. I made sure there was no citrus.

"Rose gold. I found this fabric a few years ago that is gorgeous and shimmery. The dress itself isn't complicated, but I've cut it to accent my curves, and I think it's beautiful."

"I am a fan of your curves." There's a glint in his eyes that's almost heated. It could mean anything, but to me it speaks of things that are to come later tonight.

"I'm glad," I tell him, a blush crawling its way up my neck and to my cheeks.

Five hours later, dressed to the nines, Stokes and I arrive at the Bourbon Ball, which is being held at the Marriott downtown.

If I thought the fanfare of the entrance at the bourbon tasting was a lot, boy was I wrong. This red carpet walk is that but on steroids, and what surprises us both is the number of reporters who call my name, not his. They don't have us entering the hotel straight from the curb. Instead, guests are dropped off half a block away where the red carpet entrance is placed. Against the building there is a fabric backdrop, and in three separate places there are step and repeat banners stationed for attendees to stop in front of and pose.

It feels glamorous, and I don't hate it. I'm thrilled to be here and to be photographed with Stokes.

"Rosie! Rosie! Rosie!" My name is called over and over to grab my attention.

"Rosie, did you design your dress?" This comes from a man in front of us as we stop at the first banner.

"Rosie, are you friends with Avery Layne?" comes from a woman at the second.

"Rosie, are you excited to see all of your creations tomorrow at the Derby?"

"Stokes, is Ace of Spades going to win it all?" He's asked this at the last banner, the crowd murmuring with speculation.

Of course we don't answer them, we just smile, but as we cross the threshold and enter the lobby, Stokes glances down at me, and all I see is pride, pride for me and pride to be with me.

"That was something," I whisper up at him as people are walking all around us and chatting. Who knows, some may even be eavesdropping.

"You are something." He brings my hand to his lips so he can kiss the back of it.

Is swooning a real thing? Because I'm certain that's what is happening to me. My knees feel weak, my breath has quickened, I'm lightheaded, and given the right setting, I'm certain he could make me faint.

"Come on, let's get this over with so I can get you home and out of this dress," Stokes states as if there's no other ending to tonight. I laugh but let him lead me to the ballroom. I'm not hating his plan, not at all.

The Bourbon Ball is everything I expect it to be and more. It's elegant, it's opulent, and I'm in awe of everyone's attire: the gowns, the jewels, the glitz, and the tuxedos. These men look just as remarkable as the women, but not as remarkable as Stokes. His tuxedo is a classic style, complete with a black cummerbund and a black tie. His hair has a harsh part on one side and is slicked off to the other. He looks so debonair he's stop-and-stare-worthy.

"Would you like a drink?" he asks, his hand slipping to the small of my back. I cut the back low, so low it's almost to my waist, and his fingers divide time between my skin and the dress.

"Wine would be great."

"What, no bourbon?" he teases, and I again marvel at how different this Stokes is from even just a few days ago. Between our talk at the tasting and the talk yesterday at his house on the farm, some unknown restraints that were still present seem to have been unlocked, and now he's allowing me to see him in all his glory, just him. He's relaxed. No airs, no pretenses, no expectations. It's my favorite version of him yet, one that's impossible not to love.

"No bourbon." I smile at him and think how lucky I am to be here with him.

As we're standing in line, we both spot Suzy at the same time she spots us. This time, she doesn't get all dopey-eyed over Stokes, instead curling her lip up at him with what almost looks like hatred. Beside me, Stokes tenses. The two of them have a faceoff, and then in typical Suzy form, she flips her platinum hair over her shoulder, turns on her heel, and walks away. Tonight she has a date with her, and if I could, I'd give him my condolences.

"What was that all about?" I ask him.

"Nothing. Work stuff," he says, effectively letting me know he doesn't want to discuss it.

It's at this moment that his mood shifts a tiny bit. I'm sure he thinks I don't notice, but I do, and I don't understand it. Yes, he's still charming, and yes, he's still attentive, but there's something behind his eyes that makes me feel like I should be on edge.

Did something happen between the two of them? I can't imagine that it did, but there was no mistaking the way she looked at him and his reaction in return.

Collecting our drinks, we decide to make one lap around the room for social niceties. We run into Stokes's colleague Christopher, who has been invited to sit with the family tomorrow. We find Molly and Austin, who we spend a lot of time with, and then we keep walking, allowing people to say hello to us both.

"Hi, are you Rosie May?" asks a young woman in a black dress.

I turn toward her, and my jaw nearly comes unhinged.

"I am, and you are Katy Wilde," I reply, using the most contained tone I can. Katy Wilde is the current "it" actress. This year she won an Academy Award for a role she played as the heroine in a historical romance in Cleveland during the Great Depression. There's murder, mystery, family, life, and love. It was incredible, and from what I hear, there are rumors that her next release is going to be an even bigger hit.

She smiles, pleased that I have recognized her, but it's completely the other way around. Katy Wilde recognized me! What is this life?

Stokes squeezes my hand, letting me know he knows who she is as well.

"I'm so happy to run into you here." She reaches out and clasps my arm with excitement. Meanwhile, I'm trying to not pass out. "I saw the dress you made for Avery Layne, and it was sensational. I don't know if you have the time, but I would love it if you could design and make a dress for me as well. I have a premiere in the fall. Do you think you could do it in time?"

"I can do it. With the Derby over tomorrow, things will slow down, so your timing couldn't be more perfect."

She squeals. "Oh my, I'm so excited."

I laugh. "That makes two of us. Thank you for thinking of me."

"Are you kidding? You are all my friends and I are talking about. We've seen your website, and I'm certain others will be reaching out as well."

My website! I'm so sorry Molly isn't here to hear this.

"I'm shocked, but I look forward to it. Just call the shop. I'm the only one there, or sometimes it's Molly, my best friend, but I'd love to design something with you."

"I'm so excited." She beams. "Take a picture with me?"

"Of course."

She shoves her phone at Stokes, who happily plays his part. The two of us stand together and smile, and then he and I watch her walk away.

"Did that just happen?" I look up to find him now watching me.

"Big things are going to happen for you. I know it," he

says, just before he bends down to kiss the corner of my mouth.

I lean into him and breathe in his clean familiar scent.

"Dance with me?" Stokes asks.

I pull back and look up at him. "Do you even know how to dance?" I ask, teasing him because I've never actually seen him dance before.

One corner of his mouth tips up. "Only one way to find out." He holds out his hand, which I take, letting him lead me to the dance floor.

He sighs against me, and with my body melting into his, I lose myself in the moment of the beautiful orchestra music playing and the feeling of being in Stokes's arms.

"Are you having fun tonight?" he asks, his temple resting against mine as I'm wearing sky-high heels.

"I am. What about you?" I shift back just a tiny bit to look at him.

"How could I not? I'm here with you," he says, his gaze roaming my face.

I want to make a fun sarcastic comment back to him, but the sincerity in his tone makes me speechless. There's also the fact that he tilts my chin up and lays his lips against mine.

A kiss from Stokes Whitlock is good for a girl's soul.

I lean into him, his hand shifts to gently cradle my face, and I let him deepen the kiss by sweeping his tongue against mine. Who cares that we're in a room full of people? Certainly not me when I'm his sole focus—me, no one else. My body ignites, just like it always does, every single time. It's exhilarating. It's delicious. It's addicting. It's the same burst of awe that makes me wonder how I lived so long without this. With that, I slant my lips further over his, allowing him to ease us into a fiery kiss. He tastes like salt and wine, a mix of honey and spice. He tastes like snippets of our day together, one I look forward to having over and over with him.

"Are you ready to go?" He breaks the kiss and murmurs the words against my lips.

My tongue and my heart are so twisted, yearning for more of him, and all I can squeak out is a "Yes."

The entire ride back to his apartment, we sit next to each other in dead silence. He has one hand on my lap, and the fingers of the other are tangled with mine. His thumb keeps brushing back and forth across the inside of my wrists, and it feels so erotic I'm certain if he just blew on me, I'd see stars.

At the apartment, as the door closes behind us, I walk into the living room and find the gem-crusted pins I used to secure my hair behind my ears. Stokes comes up behind me, and he gently takes them and places them on the end table next to the door.

I should turn around, I know I should, but if I do, I'm afraid he'll see every emotion stamped across my face. Although I'm certain my sentiments would be returned, there's still something holding me back. I'm not sure what it is, but I can feel it deep down in my bones, and it says, *Soon, but not yet.*

His hands fall to my shoulders, and he pulls me back

into him. I easily lean against him as he wraps his body around mine and runs his large hands down my arms, across my chest, and over my stomach to my thighs and back. He's above me, around me, and as my head falls back against his shoulder, his lips make their way to my neck.

"I want to devour every inch of you." His words vibrate against my skin. "I don't know what it is, but I just can't get enough of you. I think of you. I dream of you. When we're together, I'm having separate conversations with you in my mind. It's never enough."

I turn around in his arms, and his mouth instantly finds mine. His palms flatten against my bare back, pulling me into him, and my arms drape over his shoulders, one hand slipping into his hair to keep his head firmly locked with mine. Stokes kisses like no man on this planet. He isn't timid, he isn't sweet, he is all in, and I'm here for every second of it. His lips and his tongue are so wet, so warm, and so delicious I feel ruined and saved by him at the same time.

His hands slide up and over my rib cage until they find my face. His palms wrap around my cheeks, his fingers tangle in my hair, and he tilts my head back so he can look me in the eyes. There's something there, something that's sitting on the tip of his tongue that he wants to say to me, but his eyes turn wary, and before I can see anything else, he closes them and lowers his lips to mine.

Strings pull on my heart as if it is a marionette, but as much as I want him to speak, I'm not saying it either, so I can't push him. I can just tell him how I feel nonverbally and hope he does the same.

Reaching for my side zipper, he slowly pulls it down until the fabric falls loose and the pretty rose gold dress wisps its way to the floor. Instead of wearing a regular bra, I'm wearing a stick-on one that lifts and shapes. He groans at the sight and the heat of my skin pressing into him. Slowly and methodically, he peels it off, and then his hands run over my back and down to my butt, where he cups both cheeks and pulls me hard up against him.

As we lean back, our eyes lock together. His lids are heavy, his lashes are ridiculously long, his lips are red and puffy, and his hair is perfectly disheveled. He's so handsome one of those strings pulls hard, and my heart cries out. How I'll survive this if it ends, I have no idea, but I'm laying faith and confidence in him and in us at his feet. I know it's only been a few weeks, even though our history together makes it feel like so much longer. I'm okay with him holding back a piece of himself, as long as he knows I'm ready when he is.

Moving my hands to his shoulders, I tuck my thumbs under the lapels of his jacket and slip the sleeves over his shoulders and down his long arms. The jacket joins my dress on the floor. Next, I undo his tie and then slide my arms around his waist to the cummerbund, which I unclip until it too lands on the floor.

How many times have I seen Stokes in a suit and subconsciously undressed him? It almost feels surreal that I'm standing here with him now, and I'm getting to do just this. Granted, a tuxedo is a little fancier, but the pressed shirt, tie, and slacks make it the same. What feels even more surreal is now knowing what he looks like underneath it.

Lowering my hand between us, I cup him through his pants, and he lets out a pained sound. I understand; I do. I want him as much as he wants me. His hand covers mine and he squeezes, so I squeeze him.

"I can't," he mutters, his forehead falling to mine, his breaths coming out slightly labored.

"So don't," I tell him, and this unlocks whatever restraint he was attempting to hold on to.

Grabbing me by the hand, he pulls me down the hall to his bedroom, where he strips off our remaining clothes in record time. We tumble onto his decadent and insanely soft bed, where I let him take the lead, and he ravishes me, every inch. Sucking a little here, licking a little there, he fills the space with kisses, and all the while, I'm staring at the ceiling, trying to memorize each move he makes and how his lips make me feel. I will be returning the favor, but only when it is my turn, as this is definitely his.

Working his way up my body, he covers me completely, and his weight presses me down. Settling between my thighs, he sinks all the way in with one single push. I love his weight, and I love being connected to him. Tonight he owns my body—wait, who am I kidding? He's owned it for a while now. Maybe he always has.

Time passes as we each enjoy the feel of the other. Fast. Slow. Hard. Soft. My heart is nearly bursting as he takes me to places I've never gone. I thought our time together before was incredible, but tonight we've moved to a whole new level, and I have to fight to keep the tears away.

I love him so much.

Hovering over me, he stops moving his hips and gently asks me to look at him. My damp eyes open, and when they find his, this intangible current instantly connects us, and I know, I know he sees what I see. Reflecting back and forth between the two of us is love. It has to be. I was right about nonverbals, mine for his, and it's the best feeling in the world.

"Hi," he whispers.

"Hey," I say back, my heart free-falling into my stomach with feelings so great it's as if the entire universe has disappeared and left only the two of us, nothing else.

"You all right?" he asks, with pieces of his hair falling over his forehead. His skin is slick and flushed, and his eyes are as clear as a northern lake under a fall sky.

"Better than," I tell him.

Better than I've ever been in my whole life.

LUVU TEA
LUVU TEA'S CROWNED ROYALTY OF THE BOURBON BALL

Good evening, friends and family. I think we can all agree that the Bourbon Ball tonight was just delicious. Bourbon is known to taste smooth with notes of oak, caramel, and vanilla. It's more sweet than dry, but it's that burn going down that keeps us coming back for more, and here at the Tea we just can't get enough.

After a full evening of wining and dining, dancing and laughing, we watched, waited, and then cast our votes. Not surprisingly at all, we are unanimous in our choice for this evening's royalty. While many were splendid and divine, these two continually left us craving more. More stolen moments, more lingering touches, and a beauty so ethereal the crowns were meant for their heads. Without further ado, this year's prince and princess of the Bourbon Ball are none other than our bachelor of the season, Stokes Whitlock, and his date, Rosie May.

Felicitations, we bow to you.
Thank you for a wonderful night. We're off to get some shut-eye as we'll be back bright and early tomorrow, reporting live from Churchill Downs.

28

oday is the day.

Today is the day of the greatest two minutes in sports.

Today is the Kentucky Derby.

It is the longest continuously held sporting event in America and is recognized by all as one of the most prestigious horse races in the world. It's a top-rank, Grade I stakes race for three-year-old thoroughbred horses. The track is made of dirt and is ten furlongs, or one and a quarter miles. Twenty qualifying horses will line up, wait for the bell, and then be off. The purse is almost two million dollars.

Just thinking about it fills me with indescribable joy and glee. The gates will open at nine, and over one hundred and fifty thousand spectators will flood into Churchill Downs. They'll place their bets, sip mint juleps, listen for the *Riders up* call and sing "My Old Kentucky Home".

Spectators will socialize, they'll take photos with their family and friends, and I will be people-watching with the best of them. Will there be famous people? Yes. Do I care? No. I am one hundred percent here for the hats and fascinators.

Early this morning, Stokes left with Grayson and a few other Whitlock Farm staff members to take Ace to the track. The rule is that any horse running at Churchill Downs must be on the grounds a minimum of five and a half hours before race time. Although he isn't racing until later, for peace of mind, they wanted to make sure he was here and settled, especially with the farm having other horses racing and the large crowds rolling in.

While I have attended the Derby before, this is the first time I will be attending as a member of the Whitlock Farm team, and also with a date. Then again, I can't ever remember Stokes bringing a date either. I may have been gone over the last couple of years, but that didn't stop me from watching it on television and taking in the details surrounding my people.

It's now midafternoon, we're both dressed to impress, and I'm so excited to be here with him. Parking the car in the owners' lot, he turns to me as he cuts the engine off.

"Wait for me," he says as his hand reaches over and squeezes my leg.

I nod and watch as he gets out of the car, walks around the front, and opens my door. I can't decide if he's different with me today or if he's just nervous about the day, but he seems a little closed off and a lot lost in his head.

"You look beautiful," he tells me as he takes my hand. Moss green and whiskey roam my face just before he bends and kisses the corner of my mouth. I spent the last two days working on a hat for me. I needed it to be something spectacular—after all, this is my time to shine—but I also wanted it to blend with the colors of the farm. I'm wearing an ivory dress with a light green hat that has chic and stylish adornments. It comes from the same hue as the farm colors but is more subtle.

"So do you," I say quietly back. He is wearing the bowtie I gave him; it's Whitlock green and matches Birdie's hat. He has on a white shirt and a medium blue three-piece suit. It's not dark or pale but right in the middle, and it's cut to fit him perfectly. My gaze drops over the length of him, and I can't help but think back to last night and earlier this week when I was lying in his arms without the suit. That felt pretty perfect too.

As we make our way through the parking lot, I notice the weather has turned a little throughout the day. It was super bright this morning. Now it's overcast and cooler, but I think that makes for a more ideal day—no sweating and no glaring sun.

"I'm glad you're here with me today. Thank you for coming," he says, glancing down at me as we pass by a slew of cameras and security at a private entrance he knows about. His hand is on my lower back, but then it moves to mine and he laces our fingers together.

"Of course. Didn't we agree we are in this together? Besides, like I would miss the opportunity to see all my hats in their glory," I tease, and he smiles fondly at me, one of my smiles. So far, this is the best day ever, and I can't help but whisper, "This is so exciting."

He squeezes my hand; he understands.

It takes us no time at all to get to the Winner's Circle suites. They are usually reserved for the owners of the horses running. There are lounge seats, it's open-aired but still covered, and they have direct access to the track to get to the Winner's Circle should the horse win. Now that we're here, it seems anyone and everyone wants to speak with Stokes. I take a step back so I can allow him to shine. It's at this moment I decide now is as good a time as any to slip away and go take it all in.

Everywhere it is just a sea of color, flowers, and feathers. My hat-loving heart is so full and giddy I don't even know where to look first. I imagine this is like taking a chef to a grocery store that only carries the most exquisite food, or an art lover going to the Louvre for the first time. It's overwhelming but in the best possible way, and I give myself about thirty minutes to bask in finding some of my pieces while photographing others for inspiration. I'm staying off social media today, but tomorrow I'll dive into all the tags and comment on every single one.

As I make my way back to the suite, I see more people have arrived. I smile and wave; there isn't much that could ruin this for me today. I spot Stokes at the front of the suite, past the couches and next to the stadium seating. I weave my way through the people to get to him.

"I can't believe she agreed to this," Christopher says as I approach Stokes from behind. Neither of them sees me, fully engrossed in their conversation, and I freeze.

She? Are they talking about me?

"Me either. Especially after all these years." He runs his hand over the back of his neck then pulls on his collar. "It really wasn't that difficult to convince her either. We sat down over dinner, talked it out, and now here we are."

My heart starts to pound behind my rib cage. Who is he talking about? *Wasn't that difficult to convince.* Aside from me, the only other two women in his life that he's known for years are Birdie and Molly. Molly would have said something to me, I'm certain of it, especially since we were working together so closely all these weeks, and that leaves Birdie.

"All this time, and I had no idea. I work with you every day." He chuckles. "You could have told me. I mean you certainly committed. You played your part, you showed up to events and plastered a smile on your face—I'm impressed."

You played your part, you showed up to events.

We were playing parts, but I thought it stopped being fake a while ago. Did it not? I mean things certainly became real for me.

Dropping my head, I pull my hat down to cover my face. I can feel my muscles and bones shrinking, curling in around my heart to protect me. Did he play me for a fool?

Did he not see that I was opening up to him and falling for him? I gave him the vulnerable pieces of me. I did something I never thought I'd ever do in my entire life . . . I trusted him.

"Well don't be. I didn't like it, and I do feel kind of terrible about using her the way I am, but it had to be done."

Using her.

Oh my God.

It has to be me.

There's no one else.

I've been with him almost every day for weeks. He hasn't had time to go to other events or entertain someone else.

Seconds tick by as they are having a normal conversation, but to me everything has slowed down. Every part of me is shutting down, going numb. Shocked isn't even the right word for how I feel. It isn't strong enough. I can't breathe, and my eyes are blurring.

"So after today it's over? You'll just walk away?" Christopher asks, all nonchalant as if my life isn't suddenly imploding.

"Yeah, not today, but definitely tomorrow. I can't pretend any longer, and I need this whole charade to be over and done with, behind me."

I need this whole charade to be over and done.

I thought I knew what it felt like to have your heart broken. I wasn't even close. I'm so confused. What is happening right now? Should I be angry at him or at myself? Technically, he hasn't said anything or truly given me any reason to believe he and I were going to be something after today. I built this all up in my head. I changed the rules of the game—one I am apparently playing by myself.

Oh God.

I need a teleportation machine, an invisible cloak—something to get me out of here. I can't stay here.

"Wow, I don't know what to say."

"Not much to say. I'm just done."

Done.

I will never recover from this. In less than one minute, my whole life has changed. I no longer feel like it's us against the world. I no longer feel like I'm a part of the farm, and I've lost my home. I no longer feel proud of myself—I feel like the stupidest woman on the planet. Why did I think, after twelve years, a leopard was going to change its spots? The prince and the commoner . . . that's not real life. Splintering pain is piercing me from every angle.

"And you don't think Rosie suspects a thing?" Christopher asks again.

My head snaps up. I have to be one hundred percent sure I hear what he's about to say. I need him to say it, to kill it all, to kill me.

"No." He lets out a sigh. "But I've figured out how I want to tell her."

Train horns could be blaring, the building could be on fire, the world could be ending, infested with zombies, and

I wouldn't know it. At this moment, I'm not sure I care. I'm so hurt all I can do is shut it all off while I walk away with my head held high.

Turning around, I move to quietly slip away, but a woman I don't recognize bumps into me. She apologizes, and with the movement, Christopher spots me over Stokes's shoulder and calls my name.

I freeze.

I can't breathe and feel like hyperventilating.

"Hey," Stokes says to me. I can't look at him, can't see his handsome face, so I fumble in my clutch as he approaches cautiously. Yeah, he should be wary—at this moment I feel like a Tasmanian devil and am two seconds from whirling into a chaotic mess that takes out everyone around me, most especially him. "Did you hear what we were talking about?" he asks.

"No. Should I have?" I ask point-blank, pulling out some lip gloss I can smear over my lips. Distraction, that's what this is.

He reaches for my arm and gently pulls. He wants me to look at him, and when I do, I see his eyes narrow at my tone. Whatever—he doesn't get to look at me like that. Should I confront him? Maybe, but even I know this isn't the time.

"You were gone for a while . . . you're leaving again?" he asks, and all these years of knowing him instantly come crashing down. He might have tricked me over the last couple of weeks, luring me into donning rose-colored glasses, but he isn't deceiving me right now. I see him for what he is: a snake. Every bit of his posture, the wrinkles around his eyes, the color on his cheeks—it all screams guilty.

He is guilty.

If I had a shovel, it's quite possible I'd cut off his head.

"I walked around to look at the hats since you were busy. Now I've decided I want a drink. I'll be right back." I don't ask him if he would like one, instead pulling free to just turn and walk out of the suite.

Quickly, I make it to the restroom, find a stall, and close myself behind the door. I might have run just like I did at the bourbon tasting, but there was no way I could stand there in front of him for one moment longer. Closing my eyes, I fold over, and my beautiful hat drops to the floor.

What am I doing here? I silently ask myself. Grabbing two pieces of toilet paper, I press them to my eyes. There's no way to stop these tears, but I refuse to let them mess up my face.

Five minutes—that's all I'm going to give myself here. After that, I'm going to pull up my big girl panties and do what I always do when it comes to him. For years, I've found a way to push back at whatever he's thrown my way, and once I walk out these doors, I'll do the same. He may think he's pulled one over on me, but he's got another thing coming.

By the time I make it back, more people have come to the suite. We're getting closer to the time Ace runs, and it can't get here fast enough. His mother has arrived, along with Grayson, my mother, Molly, Austin, and other people I recognize but don't know, and everyone is so happy.

Everyone but me.

I feel like I am dying on the inside.

I make my way to Molly and use her to run interference. She chose a royal blue fascinator today and looks so lovely; it hurts to see her enjoyment in all of this. Then again, this is her family. None of this is mine. We talk about who we've seen and hats we've loved, and several times she asks me if I'm okay. Of course I nod, but anxiety has crept onto her features. Although I'm doing my best to ignore Stokes, he's stayed close by, and I've caught him eyeing me suspiciously. I let him in and he knows how to read me, which has me feeling completely exposed.

Glancing at my phone, I see it's five thirty. Any minute now, Stokes, his mother, and Grayson will head over so they can make the walk in with Ace from the barn to the paddock. It's a chance for the owners to show off their contender for the year, and it's a really big moment. They should be so proud.

I'm proud for them.

And now I feel like a traitor to myself.

I can't be here.

I grab Stokes's arm to get his attention, and when he faces me, his expression drops.

"Are you going to tell me what's wrong?" he asks quietly.

I know I should and eventually I'll need to, but I just can't right now. I am not going to cry in front of him, not going to embarrass myself or him. I've worked too hard this season for today to be recorded in the history books as the day I had an epic meltdown at the Derby.

"I think I ate something bad, or I'm coming down with a stomach virus. I'm so sorry, but I have to go."

He looks confused as his gaze bounces back and forth between my eyes. He's trying to figure out what is wrong and what to do. Unfortunately, he's done enough.

Enough of this.

"I'll be fine. We'll touch base later." I take a step away. I'm fighting tears, but again, he doesn't deserve to see them. None of these people do. With the number of cell phones up and taking pictures of every little detail, I'm certain someone would capture my humiliation and heartbreak and share it with the world, a world whose business none of this is.

"Rosie . . ." His brows pull down, concerned, and at the same time his mother calls him to go.

The noise is buzzing around us, my head is pounding, and he lets out a defeated sigh. When he leans down to kiss me, I jerk my head to the side so his lips land on my cheek. His mother, my mother, and Molly are all watching, but none of them says anything. I'm certain they too can read the room and know I'm about to lose it.

"Text me and let me know how you are," he says. "I'll check in as soon as I can."

"Great." I give him the fakest smile. "Good luck to Ace." I wave to those around us, and then I'm gone.

I was wrong about this weather—it isn't nice at all. It's

overcast, damp, breezy, and bordering on cold. It's crazy how mental health can change people's perceptions. We see what we want to see, and whereas this afternoon I thought this weather was near perfect, now it just feels miserable.

29

*A*ce lost.

Well, he came in second. It was a photo-finish win, the other horse literally beating him by a nose. I didn't make it home to watch it live, but I had set it to record. Stupid me just wanted to get to see the family clip. Instead, I watched the race on repeat. Every single time, my heart ran with him until he crossed the finish line, and even though I knew it wasn't him, my adrenaline spiked, wishing for the outcome to be different.

Just like with my life.

He still won six hundred thousand, which isn't too shabby for two minutes' worth of work, and if he does well in the next two races of the Triple Crown—and I can't imagine he won't—he'll still get incredible stud fees.

I'm happy for Birdie and for Grayson.

After the race, Stokes called me several times, but I never answered. There are always a ton of parties to attend, and I knew he needed to make the rounds. He texted a lot, and then late last night he tried to stop by, but I didn't answer the buzzer from downstairs.

Proactively, I texted Molly right after I got home to let her know I was fine, just not feeling well, and I was shutting off for the night and going to bed. That way, if Stokes reached out to her, she'd already have my alibi.

He must have spoken to her at some point, because his messages were never urgent, just said he was there if I needed him.

Yeah right.

Or they weren't urgent because the truth is he just doesn't care.

I am such an idiot. I knew better . . . I really did.

Walking through my shop, I find myself sitting at one of the tables in the center. Even though I turned the music on to break up the silence, it's still very quiet. There's a white noise in my ears that feels hollow, and it echoes deep throughout my body and into my soul. This is supposed to be my happy place, but I don't think there's anywhere in this world that could accomplish that right now.

I thought today would feel different. I thought I'd feel relief that my biggest day of the year is behind me, excitement about the hordes of social media comments the shop has been getting and in general the overall success of the season, but I don't. All I feel is sad.

Incredibly sad.

If melancholy were a color, for me it wouldn't be just black—that's too simple. It has to be a dark shade of gray with a tint of purple. It's not because I'm feeling blue, even though I am; it's just that purple feels more severe, more tragic, more me.

A knock on the shop door startles me, but I don't move to answer it. I'm closed today, the curtains are pulled, and I am not in the mood for people.

On the table, my phone buzzes.

Stokes: I'm outside the shop. Let me in.

Of course he knows I'm here. Then again, where else would I be? Anger about the last eighteen hours starts to heat under my skin.

I run my hand over my face and groan at the conversation that's about to come, one I'm not ready for. I don't want excuses. I don't want to hear his reasoning. In fact, I don't want to hear anything from him at all.

The damage, my damage, is done.

Do we really need to do this? I just want to fade into the background and pretend I didn't fall madly in love with him. What was I actually loving? If he was faking it, who knows.

Which is why no one needs to know about this. I'll let this disgrace remain private and let him off the hook the only way I know how: chin held high and as soon as I can. I'll give him his out, and he won't even have to break a sweat. There's zero need for him to fake it anymore.

If he wants fake, he's going to get it—Oscar-worthy fakeness.

Walking to the door, I look down and see I'm wearing the worst outfit possible: an old college hoodie and black leggings with a hole in them. I have not a stitch of makeup on, and my hair is in a knot on top of my head. I shouldn't care how I look, but unfortunately I do. I'd love to have an "eat your heart out" moment here, a "this is what you'll be missing," but then again, he's never cared. I'm just his little sister's annoying best friend.

Taking a deep breath, I unlock it, crack it, and then, with my back to him, move to the table. That heat rises to near boiling, and I have to remind myself to stay calm as he pushes the door open and follows me inside. He locks it behind him, just for precaution's sake. I take a seat and look at him.

I see red.

Betrayal.

He takes a quick look around the store, and I realize I never turned the lights on. He's also getting his first look at how drained of inventory I am. He doesn't comment. Instead, he turns those laser beams my way and holds steady.

"You okay?" he asks, taking a few steps closer to me. He looks tired and unsure. His hair is a mess, he hasn't shaved, and his clothes are wrinkled.

"Of course I am. Nothing a good solid night's sleep can't cure." I smile. It's one hundred percent fake.

His eyes narrow, and his nostrils flare. From the way he originally approached, it's easy to see he was feeling uncertain about what he was walking into, but with my tone right there, he knows.

Cutting to the chase, he asks, "Why did you leave?"

"What do you mean?" I play dumb and bat my eyelashes at him.

The two little lines strike. "Last night. The Derby. I know you well enough to know you weren't sick. You lied to me, and you left knowing I couldn't go with you."

"Yeah, whatever." I shrug one shoulder. "I mean does it even matter?" I'm just poking the bear to see how he might respond.

He opens his mouth to say something but then shuts it. His brows pull down in bewilderment.

I can't help the spike of confusion I feel too as we stare at each other.

"Explain," he mutters through gritted teeth.

Explain! He is not going to talk to me like this. He doesn't get to anymore. I wouldn't have ever thought it was okay for him to boss me around in that haughty tone, but in my deluded state of wanting to please him, I would have answered.

I roll my eyes before answering. "Because . . . well, this is over, and I just didn't see the point of being there any longer."

"Over." He parrots the word as if it is somehow foreign to him and he doesn't understand.

"Yes."

He runs his hand through his hair. "Is that what you

want?" he asks, as if he's having trouble understanding this conversation.

"Me?" I point to my chest. "It's literally what you have been saying to me all along, even less than forty-eight hours ago. And I quote, 'This is almost over.' 'Let's get this over with.' I'm under no illusion that this arrangement between us was ever going to be anything more. It was always ending with the Derby. That was the deal."

"That's not what I meant when I said those things. You know this." He's stiffening, feeling the need to be defensive, and this is something I was hoping to skip. He doesn't need to get all worked up; this is what he wants.

"Do I? Hate to break it to you, but that's exactly what it sounded like. Besides, this whole thing between us was set up with your terms and with the expectation of a deadline. We've reached it. Yay us!" I wave my hands sarcastically like jazz hands.

"Right," he says. As his lips turn down into a frown, he tucks his hands into his pockets and looks at the ground.

And look at that, he isn't pacing. He doesn't feel the need to argue with me. He just strangely looks like a beautiful fallen angel. But why? Ugh. It pains me to look at him.

I've always tried to think and be three steps ahead of Stokes. He's a master when it comes to this unhealthy thing between us, but this time I outsmarted him and was five steps ahead.

After all, one of the things I know about Stokes is when he says something, he means it. He said this thing between us would only last through the Derby, and I should have listened. I would have saved myself a lot of unnecessary pain, and my heart wouldn't feel as if I had laid it on the track at Churchill Downs. Forget getting run over—I let it get trampled.

"This is what you want?" he asks quietly. His voice makes me ache.

The knot that has been sitting in my chest moves to my throat. I try to swallow it down, but it keeps rising, and with it, my eyes start burning. I should answer him, but I can't. I just stare and weep on the inside. I really do love him.

"Well . . . thanks for agreeing to help me out. I appreciate it," he says, finally lifting his head. His color has drained, and his eyes look red, but that can't be. He's probably just tired from the late night.

"Of course. We did have fun, didn't we?" I mean to keep things lighthearted, but I know he hears the tinge of insecurity between my words.

"We did." He looks around the shop. I'm not sure what he's looking for, but with each second, my steely resolve is crumbling. Eventually his eyes land on the back counter, and his frown deepens. It's the counter that started what was the best night of my life.

Don't look at the counter, Stokes. I can't take it. Don't make me remember more than I already do.

It hurts. It hurts to know I'm not enough for him. It hurts to know all I'm ever going to get are just these few moments with him. It all just hurts.

"I'm going to go." He pulls his hand from his pocket

and points a thumb over his shoulder toward the door. "At least I know," he says, his eyes locking with mine, "you're fine."

"Yep. I'm great. Thanks for stopping by."

He stares at me for a few more moments, lets out a rush of air, and turns around on his heel. Without saying another word, he's out the door and gone. As it closes and the ringing of the bell dies down, my spirit howls.

I don't know how to recover from this.

How do I look at him after knowing all that I know?

I really did think there was something there.

Collapsing back in my seat, I lay my head on the table and cry. I can't stop the tears that fill my eyes and silently run down the side of my face. I've always said I know Stokes better than anyone else. I've gotten to see the good and the evil, but now I can add his loving side to the list as well. He may not have meant to have shown me this side, but he did, and after this, I'll be forced to stand in the background and watch as he one day gives all of himself to someone else.

Someone who's not me.

30

I've decided there are only two things for me to do today, sleep or clean, and since yesterday after Stokes left I went straight up to my apartment, climbed under my blankets, and shut out the world, today I must clean.

I'm down in my shop. All the inventory has been moved, and I am scrubbing floor to ceiling: the walls, the shelves, the windows, the baseboards, and the floors. You'd think since I've only been open for a few months, it would still be pretty clean, but nope. With the winter and spring weather and the traffic in and out of the shop, it's dirtier than I expected.

I'm on my hands and knees when the door opens and Birdie pops in looking as fresh as a daisy in white linen pants, a deep green sweater, and gold sandals. I went ahead and left it open; after all, I'm in here, so may as well not miss any potential sales.

"Hello, darling," she calls out, and I hop up from the floor.

"Hi." I smile at her and wipe my hands on my already dirty shorts. "I didn't know you were coming by today." I walk toward her and let her wrap me in her arms.

"I had some business in town and thought I'd stop in and say hello."

Her arms feel so good. She gives me the most needed hug I think I've ever needed in my life then pulls back, keeping hold of my arms.

"I see," she says as she studies my face and frowns. "This explains a lot." Her words are cryptic.

I understand what she's looking at—I look dreadful. There are bags under my eyes, my hair is flat and gross even though I've wrapped a scarf around it to keep it off my face, and well, I am a hot mess.

Stokes used to call me that frequently. I guess he was right.

Letting go of me, she begins to walk around and observe. She sees the small selection of remaining inventory and smiles. "I can't get over how successful you've been here. Don't get me wrong, I've known your talent since you were a young girl, but what you've done here . . . I'm just so proud of you."

Tears well in my eyes. Yes, I have a mother, but Birdie has been such a constant and an inspiration in my life. She is a second mother, and her praise means something to me.

"Thank you. And I can't say thanks enough for the tip

on this space. It's worked out so well, and I love it here." I glance up at the chandeliers and smile. They were my big splurge, and they were so worth it.

"I really can't take the credit for that. Stokes was the one who told me I should pass along the information to you." She eyes me knowingly.

My eyes widen. "What? Stokes?"

I'm shocked. I specifically remember having a conversation with my mother right after I moved back about real estate, and Birdie randomly chimed in. She said she heard through the grapevine this spot was opening, and she thought the neighborhood would be perfect for me. I had no idea any of it was his doing.

She gives me a look that says, *Y'all were fooling no one.* "He knew you would have rejected it immediately on principle if he suggested it, so he asked that I tell you. I guess he had been watching the inventory around him closely to see when something was opening up."

"Oh, for sure I would have," I tell her. There's no point in trying to convince her otherwise. She knows me—and apparently Stokes does too.

My stomach dips as I think about this. He went out of his way to look at real estate for me, and near him. I swear he is the most confusing man on the planet.

Moving to one of the tables, she pulls out a chair and sits down. I follow as I know she isn't here for just a social call.

"Would you like me to make some tea?" I ask her.

She shakes her head then takes a long look at me; it's

half curious and half loving. Finally, she lets out a long exhale and says, "My son . . . he had to grow up way too fast."

Okaaay. I have no idea where she is going with this, but I don't want to talk about Stokes with her, at all. I'm not ready. I sit down across from her and do my best to make a blank face and not one that scrunches up in devastation at just his name.

"When you and your mother moved to the farm, it was the first time in months my family smiled. Molly was over the moon, and Stokes . . . well he came in one day and, at fifteen years old, told me you were the most beautiful girl he had ever seen and one day he was going to marry you." She pauses to see how I'm going to react.

My breath catches, and I drop my gaze to the table. I can't look at her. Maybe she isn't aware that he doesn't want to be with me. It's not like we've had an opportunity to really tell people yet. Then again, she knew all of this was for show, just to get through the season.

But knowing what I know now about that day so many years ago with the horses and how things might have been different, it's like pushing on a bruise that has no intention of healing. He thought so much of me after barely meeting me that he thought he'd marry me. If my heart were able to break all over again, it would. Instead, it withers up even more as it prepares for its imminent death.

"I just recently learned that Stokes thought I was snubbing him on one of those early days. He wanted to take me for a ride, and I told him no, said I didn't want to ride with him. He didn't understand that it was not about him, but about the horses. He didn't know about my father."

She leans back in her chair. "What do you mean he didn't know about your father?"

"He didn't know what happened. He thought it was just a heart attack."

Birdie reaches up and rubs her forehead while she thinks. "Rosie, I don't remember what I did or didn't tell them back then . . ." She drops her hand. "But I assure you, nothing was intentional."

"Oh, I don't think it was. It's just been a twelve-year misunderstanding." Twelve years of torture when I could have had twelve years with the love of my life. I sniff to attempt to ward off the tears threatening to come out and start fidgeting with the hem of my shirt.

"Well, this is an enlightening piece of information," she says, almost a little cheerful, as if this answers a question I didn't know she had.

"I don't know. I'm not sure how. I thought things were changing between us, but I was wrong. Ever since that dinner in New York, he's been different. Or maybe it's me who's been hoping for something different."

"He took you to dinner when he was in New York?" she asks, tilting her head as she watches me.

My eyes find hers. They are also hazel and feel like a punch to the stomach. "Yes. He said he had to, or you would be disappointed in him."

A smile pushes the edge of her lips as she crosses one leg over the other. "Darling, I had no idea about him taking you to dinner. That was never discussed between us —that's something he did all on his own."

What?

This whole conversation is throwing me for a loop.

In five minutes, I've learned of two instances involving him where I had no idea of the truth. This makes me think of other interactions with him, and there are many. Despite what Stokes has said to me over the years, I'm coming to realize his actions always spoke differently. But why? Why did he do these things? The lease availability for my shop, the dinner in New York, him bringing Molly to my college graduation in Savannah, helping me move in, the champagne for my grand opening, wanting to support me in promoting the store . . .

"Wait." I sit up straighter. "Did he somehow bring Avery Layne to me, too?"

Birdie gives me a look that shows she has the ability to look sheepish and proud at the same time. "At our level, it's a small world. You know this. He is friends with Will Ashton and was at a Super Bowl party with him in Nashville back in February. I'm not sure how the topic came up, but from what I hear, he pitched you hard. He always has."

What do I say to that? I knew he went to Nashville to visit friends, but I had no idea it was friends like that.

Dread sinks into my bones. I'm going to have to thank him. I'm going to have to put aside my wounded pride and weeping heart and say thank you. Regardless of how I'm feeling about us, he at least deserves that for everything he's done for me.

"Rosie, I want to tell you something, and I'm hoping you won't be upset with me." She shifts her weight in her seat, almost like she's nervous, but then it's gone. The confident woman I know stares me down.

There's nothing she could tell me that would upset me more than I already am. I start shaking my head, but she just holds up her hand to stop me and continues.

"You know I love my son, but he was stuck. He's been stuck for a while, and as you and I both know, life can be unfairly short. For years, I've watched him be what he thinks he needs to be. He put me first, put the farm first, and while I know he's happy with his choices, very few of them have been for him. He's selfless in so many ways, and this is where you come in. It's always been you. Since you moved back last year, he has been someone else. It's like he's been more alive. He came out from behind his expectations . . . but again, he was still stuck.

"Stokes is about to turn twenty-eight—we're going to blink and he'll be in his thirties. There's so much more to life than just work and the farm, and he is in his prime for the best parts of it. He needed a shove out of his comfort zone. I know how much he hates the spotlight, and the Tea was the perfect opportunity."

"The Tea?" I'm shocked. Is she saying what I think she is?

"I reached out to LuVu Tea and pitched Stokes as their bachelor of the season. It didn't take much convincing—after all, he is Stokes Whitlock—but I gave them a donation, and they ran with it."

"You set him up?" My head tilts, and I scoot to the edge of my seat. Suddenly, I'm angry for him, and she can upset me more than I thought. He was so bothered by all the constant harassment and the random people; this was not a very nice thing she did to him.

"Yes, and I'm not sorry for it. I knew it would send him into a tailspin, and although I wasn't certain how he would respond, I was hoping it would push him right in your direction. You've never noticed how he looks at you. It doesn't take a genius to see that he thinks the sun rises and sets with you. He's completely in love with you, and since that night at the party, he hasn't just been a different person. He's been determined, and I've enjoyed every second of watching him become this elevated version of himself."

"Since the party?" The party where he kissed me senseless and changed the trajectory of my life.

"Oh, yes. It's like a light switched on in him and he finally started making the changes that put him first. He started planning for himself, doing for himself, thinking about what makes him happy."

She keeps going in her adoration of this new and changed Stokes, and maybe I've seen a little of what she is saying, but none of this changes the outcome for us.

And then my ears pick up her saying, "I am so proud of him for quitting the law firm."

"He quit?" I almost shout. My eyes have widened, and where I felt speared in the chest before, now I feel like a cannon has rammed through me.

"He didn't tell you?" She looks completely confused and surprised.

"No. Why wouldn't he tell me that? I saw him almost every day." My hands find their way under the table, and I start squeezing my fingers.

I thought we were friends, or had at least become friendly. This is such a huge piece of news, and he didn't share it with me.

"I don't know why. I just assumed you would have been the first person he told. Weeks ago, he came over for dinner and laid out his plan. I was completely on board with it—after all, it was his choice to go work for that firm in the first place. I've always wanted him at the farm to learn the ropes and take over."

My ears start ringing.

Came over for dinner and laid out his plan.

Wasn't that difficult to convince.

"When is he taking over?" My voice is hoarse.

"He starts this afternoon. He had a few loose ends to wrap up this morning at the firm, but he's meeting with me later today."

"I had no idea." I'm realizing I might have had it all wrong. Not might—I'm certain of it. He was talking to Christopher from the firm, we went to firm events where he could have been faking it, and when they talked about me, he said he had a plan.

What is this plan?

My chest deflates.

Why didn't I just ask him?

"But enough about Stokes." She waves her hand in the air to wipe that conversation away. "The real reason I stopped by is I wanted to say thank you for what you did for Ace. Dr. Miller was found guilty."

The word guilty clears the Stokes-induced fog in my head.

"He was?" I'm shocked but not at the same time.

She nods and shifts to recross her legs. "Turns out he is a very bitter man. Detectives reviewed the film from when he was on the property as well as the day we found the random girl outside Ace's barn. Turns out that is his granddaughter. They brought her in for questioning, and the poor girl sang like a canary. Then the detective reached out to the farms on the list we provided and began additional investigations.

"Here's what happened. The first horse you mentioned, from Sterling Bells Farm, came down with laminitis. Two days earlier, one of Dr. Miller's staff members was out at their farm doing a routine visit. Once the horse became lame, Mr. Rupp went into a tailspin and went over the barn from one end to the other, and they discovered black walnut shavings in two of the stalls. Was it in more, maybe, but by the time they found it, not much remained because the stalls had been cleaned. However, not that much is needed. Just a small percentage of the shavings is enough and is very toxic bedding to horses. Within twenty-four to forty-eight hours, they can show signs of toxicity, and laminitis is a side effect. Of course they were told the veterinarian couldn't determine the cause, when actually he knew and lied."

"That is just awful." I lean back in my seat to try to loosen some of the tension that's built up in my shoulders. I don't understand people who don't have a conscience when it comes to animals and cruelty. He hurt those poor horses.

"It truly is." She frowns. "The barn fire at Shaded Oaks was determined to be arson. Fire and arson investigators declared this pretty early on, but the evidence was kept quiet and the truth wasn't discussed. You know how these things are—reputation is everything, and they didn't want it getting around that it was potentially them looking for an insurance payout. Who started the fire, no one knows, but apparently Dr. Miller isn't being very subtle in his lies at the station. His tics and tells are giving him away, even though his words aren't.

"For the horse with laminitis from Bluegrass Fields Farm, they were told the same thing—that the cause was unknown. Turns out the horse was given large amounts of sugar through its water trough. They didn't know this, and it wasn't until after the horse was moved to another barn and the water trough began to dry that they saw the sugar deposits left behind. Sugar and horses is bad. They can quickly become insulin resistant, which, as you know, can lead to laminitis. Guess who was out at the farm that same week?"

"Dr. Miller." I shake my head in disgust, and Birdie's cheeks flush with anger. She loves horses, loves them like no one I've ever known. All of this must have been so hard for her considering he's worked on her farm for so long.

"Yes, ma'am. Horses love sugar, so as soon as he tasted that water, you know he took in way more than he should have. Who knows how long he had been drinking that sweet water."

"What about the stolen horse?"

"He was found."

My jaw drops, and she smiles at me. She's loving telling me this story.

"Where?"

"At Red Star Ranch. It seems Dr. Miller felt slighted all these years. Since he was taking care of the horses who were earning everyone else so much money, he felt he should have been awarded a portion of each purse as well. After so much time, he thought he would be sneaky and opened a shell corporation, DRM Enterprises, and bought Red Star Ranch a few years ago. While it has been growing and last year had its first big payout with the horse who won the Belmont Stakes, it seems the management crew began to suspect there were shady dealings occurring, most recently a new addition to the farm who looked like the stolen horse, even though he had undergone surgery on his neck for a supposed tumor, according to the ranch's veterinarian."

I inhale sharply. "He cut out the tracking chip."

She nods. "Yes. It's not easy to find either. It's an invasive surgery, but hey, stud him with a ranked filly and guess what you have in three years . . . a Derby contender. The farm crew started talking, and whispers spread from the Blantons' farm to Shaded Oaks. When the detective approached Shaded Oaks, it was the staff who alerted him to the possible dupe."

"Unbelievable." I shake my head in complete bafflement.

"The detective said there has been an increase over the last couple of years in suspicious activities in the Louisville area, but none of them could be linked. Unfortunately for Dr. Miller, this year he became even more greedy and left a trail."

"So what was in the syringe for Ace?" I ask, now leaning forward with my arms on the table. She matches my posture and leans on the table, too.

"Remember he claimed he was giving him vitamins to help with the inflammation? Turns out he was attempting to inject him with betamethasone. While it is not illegal to use on horses and it is an anti-inflammatory, it is illegal to be found in the bloodstream on race day. It is considered a doping drug and would have disqualified him."

"Wow." I shake my head again. This is nuts. "So he was wanting his horses to place higher, or better yet win, so he'd have a bigger payday."

"That's right," she says, annoyance showing through as she presses her lips together.

"I have no words. This is all . . . too preposterous to even make up."

"Thanks to you, the mystery is solved." She leans forward more and places her hand on my arm.

Heat rushes into my cheeks at her appraisal. "Well, I don't know about that. They eventually would have figured it out."

"Not before Ace would have found himself disqualified and a black mark would have been put across Grayson's name. We are extremely grateful." She pats me and then squeezes once before sitting back in her chair.

"I love you and the farm. I just didn't want anything to happen to him," I tell her honestly. Regardless of how things are at the moment with Stokes and me, my love for them hasn't changed.

With an appreciative and affectionate smile, she says, "And it didn't."

ot long after Birdie leaves, I end up locking up the shop and heading upstairs to shower. If they have work to do this afternoon at the farm, I may as well head that way to find him. I do need to thank him for all the things he's done for me, but I think this time, instead of trying to sage the room and ward off anything unwanted, I need to ask the hard questions and get some answers.

Especially because my gut is telling me I'm in the wrong.

I was so convinced he and Christopher had been talking about me that I handled this all wrong. I've hurt myself and him in the process. A levelheaded person would have taken a deep breath and asked for clarification or answered yes when he asked if I had heard him, but apparently I'm not levelheaded—I am an idiot.

Poor Stokes. He's been so good to me, and I was awful.

This is going to take more than just an apology. I'm going to have to come up with a grand gesture.

Just that thought has me gasping.

All these months, the big and the little things he's done, all of it has been his big grand gesture, his Hallmark moment to try to make up for all those years. I now know the bachelor of the season was because of Birdie, but she's right—he didn't have to handle it the way he did. He didn't have to use his unfortunate circumstance as an opportunity to help me promote my name, to push me into the spotlight. But he did, and he did it for me. He could have slunk off into the background until the season was over, but he didn't. He went out of his way for us to be known.

In addition to that, the coffees, the food, driving me to the family dinner, working in the shop—I mean he's had a lot going on in his life too, but he went out of his way for weeks to make sure I felt like I was number one, like I was important and taken care of. All of this has been his way of trying to make amends and be the man I needed him to be —the man he is.

I'm not even sure the word idiot covers it. He is the best thing to ever happen to me.

Wanting a few minutes to gather myself, I head out to the back of the property. This has always been my go-to spot when I need to think, and well, if any day qualifies as a day for thinking, it's today. I might have been here for thirty minutes or so when I feel and hear behind me the familiar canter of a horse as it comes closer and closer. The ground vibrates, the leaves on the trees shake, and with each breath, I know there's only one person it could be. A lump instantly crawls its way up into my throat.

Eventually the canter slows to a walk. I know he's there, and he knows I know, too. I wasn't expecting to see him yet, thought this conversation would take place later at his house and I'd have more time to think, but apparently not. Now here we are on a secluded part of the property, under the trees where the stream runs through it.

Standing, I shake off the dirt from the skirt of my dress and turn to face him.

He's wearing dark brown slacks, a black belt with black shoes, and a pressed white button-down with the top undone and his sleeves rolled up. He's so handsome I have a visceral reaction to seeing him, and my whole body sags in relief. My muscles and bones relax, my heart thumps hard with recognition, and my soul shouts, *Mate!*

Only, I'm not sure if I'm his. At least not anymore.

Did I screw this up?

I watch as he slides off the horse and loosely ties the reins to a low-hanging branch of a nearby tree. He turns to face me, and his ever-present scowl is locked in place. My stomach falls, and I suck in air through my nose to try to calm my breaking heart. It is over. We're back here, in this place where we started, where he looks at me as if I'm gum stuck on the bottom of his shoe.

My chin quivers. I'm trying so hard to keep my feelings hidden away, but I'm failing, and he's going to see it. He comes to stand in front of me and just studies my face. The tension is so thick between us I could cut it with a knife, and I blurt out the first thing I can think of.

"How did you know I was here?" It's a place where we've had a few moments and a lot of bad.

His scowl turns wary as he pulls his phone from his pocket and holds it up.

"Oh," I say, remembering he somehow added a tracker to me.

"It's not like that," he says. His voice sounds so good it's like the angels are singing just for me. "I was in the security house and saw on the monitors when you arrived. This told me where to find you." He shrugs one shoulder.

"It's okay," I tell him, and it is. I don't mind him knowing how to find me. I mean really, it's smart. At least one person in this world should know.

He runs his hand over his face, lets out a sharp exhale, and then steps away from me. He shoves his phone back in his pocket and starts pacing. My heart trips over itself watching him try to come up with the words he wants to say to me when it should be me saying all the words. Then he stops, turns, and looks devastatingly vulnerable. The scowl is gone, and he's giving me his true self. He looks miserable, and I want to stop whatever he's about to say before it has a chance to be released into the air. I don't want him to be miserable, and I move toward him.

"I saw you that day . . . here in the woods," he says.

I stop walking, inhale quickly, and wrap my arms around myself.

"Well, not at first, and I guess technically I didn't see

you at all, but after a while, I knew it was you who was there. I didn't realize it at the time." He glances at his feet and then back at me. "There's this feeling I get whenever you are near me. It's strange to describe because it doesn't make any sense, but you calm me. Without even realizing it's happening, my muscles seem to un-bunch, the noise in my head dulls, and I feel like I can breathe deeper. Of course, that day I didn't know what was happening to me, just knew I felt safe to be me and I wasn't alone. That's the feeling I always get, since that day, and only with you. When we actually did meet on the porch, despite all the horrible things that had happened and what I'd gone through with losing my father, when my eyes landed on you, my world shifted."

"That is not what I took away from you that day." I could add more, but it's irrelevant now, and I don't want to hurt him or make him feel bad.

"And that's unfortunate." He gives me a sad smile. "I told myself I was being ridiculous. I was fifteen and you were thirteen, and then I turned sixteen and you fourteen. I know two years doesn't seem like a big deal now, but then it was. I was driving, playing sports with my friends, doing the things teenage boys do, and yet I couldn't stop thinking about the fourteen-year-old middle school girl who was friends with my sister, who didn't want to spend time with me. I was angry with myself and angry with you." The corner of his mouth tips up just a little bit more, his sad smile now also mournful. "Sometimes, it's easier to direct anger at something or someone else than to admit you're just angry with yourself about something or someone you can never have."

"But that wasn't true." I shake my head.

"At the time, I didn't see things that way. I'm not making an excuse, just trying to explain more of why things were the way they were between us."

I think back to the boy I knew and then to the man I know now, glimpses of him over the years as he grew into this person who seemed so large when I saw him next to others, but next to me, he was always just Stokes—untouchable, unflappable, uninterested in me. I think that's what really got to me year after year. There he was, living his life, becoming more, and I've felt exactly the same.

"At the beginning of all of this, you asked me several times why I wanted to do it, why I wanted to make you my 'fake girlfriend,'" he says with finger quotes, "and I never answered you. The truth is, I didn't know how to move us out of the place we had found ourselves in. I couldn't think of anything that would make you see me differently. So, although the LuVu Tea article was irritating and inconvenient, it was also a blessing in disguise. This idea sprung up to force you to spend time with me, so you could see I'm not the man you've made me out to be."

"I'm glad you did." I take a step forward and look up at him. "I love the man I've discovered you to be."

His eyes widen a little, turning glassy, and then he rubs his hand over his face. My poor sweet man. We're still a few steps apart, and as much as I want to close this distance between us and take him in my arms, it's now or never. I need to eat crow and explain my part in this, too.

"Stokes, all of this is my fault." He drops his hand and looks down at me as I speak. "We wouldn't even be here having to go through this if I had just been honest with you at the Derby. I did hear you talking to Christopher, and I thought you were talking about me. I was so shattered and wrecked at that moment that I couldn't see the forest for the trees. I should have asked you, not assumed the worst, and I'm so sorry I didn't."

"I knew it," he says, shaking his head and letting out a deep breath. "The way your mood flipped that day, I had no idea what was going on, but I should have known. It's the only thing that makes sense."

"Birdie stopped by the shop this morning. I didn't know you had dinner with her, not that you have to tell me everything you do, but I couldn't come up with anyone else the 'she' could be but me. To my knowledge, I was the one you were spending your time with."

"I'm sorry, Rosie."

"No, I'm sorry. You've been nothing but amazing to me these last two months, and I hate that I didn't give you the benefit of the doubt and I hurt you." My eyes fill and overflow with tears.

Upon seeing them fall, he's done with the distance between us and wraps me in his arms. His head drops to mine like it always does, and he breathes me in as if I can set everything right in his world.

"No, I'm sorry. I unknowingly hurt you, and I didn't mean to."

I love how he's trying to claim some of the responsibility in this, but it is all on me. Then again, maybe his apology has more to do with the situation in general than this one specific moment. How did I ever peg him so differently?

"Stokes, this, us . . . it wasn't fake, was it?" I feel more hopeful than I have in a long time but also fearful at the same time.

A chuckle breaks free in his chest. Pulling back, he looks down at me so I can see him, really see him, and he says, "It was never fake for me, not one second of it. To me, it was like finally having a dream come true."

"Stokes . . ."

The lump in my throat cuts off my words. My whole body is shaking, and I grip his shirt to hold myself steady. He raises one hand, tucks some loose hair behind my ear, and wipes away the tear tracks that he sees. His gaze is adoring as it touches upon features of my face I know he knows by heart, and, needing more of him, I rise up on my toes, press my lips briefly to his, and then drape my arms over his shoulders so I can hold him tight. He returns my embrace, and I drown in the best smell ever—him.

Those butterflies that grew and grew over our time together . . . there's no flapping of their wings today. Instead, they are sitting and enjoying the show. They've sighed with relief and feel not anxious but at peace.

Loosening my hold on him, I ask the question that's been bothering me for hours.

"Why didn't you tell me about quitting the firm? Taking over here? I had to hear it from someone else when news of these exciting life changes should have come from you. All this is happening, and I didn't get to share these moments with you."

He pulls away from me but holds on to one hand to keep us connected, and he shakes his head. "It's not that I didn't want to tell you. I did, but I had a plan. In my mind, all of this was coming together perfectly. In retrospect, it's dumb."

His plan.

"What was it?" I ask as a breeze blows by. The air isn't cool; it's pleasant as summer is just around the corner, and it ruffles his hair, somehow making him more real to me.

Taking a deep breath, his gaze affectionately sweeps over my face, and then he takes a small step backward, still holding my hand, and kneels. He's kneeling and looking up at me in a way that only means one thing.

I gasp and pull my hand free from his as both of mine fly to my mouth. My poor broken heart starts to rewind as the pieces float back together, making it whole.

Should I say something? Should I do something? I don't know, so I stand here frozen, but I am loving the blazing sparks of complete adoration shooting from my head to my pinky toes.

Silence stretches as he continues to gaze up at me. The

emotion in his eyes is raw, exposed. Whatever he's about to say, his vulnerability is back and rushing toward me.

"It was never a secret that I would one day be taking over the farm. When I was going to do so was never discussed, and as it turns out, it was my mother who was waiting on me all along. She was waiting for me to be ready, and over the last couple of weeks, this desire to do so has been all-consuming. I want it so badly. It's like that kiss at the party woke me up, and I knew not only was it time to make a change, it was also time to claim my life, and that meant you too."

He holds out his hands, and I lay mine on top of his. His thumbs gently brush over them.

"Rosie, I love you. I have loved you for over twelve years. I know at times it may not have seemed that way, but I did, and I've always been in the background hoping one day you would realize it too. For some, this may seem fast, but it doesn't feel that way to me. I've always known. I'm not suggesting we get married tomorrow, but you are it for me, all I have ever wanted. It was important to me to go all in with this, because I'm all in with you, and I was hoping you'd appreciate how serious I am."

He lets out a deep breath but continues to watch me.

"I wanted to surprise you. I wanted the transition to be complete, wanted to show you I'm ready for a future, a future that is for us. No more law firm. No more trying to prove to others that I'm good enough. Just no more. It's like one day I no longer cared about what anyone else thought, just you. Maybe I shouldn't have waited to tell you, but I wanted to show you the kind of man I am and the one you inspire me to be. In my mind, I wasn't just giving you me .. . I was giving you our future, too."

I stare at him and process what he's just said. It makes sense, and now I understand.

"When you put it like that . . ." I whisper, feeling in awe of his declaration.

His eyes are shiny, his heart is laid bare at my feet, and not once do I tear my eyes away from him. This connection is one I want to grasp onto, bottle and keep.

"I know I'm not the easiest person in the world, but I told you at the beginning of all this that I would do better and be better, and that is my promise to you. For you, I would do anything. I love you, desperately. Do you love me, too?"

"Oh, Stokes." I fall to my knees and wrap my hands around his face. "You know I do. I love you so much that sometimes I don't even know what to do with myself. You're not alone in this. I loved you when I was younger, I love you fiercely now that we're older, and as for the middle part, you've always been my person, too."

Stokes's arms band around me, he pulls me flush against him, and we're hugging so tight it's as if we've fused ourselves together to become one. I want to hold on to him forever, and a bubble of laughter rises up in me, because now I know I can.

"Marry me?" he asks. "Spend your life with me. I promise I'll give you the best life I can." He speaks the words into my skin with his lips brushing my neck. They feel tattooed, imprinted, permanent just like he is.

"Yes," I reply breathlessly. "Yes, I'll marry you, but Stokes, I already have the best life because I have you."

A tremor runs through his body and straight into mine.

Who would have thought when I woke up today I'd end up engaged to marry the man of my dreams? Certainly not me. Have I thought about marrying Stokes? Absolutely, and definitely more over the last couple of weeks as I found myself wanting to merge our homes. But did I wish for it? No. I think I was worried I would jinx a good thing, and a good thing is what we are—the best thing.

"You always smell so good," I tell him.

He laughs and pulls back to look at me. "What?"

"You do. I don't know what it is, but I want to bury my face in it. I can't get enough." I run my face across his shirt and inhale.

He chuckles again then says the three little words that have more meaning than any others ever.

"I love you."

Every nerve in my body responds. Little zings fly every which way under my skin, and those butterflies, the ones who are now grown, large, and watching the show, they flap their wings to stand and cheer.

"I love you too," I tell him, so happy to be free of these words that have been heavy on my heart.

Shifting us both so we're sitting and no longer on our knees, my eyes find his just before his lips find mine, and at this moment there is no trace of my broody, grumpy, boring guy. Instead, I find happiness, contentment, and a lightness that is all for me and envelops us in the best way.

"You know it was supposed to be me," I tell him, my hands greedily clamping on to his forearms, just wanting to make contact with him somewhere.

"You what?" His warm mouth kisses from my jaw down my throat, across my collarbone and between my breasts.

"With the grand gesture. I messed up, and yet here you are, giving me the grandest of them all."

He pulls back and looks at me, his face is so precious and dear to me it's hard to believe that I ever thought it differently. "Actually, I haven't given it to you yet, it's back at the house."

"What is?"

"Your ring. I didn't plan on proposing to you just now, but I felt it and had to ask." He runs his fingers through my hair and then down my arm to the fourth finger of my left hand.

"You already bought me a ring?" I'm shocked.

Pink dots his cheeks. "Yes."

"When?" I pull back a little and sit up straight.

"The day after we had dinner together in New York."

I inhale sharply. "But, that dinner was terrible."

"Was it?" He tilts his head, and a small smile creeps onto his lips. "I thought you were endearing."

"Endearing? More like appalling. We were awful together."

He chuckles and sunlight glitters over us as it peeks through the leaves.

"No, we weren't. But that night I went back to my hotel room, and I had to force myself to stay there. All I wanted was to be with you at your apartment. We might have argued a lot, but that didn't change how much I just wanted to be near you. The next morning, I went out for a walk and found myself standing in front of a jewelry store window. I embraced the moment, knowing one day soon this would be happening."

"Stokes . . ."

I'm at a loss for words. That was over a year ago. This man. Will he ever cease to surprise and amaze me?

Cradling my head in both of his hands, he looks me in the eyes and says, "But you've got it wrong. There's nothing grander than you saying yes to me and giving me your forever."

"I think we'll have to agree to disagree about this," I tell him as he makes my heart pound harder in my chest.

"Won't be the first time." He grins. "Or, I imagine, the last."

"Probably not." I smile at him as I lay my forehead against his.

"Should we head back to our house for a while?"

He said *our*. As if he hasn't already melted my heart six ways to Sunday, here it is, folks—complete mush.

"You know I'm not riding that horse back, right?" I ask while glancing its way. Poor thing is just standing there.

"Oh, Thorney, I do know, but I wouldn't be opposed if you decided to ride me," he teases, wiggling his eyebrows as I laugh. He runs his hand up under my skirt and squeezes my butt.

"Why do you call me that?" I ask, watching as he smirks.

"Because you've always been a thorn in my side." He says it as if that's the most obvious thing in the world.

My face drops to an expression of complete lack of amusement. "Are you trying to ruin this moment?"

He tips his head back and laughs, the sound giving me life. Then he grabs my face and kisses me hard.

The next thing I know, he's on his back, and I'm on top of him. My knees are digging into the grass that's still coming in from spring, my hands are dirty, and his clothes are surely going to look worse for wear, but the bliss in his eyes says, *Bring it on.*

"You know we're getting filthy right now," I say to him, and he just grins with his lips against mine.

"Do you think I care?" he asks. I already know the answer.

Another breeze blows by, and the leaves on the trees sway, casting different shadows across his face. I snuggle into him as his arms wrap around me, and then his palms rub up and down my back. My eyes roll back in my head at the sensations it's giving me, but then I remember.

"So, you quit your job?"

His hands pause for just a second then resume their journey. "Yep. I had just turned in my formal complaint with possible notice the day security called about Dr. Miller."

"Formal complaint?" I sit up to get a better look at him. "And possible notice? Aren't they expecting like a two-week notice or something?"

"Nope. This morning I made it effective immediately, and all parties agreed. When we added the cameras to Ace's barn, it got me thinking about my office as well. We do have them positioned here and there, and well, one call to maintenance and I now had one aimed directly into my office. Every time Suzy came in, I wrote down the date and time. Her sitting on my desk, her leaning over, her touching my arm—you name it, it's all there, and in every one of those videos, you can see me looking extremely uncomfortable, asking her to leave, or something along those lines. Plus, they know about you. All I did was toss out the words hostile work environment, and Dean practically helped me pack."

"That explains her murderous glare at the gala."

"Yep. I wanted to give them a few days to review the footage. This way my complaint is valid, and they had no choice but to honor my request."

All these things and I just didn't know. I swear, if I ever see her on the street, she is going to get a piece of my mind. It's completely unacceptable. He sees the frown, even though I try to hold it off, and his thumb reaches up to push on my lips.

"Tell me," he says.

"I don't like not being included." It hurts my feelings, and I know that is stupid, but she was legit harassing him more than I thought, and I could have helped him.

"Never again." He shakes his head. "I'm sorry. My plan was stupid." His fingertips dig in, adding a little emphasis to his words.

I run my hand through his hair then down the center of his chest over the buttons on his shirt to ease some of his tension. "It wasn't stupid. I love the motivation and thought you put into it. That means more to me than you will ever know, but going forward, we're a team, okay?" I place both hands on the center of his chest then stick my fingers in his armpits to tickle him.

He clenches his arms against his body then gives me one of my smiles that I love.

"One hundred percent. You should know that Christopher is also on our team. I hired him to be the farm's new lead counsel. Today he is setting up his own LLC, and we'll be transferring our legal affairs from Collier, Pierson, and Bilella to him."

"Wow, that's great!" I tell him and mean it.

"But don't worry, you can be the team captain." He smiles, and little crinkles make an appearance around his eyes.

"Ohhh, I'll need a T-shirt with a captain's patch," I mock.

"As long as it says Whitlock across your back, you can have anything you want."

Whitlock—why does that sound so sexy coming out of his mouth?

Moments pass as we stare at each other. Underneath me, he hardens, and his hands again find their way up under the skirt of my dress. He dips them inside my underwear, and I realize he wasn't kidding when he mentioned me riding him.

"Out here in the open?"

"Why not? There's no one out here," he says.

I look around, and he's right. No one comes to this spot but us. It's our spot.

"I guess it's fitting . . . after all, this is the place where I first saw you."

Remorse splashes across his features. "I wish I'd known. I'd have liked to see you too."

"Yeah?" I ask as I stand and shimmy out of my underwear.

"More than you will ever know," he says as he reaches for me to sit back down.

Settling on his thighs, I run my hands over his shoulders, his chest, and across his washboard abs. I stick my finger between the buttons on his shirt to poke my finger in his belly button, and he grabs my wrist. His expression says, *Not now—play later*, and I give him the most sultry look I can. He pulls on my wrist to get me to come closer, but instead I pull free and use that same finger to undo his belt. A small gasp leaves him, and his chest starts rising higher and faster. Unfastening his pants, I slide the zipper down, push his shirt out of the way, and pull him free. He watches me with rapt attention until I run my hand up and down, then his eyes slip shut, and he groans. Needing him like I know he needs me, I rise up on my knees, position him at my entrance, and lower my way home. That's what this is, what it's always been—he is my home.

These are the kind of moments when I realize that although I have been focusing on words, words he's said all these years and words I so desperately wanted to hear, I missed the words he was telling me through his actions. His words and his truths, they were always right there, and at this moment, I finally hear them. His words are all over me and all over us. They're in his steady and sure touch, they're in his gaze every time I feel it straight in my soul, they're in the way he breathes me in and the way he gives himself to me. I hear him. I hear all of him.

"I love you," I tell him, and his gaze finds mine. His eyes are greener than I've ever seen them, and they're reverent, devoted, and bordering on having a tiny bit of wonder.

"I love you, too," he says softly, knowing deep down that I've finally heard him too.

Maybe fairy tales can come true. After all, I am just a commoner, and look at us now.

LUVU TEA
HATS OFF TO LOVE

Dear Louisvillians, although the Derby season has come to an end, we are elated to report that love is in the air. A little Birdie just left us the most extraordinary and delicious morsel of all. Did we lend a hand to Fate's magical plan? Maybe or maybe not, but I'd like to believe their future was seen in the reading of the Tea's leaves.

What is this grand news? Well, here at LuVu Tea, we are delighted to be the first to let all of you know that our beloved bachelor of the season, Stokes Whitlock, and his rose, Rosie May, are officially ENGAGED!

Sources tell us Mr. Whitlock proposed on the farm while the two were out for a quiet late-afternoon spring walk. Down on one knee, our dashing bachelor presented Rosie with his heart and then later a three-carat solitaire diamond ring that will send hearts all over Kentucky aflutter. Are there any wedding details? Not at the moment—it seems the two are looking forward to some time spent out of the spotlight. Think again,

Mr. and Mrs. to be. We here at the Tea will be anxiously waiting to announce and document every step of the marital way. From the colors, the venue, and the bridal party to what dress Rosie will be wearing, you'll hear it here first as we report on what will be the most anticipated wedding of the year.

Enjoy this time, Stokes and Rosie. From all of us here at the Tea, we shower you with many congratulations.

So, come one, come all, grab your teacups and raise them high. Instead of saying, "Hats off to you," our hearts are full as we toast and say, "Hats off to love."

ACKNOWLEDGMENTS

To my family, thank you for allowing me to be me. You understand my need to write the characters that speak to me and you love me for it. I am so lucky to have each of you. You make my world go round and my cup runneth over.

To Kelli B, I'm not sure if this should be a thank you note or an apology letter. You've had to listen to me talk about this story ad nauseam for the last year and you've always been my biggest cheerleader. Thank you for brainstorming, plotting, laughing, and just being my person who has to listen to me endlessly talk about fictional characters. I am so grateful for you and look forward to bombarding you with more all over again. Hope you're ready. xo

To Kelly L., thank you for helping me the horse scenarios and our villain. What was meant to be one, turned into many because I loved all the different ideas you gave me. I hope you enjoyed the story, it wouldn't have turned out the way it did without you. <3

To Megan C., thank you for being my person. My person who I always trust first with my words, who pats my head, and gives the best feedback. I don't know what I would do without you and I love you. Thank you...

To Karla S. and Kandi H., thank you for always being my inspiration to keep going. Watching the two of you succeed has been a highlight of my author journey. I'm so proud of you both and blessed to call you friends.

To Taylor R., thank you for loving my stories. Thank you for reaching out, being my friend, and always being willing to help me with whatever I need. I've said it before, but all my social media pages should definitely be renamed to Kathryn and Taylor. I am grateful for you and I hope you loved Stokes and Rosie. xo

To Julie, Caitlyn, Julia, and Shauna, thank you for helping me clean up, package, and promote my new book. It takes a team and I am so happy to have all of you on mine. Thank you. Thank you. Thank you.

To the readers, thank you for taking a chance on Hats off to Love. For those who have been with me for a while, I am forever grateful for your loyalty. For those of you who are new, I can't wait to give you more. More words, more magical moments, more stories. Happy reading . . . much love, Kathryn.

ABOUT THE AUTHOR

Kathryn Andrews loves stories that end with a happily ever after. She started writing at age seven and never stopped. Kathryn is an Amazon Bestseller for her much loved Hale Brothers series, Chasing Clouds and is a chick lit, contemporary romance, and Southern fiction writer.

Kathryn graduated from the University of South Florida with degrees in biology and chemistry, and she currently lives in Tampa, Florida. She spends her days as a sales director for a medical device company and her nights lost in her love of fictional characters.

When Kathryn is not crafting beautiful worlds that incorporate some of her most favorite real-life places, she can be found with her husband and two boys while drinking iced coffee and enjoying the sun.

Website: www.kandrewsauthor.com
Facebook: Author Kathryn Andrews
Instagram: @kandrewsauthor

ALSO BY KATHRYN ANDREWS

Starving for Southern series

The Sweetness of Life

Last Slice of Pie

Lessons in Lemonade

The Hale Brothers Series

Drops of Rain

Starless Nights

Unforgettable Sun

Other Titles

Chasing Clouds

Blue Horizons

Where the Light Shines